17 Dresses

a novel

PAMELA KLEIN

17 DRESSES
a novel

Pamela Klein

ISBN: 97809906966-9-8

First published in 2018 by Padaro Press
A subsidiary of Huqua Press, an operating division of
Morling Manor Corporation
Los Angeles, California

Cover illustration by Yoko Matsuoko
Graphic Design: designSimple

PADARO PRESS

huquapress.com

For Maria Giacosie, whose teenage years gave me something significant to write about, and for Esther Ginsberg, an expert on vintage clothing whose enduring friendship stirred me to look closely at style and consider what may be stiff there at its fraying edges.

Tender Buttons [A Long Dress]

What is the current that makes machinery, that makes it crackle, what is the current that presents a long line and a necessary waist. What is this current.

What is the wind, what is it.

Where is the serene length, it is there and a dark place is not a dark place, only a white and red are black, only a yellow and green are blue, a pink is scarlet, a bow is every color. A line distinguishes it. A line just distinguishes it.

—Gertrude Stein

Acknowledgments

Just before my daughter Maria began college at Brown, we struck up a light conversation about dresses with my oldest friend Barbara and her teenage daughter Arianna. It began as light, at any rate. Not about where to go for dresses, or the sorts we each liked, but more about their places in our lives. On our way to a shop in Manhattan Beach, and excited to be all together for a few hours, Barbara told me she liked how I wrote about dresses in my first book, *Some Feet Not Meant for Shoes*. She said I made the dresses come to life as I wrote about reincarnation and the wounds of slavery. In a world with far more pressing things, I was not intending to write anything about clothes, but something of our exchange stuck and would not let go of me. We all have moments in our pasts that we remember though what we wore, Barbara said. And there are stories in those garments. "Why do we pick the clothes we do?," Ari asked. "And how do we feel in what we wear." Of course I had thought about these things before, but not in the way I was reflecting on them then. " You will have lots of time, Mama," Maria said. Dreading her departure and the distance, I kept thinking how a book might fill me when she left. And when we went to prepare for her time away, I found that shopping with her for some dresses at Valija in San Juan was as fulfilling a moment as taking a hike with her in the Puerto Rican rain forest near where we lived at the time. When she went off to Providence, I sat down to see what might come out, and how that might shape itself into a book. I could have just one character, or several, and weave their t-shirt tales around a larger story, Barbara suggested. For a writer, it was almost a dare. That was over five years ago. I want to thank her for the prodding, and the dialogue struck up over the years while I was working. And I want to thank each of them for the tender encouragement. As the book grew and sorted itself out, my memory of that August day never drifted very far.

Summer sundresses at Target, a yearly get-together with family and friends at Polkadots & Moonbeams, then tea at Chado after, boxes of outgrown garments sent with love and care to a cousin in Bulgaria, clothing has organized me in countless ways I will dwell upon always. I have made lasting friendships with shop owners, have spent hours talking with them about all sorts of things other than clothes. I even found a new friend El-len at a garage sale in San Juan when I picked up a berry-colored shirt of hers that she hardly ever wore. She introduced me to her book club, and for three years we all read and cooked together from the world's literature.

Gathering and collecting vintage has turned weekends into passionate escapades. Thank you my dear sweet husband Robert for all your indul-gences. They resonate still.

To the young women (and men) who have lived with and are living with eating disorders, I urge you to find your way to counsel and healing. The root of the disorder is tangled and varied. Societal pressures, family dynamics and abuse can all be factors but there's nothing textbook about the how and why of the disorder. It's a painful and lonely life and I hope, like Paulette, you can find your way to peace.

Each of the 17 dresses in the book is a real one, while the stories around them are fiction, for the most part. Thank you Golyester for the photos and the research assistance. I did not intend on becoming a scholar of vintage, only a devoted patron wanting to share with the cosmos the exquisite nature of old things.

And to my family, who has not seen much of me recently, thank you for your patience. It takes a long time to write a book, and it is not easy being part of the consciousness of a writer. I am sure they cringed with worry at the thought they might become part of my story. Well not so much this one, Mother and Sis, but for some backdrop. This one comes from the sting of raising a teenager, and summoning up the teenager in us all.

Finally, to my publisher Judy Proffer, you have been a dream to work with. I have been blessed by your support and guidance, and by your willingness to keep at it until we were each pleased. Thank you for the care with which you handled and presented my manuscript. If it touches others the way it did you, then I will have done my very best job.

Table of Contents

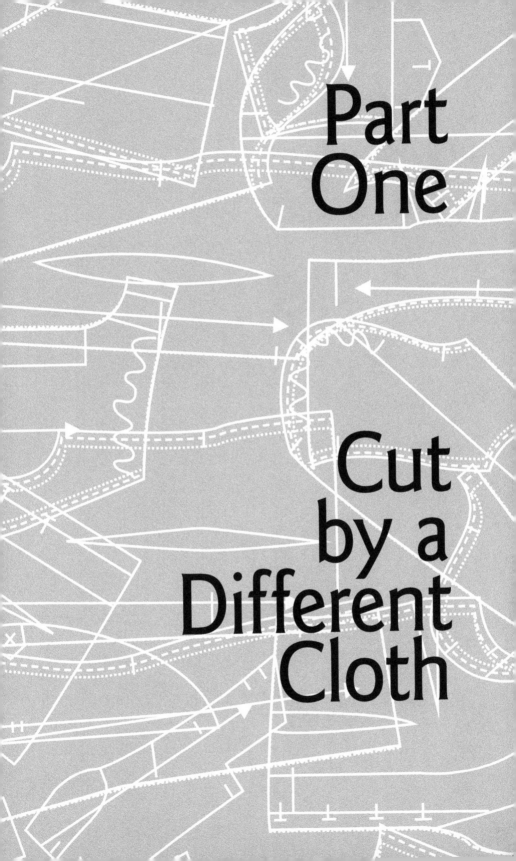

Part One

Cut by a Different Cloth

1.

Beltless and Bangled

Paulette, her long yellow hair textured and coarse and thick as a lion's mane (not yet dyed, for she does not even think of such things, as few did in the mid-1970s), takes in the clean mountain rays. It's the original Sun-In, that sparkling light, and on the wane in much of America. On the wane elsewhere too, along with baby oil tans, women in dresses, and that carefree, mindless living. Her bare feet grip scuffed up and black-as-a-panther clogs—the same wooden heels a Swedish girl would wear generation after generation. USA flag patches are sewn into the knees of her baggy high-waist jeans, and their half-an-inch-too-long hem drags dirty along the two-lane street blocked off from traffic for a weekend community yard sale. Card tables covered in folksy embroidered vintage cloths flank the road, sheltered from the sun by great old pine trees full of charcoal squirrels and swathed in deep-green needles. The repressive Playtex bra in eggshell she'd worn when she left the two-room log cabin just outside town is now tucked inside her red silk purse, the Chinese one, along with a vamp-colored lipstick from England, a brush for her gypsy shag, and $20 itching in a wallet, money she'd saved up of her monthly allowance. Aged glamour all around her, of the sort she'd seen in the silent movies her grandparents took her to, it is cheap and swanky, and for Paulette, it calls up images of pink garters with little rosettes on them, cigar smoke and Asti Spumante, artificial jewels that shimmer blue and yellow exactly like the real stuff. Well, not exactly. There's defiance in it too, of sorts, and possibility, revolt, like going braless in a thin leotard with the crotch scissor-cut.

When Paulette spies something folded and stacked up neatly on a table full of used Levi's and thick Pendleton shirts, she heads right for its little winks, right for its cut-on-the-bias timeworn soul. It is a challenge for her to sort through and discover the pencil skirts among the short A-lines, the lace hankies among the ironed bandanas, the jackets with square shoulders among the heavy woolen sweaters that all seem the color of oatmeal. It is like panning for gold in a stream full of pebbles. Heart pounds and palms sweat when she sees something shiny in the sediment, this prospector. Nothing like this had ever happened keeping near her mother and sisters when shopping at Sears.

There are lots of sophisticated older folks in the small rustic town of Idyllwild, artists and playwrights and retired company heads from rousing faraway places like London and Paris and New York City. Some, like Paulette's family, flee the cities of Southern California for the mountains on weekends for snow come winter and bragging rights come summer. Others manage to find a way to live here year-round. Closets overfull of clothes, some here, some there, some awaiting that sad day when things bought full price at I. Magnin for that fundraiser at the country club down the mountain no longer fasten and take up entirely too much space, even when relegated to the tiny cedar closet down the hall. Give it away for goodness' sake, to Goodwill or the cancer thrift shop; put it out on the town tables twice a year for pocket change. Lots of quiet second-hand that is hardly second-rate. Magninique, Paulette had heard it called and long before she ever knew what it meant, oh, not even close to second-rate.

"Hey Sunshine," shouts Tony, waving frantically from across the street, the bright morning glow behind him and his green-tinted lenses. He's a Hells Angels motorcycle-type guy who unwearyingly taught Paulette to play pool. Not much else a precocious 15-year-old girl can do Saturday nights up on this mountain. Well, there's a little LSD, and nobody has OD'd yet from various substances, not her sort-of friends from home Dee or Fern or Larry. She's tried a few things with the hippies up here, since she feels quite in sync with them, and back home too, after school in the backs of various vans, been to second base, but in most ways that count she is still a virgin. You'd never know it though by the way she sits so decidedly un-selfconscious on boys' laps. Normally restless, anxious and in need of some shape, of some purpose, she'd burst across the street to offer up a quarter for a game of eight-ball in the smoky hall beside Tony's little country cabin with the cute gingerbread trim. A quick learner, Paulette, when she put her mind to it, with fairly good hand-eye coordination that seemed to her slow in developing. Two dozen Harleys are parked haphazardly outside the pool hall, their riders still asleep. They will sleep till noon most likely, and wake up to poached eggs and thick-cut smoked bacon with buttered white toast at the small café on the corner with a pine wood porch. Wake up to buttermilk pancakes with real maple syrup too.

She waves to Tony but does not fasten herself on him. An Italian from Chicago with bronzy skin like native copper who seems to Paulette about 25, Tony rode his bike across America with a group of leather-clad others, landed 5,500 feet up where the California winters are mild and only last four months a year. He brought his Midwest accent with him and his wide endearing grin. Good manners too, just oozing, like most of the town's. There's a small market, a movie theater, a bar, a couple Alpine diners loaded with fretwork, a church or three, Palm Springs at the other end of the aerial tram, from forest to desert in 12 and a half minutes. It's magnetic enough to keep him for a while, long enough to grow out his substantial black ponytail and become a natural mountain man. He's taken up painting living landscapes in purples, yellows and oranges. "Earthworks," he calls them. His mother and grandmother were artists as well. "Way decent ones," Tony likes to boast.

On a table filled almost entirely with pale old cowboy shirts washed and hung, washed and hung, and boots and etched leather belts that bear no tags and resemble rat snakes and lizards, there's something scarlet and daring and delicate and dramatic that waves to Paulette as frantically as Tony. It is that which she fastens herself to. It is the girl emerging sharp and independent inside Paulette who sees it, the not-quite woman, but the longing to be one nevertheless that she finds embedded in the firm shoulder pads. It is breath-taking and fragile and she clutches at something near her chest. Blue-red and like new only better, after maybe 20 years, she imagines, and nothing resembling whatsoever the boring school clothes that were always so much the same—the dirndl dresses from the Sears in Santa Monica, two for $7.90 that her mother, with three girls, put on layaway for each September, or the J.C. Penney catalogue washable plaid kilts that made her look exactly like everyone else. It is a culotte dress of light cashmere, with a rounded neckline studded by rhinestones and little white clam shells beside imitation pearls that reach around like a necklace of the sea. It is playful, ritzy, gathered at the waist, zipped all the way down the back, with full dolman sleeves and wide, elephant legs that make it look almost like a maxi. And that blue-red running in your veins, she thinks, almost gasping.

Outta sight, she says to herself, fondling it, admiring it every which way. She sees the red belt loops yet the actual belt itself seems to have gone missing. And the belt, that is the essential thing that gives the whole its hourglass shape, the real curve in the equation that is the jumpsuit. Not that Paulette really understood the math. Passed pre-algebra only barely, with nearly no help at all since her father mostly barked when she went to him asking for it. Got an A in English lit though. Read *The Great Gatsby* twice. It was the slender drive for reinvention that thoroughly charmed her, and all that fuss about the '20s that just roared. Roared and roared, like a tropical storm, like a hurricane that tore things up, category 4.

"Oh, but where's the belt," she asks the woman with soft bluish eyes sitting behind the table. Her brown hair is pulled back into a thick braid. Her skin is buttery golden and well-lathered in moisturizing lotion. Lipstick more coral than pink, Paulette notes. "There should be a red belt some-where," Paulette frets, disappointed, searching carelessly through the folds of green plaids and grey paisleys, "maybe made of the same wool?"

The woman rests her coral-tipped cigarette in the ceramic ashtray on a nearby log and helps Paulette to search. Not quite old enough to have worn this jumpsuit in its day, a day in the '50s sometime, the woman tells Paulette it was most likely her aunt's, though she couldn't really be sure of it. "A Robert Rosenfeld Original," she says, reading from the white label inside the garment's neck, using the glasses she pushes up from the bridge of her flat nose, navy blue frames fixed on a thick silver chain. "My aunt was a wild one," she says, blushing just a little.

Wild. Why, nobody Paulette knew was really that and it made her heart speed up even faster. She has red wooden platform shoes, brand new, the kicks her dad took her birthday shopping for in Manhattan Beach that just might match, Paulette thinks, randomly unfolding and folding shirts, shoving things violently aside, hoping to get lucky and find that belt. They crisscrossed at the toe and were trimmed in white, those shoes. Matched nothing she owned at the time but her mood, of that same red—bloodshot and enflamed.

Now and then she felt that way, lucky. Felt unlucky too. The lady with a weekend cabin next door to her parents' had a trunk she brought up from Brawley full of some old velvet jackets jeweled with sequins that she was aching to be rid of. "Hand-me-downs," she'd called them. Now that was a good day, Paulette remembers, even with the cold snow outside that sometimes hurt her chest to breathe in. She felt luck deep in her bones, that day. Nothing trendy in that trunk, she'd thought, nothing mass-produced. Classics, she'd felt of the jackets, some of them even with sleeves of bracelet length, authentic, and like nature, endangered by technology. When she could get her hands on garments so full of grace, pieces that nobody else in the world would likely have anymore, well, it perked her up like grass in the wind. Just the sensation of hanging something so beautiful in her closet, a dream she could creep into and hide inside, a refuge from the nowhere, like an old hotel with a distinctive name.

"Twelve bucks, without the belt," the woman says, still rummaging around. "It's double that, if we can find it." All items for sale are negotiable since nobody is trying to get rich. Cleaning out the spot is all, the musty smells, the cramped quarters. Even the tables of candles and locally made ceramics from Idyllwild merchants are full of the old, polished up with verve, making way for the new. Fringes, tassels and synthetic fabrics are all the rage. And for the office, the pantsuit, no longer a wardrobe basic solely for men. One day it will become hugely political, but right now, it is a staple that does not flicker on the stick of wax. Style over substance, right now, and in need of some breathing room.

It's not perfect, Paulette thinks. It's missing something key. She'd much rather pay $24 to have it just right. But all she has is $20 and she had planned to buy that eyeshadow at the village drugstore, had saved up a while for it, the taupes and the greys in a shiny black compact. She could owe, run home, plead with her mother and head right back. She might even hitch a ride since the world is innocent yet and up here on the mountain people are decent, Friday through Sunday anyway. The woman would hold it for her, she was pretty sure of that. And really if she had to, well, she could simply kipe that eyeshadow. She'd done that sort of thing a few times already and never once got caught for it, fear being kind of a pick-me-up and all, like water for a parched plant. Panic, and the dare of some bored, bad-seed girlfriend that couldn't give a damn who lost so long as she got just what she'd wanted. Like some girls her age, Paulette had not yet learnt to take "no" for an answer. Perhaps she never would.

Well, she could snip off the belt loops, but that would be altering the garment and she did not like the idea of that, changing the drape of the thing, of its intention, violating it in some strange way. Not even a shortened hem. This would become a maxim for her later, but right now it just does not sit well with her. Oh, but she could use a rhinestone belt from another dress. She had seen those before, at thrift shops she passed when she and her father walked along Pico Boulevard near the Jewish delis where he shopped for pastrami and rye bread. Rhinestone belts that seem to have gone missing from their loops upon dresses. Maybe she could rescue one.

She'd seen them sparkly in baskets before, arranged like coiled snakes awaiting opportunity. Orphans, she'd sometimes thought of them, pining to stay and touch, smelling corned beef and pickles and something else sweet as she wandered along the sidewalk just behind her father, who almost never looked back to see if she was there. Once, when she caught a glimpse of a mannequin modeling a fab black sequin-covered dress, she begged her father to stop. Captivated by the mannequin's deep red lips, and by another era that her wavy silhouette conjured, Paulette looked her over some while her father walked twice around the block. Plenty of time for pastrami, but he had none for what fascinated Paulette. She made a pal at least, that mannequin, that day.

"Can I just go try it on?" she asks the woman, knowing full well that it would fit. She weighs 110 pounds, is 5'7" and still growing, the doctor says, will be growing for another year. Everything just seems to fit so long as it does not cling too tightly around the hips. She has the shape of a Gil Elvgren pin-up girl from the '50s, though she does not know it yet. Thin waist, thick ankles, winsome pout. Girly; Miss June or July. Paulette supposes the word "zaftig," used by some to define her body, means pleasantly plump and grandmotherly, though she has not once thought to do anything about it. And she did not yet loathe being compared to the deliciousness of some full-bodied ale. "Go," the woman tells her with a flick of her hand.

She runs across to Tony's place and tries the culotte dress on in his little bathroom full of land art, placing her jeans in the corner to give herself some extra room to move around. It hangs sweetly and makes her feel glamorous, frees her from the tight space, grows it even. She sees herself wearing it that night at the pool table leaning against the cue, a beer in one hand and a Virginia Slims menthol in the other. She almost looks old enough to pass for 21, and anyway they are not always checking ID.

Well, if this thing could only speak, she thinks, examining the soft folds of fabric and all the rhinestones to be certain they are each one still there, in place. Perhaps it can. That chance, that lexis she has yet to absorb, that wildness of the woman who wore it before her, oh just the hint of it makes her smile, the way finally getting her driver's permit makes her smile, but only for an instant, and only inside, like intuition is only inside. Outside she is a coloring book still wrapped up tight in clear cellophane, buried beneath all the successful fashion magazines showing us a world that ought to be.

Tony stands at the cracked-open door, bushy eyebrows raised up and stroking his heavy black handlebar mustache. He is smoking weed, as he often does, rolls it up skinny in papers himself, and he offers her some. She declines, but just for the moment, since she's quite occupied trying to view herself in the small mirror above the sink. She has to move in really close and stand on her toes to get the fullest perspective, struggling to ignore the gloomy lighting. She's partial to getting high, though, more so than being drunk. It goes better with the surrounding peaks, is sadder somehow, seems more genuine, more flower-power. At least to her.

"Hey, right on, like from an old Hollywood flick," says Tony, blowing out smoke and coughing a bit. "Ever heard of Anne Francis?" She hadn't, though she's flattered and flushed some. He's paying close attention and she is fed by it. Hungry all her life.

"You bone jacked Honey West," he says, grinning, fanning the air. It's far too early yet to be stoned but Tony, he is well on his way. Too early yet also to light the room with candles but he takes a match to one anyway, then to another, for atmosphere, goes along with his trippy Grateful Dead music playing on the stereo. He'll sometimes make Paulette spaghetti with red marinara sauce, or fluffy omelets with white cheese, sprouts and mushrooms. Brews Red Zinger tea and sits drinking with her on the wooden deck when it is warm enough and the June bugs are not out. They behold the squirrels and the jays and the clear afternoon sky. Behold the stars too flickering in the utter darkness. "Unreal," they often say to one another when the moon is full. "Far out." Scarfed down a whole box of Doo Dads, not only once.

Even with his age, her mother and father would be keen on him, the pureness of his ways, his gentleness, right from the get-go, solid on down, though they have never met. He is shy with parents, he says. In such a small town you'd think they would cross paths, yet Tony keeps a low profile and her parents are only just barely social here. Plenty of hobnobbing in L.A., the mountain, without so much as a television, it is their escape. And anyway in his leathers, Paulette herself couldn't tell Tony from the next guy.

"But what about the shadows under your sad eyes?" Tony asks Paulette somewhat tenderly as she struggles to stand on the very tips of her toes to see herself in the mirror. "What about them?" She is busy with her reflection, and not really listening to anything much he tells her, ignoring his scrutiny. He would like to peel away the wrap, become a crayon and start filling her in. Amber, maybe, like that of his solitary walks at sunset. The ones he never asks her to join, but imagines her alongside him anyway, hands kept down deep inside the kangaroo pockets of his Baja jacket.

Stepping back and away from the mirror her head really hears the "shadows" and "sad eyes" remark, now playing on a temporary loop. Over and over and over. *Why does the mind work like this?* she wonders. If she didn't hear it the first time, if she was distracted and didn't really hear the sharpness when he just spoke it, why must her brain replay it again and again?

Probably everybody looks wretched in that bad light, she considers, finally dismissing the comment and shutting the door to the bathroom all the way until it clicks, taking the jumpsuit off carefully so as not to rip it. These older guys can be such a drag. She makes fun of Tony's Canadian tuxedo, though his studded belt is okay, she admits. Just okay.

"I'll take it," Paulette says eagerly to the woman sitting behind the table, thinking that if she went to the senior prom or to a concert at the Forum, and if she could find a belt, oh this certainly is the right outfit. Handing over the wrinkled $20 bill, she waits for the change with her wallet still open and thinks that she might even have enough to pay for the eyeshadow. This is the very first time she has decided on something to wear entirely without her mother's consent, and paid for it even with her own money. She feels quite the grown-up because of it, exhilarated because of it, is pleased with herself because of it. It's not like taking off your bra. Everybody was doing that. Well, not everybody, but almost. She had rolled up her skirts, snipped her sleeves and her neckline, worn her button-downs turned inside out and tied, backwards even, patched over this and that before, worked with and over what she had been given. This was entirely different, off-trend, sort of like cutting out a garment sans a pattern. Now if only she had the patience and the temperament and the inclination to sew. Well, her mother didn't and so Paulette, she followed suit.

A man with his black dog stops to look closely at a cowboy shirt. He's a weathered-skin local with almost midnight-colored eyes and everyone around seems to know him and Raincloud, ask about how he's doing, about how his mother's doing too. The *Town Crier* said it was a broken hip? "True, true," the man answers, stroking his dog, passing on the shirt with a horizontal hand and turned-down lips. "Looks better on the kids," he says, eyeing Paulette, remembering back when his younger sister was almost that blonde. Still has her old Girl Scout uniform in the attic, he recalls, the sash with all the badges too, the courage, confidence and character that any young girl these days might use a little of. Raincloud wags his tail in circles, barks shrilly when somebody calls out to him.

Now maybe she'd have her hair set in curlers to those Victory Rolls, Paulette thinks, totally stoked, putting the uncounted change quickly back into her wallet and that into her purse, heart pounding as though she were in some kind of serious trouble, as if she had broken every window in some old abandoned house, shattered all of them to smithereens. With deep rouge lips and cheeks, she muses, chandelier earrings of fake diamonds, nails and toes manicured a red purple. She'd for sure recruit her grandmother's help, the one on her mother's side, the one with some self-knowledge, a half-beehive of bashful blonde and gobs of attitude. So should Gary ask Paulette to his prom, which she hopes that he will do, which she crosses her fingers on both hands that he will do and crosses her knees too, well then she'll be a flaming starlet with a purple orchid wrist corsage at the *Hôtel d'Arrivée*.

2.

Shrouded

Veiled in mystery, the French chanteuse Edith Piaf performed on the gas-lit streets of Paris in a black sheath dress. She was nicknamed the Little Black Sparrow because of it. She is Paulette's favorite icon, even though the French language is Greek to her. She can feel Piaf's chanson though, her passion and her loss and her sorrow. Sings to her physique every time she hears it on the family stereo in their beige upon beige living room, commands every little and large bit of it, an ecstasy she had not yet known. Like a half-truth, it drowns out the anxiety of life and its knots in throaty, showgirl style.

So as a painter reaches across the quiet world of line and color, at 16 Paulette steps into the very back caverns of her mother's walk-in closet, searching for the courageous ebony garment that might let her experience *La Vie En Rose*. She wanted to know it the way a tiny cut to the wrist lets her pain out. The way it lets her see the very *rouge* of the throbbing sting. Mysterious as the French tongue, she does not know what drives her to nick herself. It was in a dream. It was in a nightmare. It was in some novel she got from a used book store. What she does know is that it gets the job done, a sort of release into some kind of rose-colored vacancy, where Piaf's rapture touched Paulette in a manner that she so very much wanted to dwell in, for it gave value to her futility. *How to make that torment into something like her everyday skin?* she wonders logically, only sometimes, and in a manner like the subversive supermodel Grace Jones, become the torch song.

She knew exactly the hanger it was on, the hibernating dress, and went right straight to it. It had not been worn in years, had been to the dry cleaners and was covered halfway in plastic, but oddly it still smelled of Chanel No. 5. In fact, everything in her mother's closet smells that way, powdery and musky and flowery, even the polyester pants with those cheap elastic waists. Doesn't everybody's mom smell that ooh-la-la French way? She recognizes immediately the hand-done embroidery, the stylized flowers on the bottom of the wool dress that whisper the Kashmiri, its mustards and lilacs and greens, and even in the near-darkness of the closet's cavity Paulette just about swoons. Psyched about it, her heart races fast and sharp and nervously at the presence of such loveliness among all that is dank and mundane.

Fondly spoken of still by her father, yet abandoned by her mother the way Paulette sometimes herself felt, the dress will be resurrected and worn to the Troubadour in West Hollywood. She's planning to go with her buddies to see Joni Mitchell there the week after next. It will stink of smoke afterward though, of sweat too and maybe some spilled beer, but at least it will have some new life again. Out of the closet and hardly sluggish, at least, like a train set with a change of battery, the Starlight Express perhaps.

Mitchell had been touring around with Jackson Browne, whose lyrical idol was Leonard Cohen. None of these storyteller/poets made whistling tunes, yet they had you thinking, feeling and growing just the way that Piaf did. The stanzas and music, Paulette thinks, it will all seem like prayers, and when it mingles with that smolder and that wetness and that sexy, well, she will be on cloud nine. Heaven on Santa Monica Boulevard, that is, where for only a few dollars there's solidarity and hope and good vibes for everybody. Raza Unida, and relevant, worth every penny Paulette saved up for it babysitting, and weekends spent as a mother's helper across her street.

"And you want to get moving
And you want to stay still
But lost in the moment
Some longing gets filled…"

There are lots more extravagant temples. The Sunday ones, the Saturdays, the Friday nights, some golden, some bearing crosses and others colored in glass and marble. She had gone with her friends to quite a few, heard their old-world sacraments and scanned their pious texts, but none were more germane to Paulette, none more holy. And honestly, she couldn't really wear anything low-cut to church. For Paulette, decrees and decorum were hard to blindly follow. Some folk music though, it plunges Paulette to her knees where she might crawl on cobbled stones to reach the altar.

"The Circle Game," it lives like a messiah inside Paulette's heart. "Fearful when the sky was full of thunder. And tearful at the falling of a star. And the seasons they go round and round…" Paulette's father will drive her and her friends to the Troubadour, and Gabby's father will pick them up when the music stops. That Paulette had got her license now, that she recently passed the driver's test on her first try, it did not mean she had the car. To go out late into the night, with or without companions, the car would take some coaxing. Independence seemed quite close, within an inch of her life, and she was quite motivated. "And they tell him, take your time, it won't be long now till you drag your feet..." It anointed her, those words, delivered her soul to her body, did just what a messiah was supposed to do.

The last time her mother wore this dress was when the ship sailed home to California from Manila, where Paulette was born and had lived for a couple years. It had been a court robe from the barren cold desert of India once, where Paulette's father traveled in the Air Force during the Korean War. The robe was made for her mother into a dress in the early '50s by a Filipino craftswoman, at a time when people still sewed well and coveted the exotic textiles. There's a sepia photograph laying around somewhere with her mother wearing it, Paulette recalls, bringing the dress out of the long closet and away from the melancholy baby-blue powder room with the matching coffee-stained shag carpet. She hates that blue, miles away as it is from turquoise. It's cold and rational and quite aloof from yellow. Hates that shoddy, striped, flocked blue wallpaper too.

And while she's emphatically at it yet, she hates the Ford Galaxie her mother drives. She's learned to drive with it but is quite embarrassed to be seen behind the wheel. Even shotgun. Skylight blue, when it's paired with chocolate cupcake for the woodwork, it is perfectly acceptable maybe for a bathroom. The long blue days that last forever and never, the hue is downright depressing. And unless it's a Mustang in raven black like the girl 'round the corner has got, she'd throw it out the window, whatever color it is. Park up the street or down the block where nobody would notice your set of wheels, as it might jeopardize your reputation. Now if maybe she had a dark green TR4, like the sound guy from Queen, she might be able to love her car too. Cars in L.A. can be metaphors for your soulless body, for your basic human drives. The muscle ones with galloping horses or unleashed cougars used to lure girls have got some dick with their electric shaver grilles, and Paulette was unsuspectingly after a bit of that. After something untamed and beyond blue, too.

Yet at it, nonetheless, still, since it is like the whole sky, the backdrop to everything: I am ugly today. Fat, with bulging thighs, big butt and bad skin to boot. Ashamed down deep in every way. I am just okay today, greasy hair, bloated belly, hanging by a thread. Tomorrow will be better. Yesterday is forgotten. Alone, as Paulette is, and sad, inside, with her Russian literature books, with her Dostoyevsky and her Tolstoy and her Chekhov, with her Bob Marley and his OneLove reggae music. Swing high. Swing low. Love and hate in equal measure, some of the West Coast girls her age. Mellow out already; if they are not careful they will grow up this way.

Alone too in the house just now, Paulette goes inside her mother's dresser drawers, among the complicated lingerie and the packages of Trojans and other things she thinks might be sex toys, to find a full black slip, a padded bra and some dark stockings. If she is going to try this dress on properly, she wants to do it all up right. She had worn pantyhose and tights before and knows to put them on carefully, all the time feeling light-headed and dizzy, drunk on some forbidden luxury—this time alone in a place she almost never goes, the touch of the nylon silky against her skin and the sensual whiff of her No. 5 mother emanating from that drawer. There is some electric static from the nylon carpet and she is literally shocked by it. The white hairs on her arms, they stand right up, the ones on the back of her neck too. Something is charged more positively than negatively, and separating fast.

Some turn up their noses, say that used clothing has got stigma, that it is for people who cannot afford new, but she does not listen. If she can herself become a quilt of the past, a global one, with all the aromas and the music and colors and the drama, with all the stories, then she willingly offers herself up to that. If things of such beauty that are dead and buried can be born again, oh if. "Into my heart has entered a little bit of happiness…"

Her grandmother's black wedge heels, oh, she'd happily borrowed them before, the ones with the peep-toes, they would suit the style, the capped sleeves and thin waist and elegant gathering at the middle where the artful embroidered belt goes. The bare arm, why, it needed the exposed toe to balance, the way a gladiola does a tall vase, the way purple needs orange to distinguish itself and all that it might be, and pink, green. She has to inhale deep and hold her breath to get the dress on, to pull the zipper up at the side.

The old zippers, well, they don't make the curve over the hip very easily. She will have to starve herself to wear the dress svelte, the way she wants to. She vows right then to skip every lunch at school until the concert, and to cut out McDonald's, which hurts, the cheeseburgers and the fries. And anyway, her parents don't pay attention much to what she eats, or doesn't. *How did her mother ever fit this tiny waist?* she wonders, remembering how very pretty she once was. A bit like Barbara Eden, her mother, when she was Jeannie and set free.

In and out of that bottle, her mother, from comedy to tragedy. When Paulette was a small child, her father's anger scared her. For this and that—

for something, for nothing. You just never knew. Her mother was scared too and cried a lot. Hands shook so that she couldn't steady the wheel of the car when she had to take the girls and leave, stay a night or two in some Venice Beach motel. Ice buckets, vending machines, the safe murmur of the television all night long. The tears in her mother's hair smelled good, like ripe plums. She smoked one cigarette after the other, Virginia Slims, almost all the time, midnight and morning. Perhaps that's where her pretty went, Paulette thinks, feeling the pinch of her underarm as a bit of flesh catches in the zipper. Ouch, she cries out. The bodice is tight and obliging, even for her.

Paulette admires and tries to copy her mother, in some ways. Smoking, for one. She had a preference for Lark though. Some older boys at school thought they were cool; Lark and Leonard Cohen too. Hopeful that one day very soon the sun would cover her in gold dust glittering with significance, Paulette developed little patience for lightweights, and a penchant for brooding solitude. Like her father in that way.

The not unfriendly mirror on the back of the door to the rust-orange master bath is in a dark wooden frame and a lavish full length. Paulette can see all the way down to her feet and most of the time when she showers there to shave her legs she hates to look at herself naked. Legs too squat, hips too wide, thighs too thick and tummy bloated. She prefers much more to examine herself clothed. When all the ugly is fully clad, she finds that even her ski-jump nose that's a bit on the big side looks better. Indifferent yet to boys and what it is that they desire of her physically, Paulette is drawn to layers of textiles that move through the air like fog. And when the mist lingers heavily, you simply cannot ignore it. Looking down at her normal-size feet, she decides to paint her toenails grape later in the week, since they will show in the shoes. The dress thankfully covers up her foul knees, and comes down mid-calf where her leg is decent. The near-black stockings bag at the ankle some, and are much too big for her, but the look is careful, in a distinctly careless way. With lots of skin at the arms, too black and bulky an opaque would throw off the equilibrium completely, she reasons, and quite confidently, calmly even. The gladiola would simply fall.

She will need a handbag that's small and plain with a sturdy shoulder strap and some hint of India, she thinks, and chunky jewelry of onyx or jet, her hair loose and without a distinct part, pale ends curled up tight in jumbo sponge rollers with setting gel. She is walking around the bathroom parading before the mirror, *the long cool woman in a black dress*, watching the garment move as she does, dance as she does, vaguely aware of her parents' romance back when it was still perky, like her breasts. She is hardly breathing with the embroidered belt clenching her middle, wondering if she feels worthy in the dress, if she is appropriately cheery. If she has got some nerve, even some wings. Just five pounds less, she tells herself, imagining her arms morph, lift her up up up.

With so much night and day in the way she sees the world and herself in it, and quite on her own among her peers who seem far more intent on impressing each other and the opposite sex than on fully expressing themselves, it is a wonder she can transform into herself with anything close to authority. Fitting in, now isn't that what every teenage girl wants, become one of the heads, jocks, bunnies or nerds? Well, not Paulette. Conformity, oh, for her that was the real poverty.

Her saucy grandmother, named after a gust of wind, well, she is a different matter. She wears those cotton print housedresses like they were satin lounging attire, like they were va-va-voom. Hardly any hint at all of that Nordic ice. She must have been a real outlaw when she was a teenager, Paulette imagines. Wayward, when she married that French Jew. At 16, no less.

Earlier this year when her parents were away on a cruise of the Panama Canal, Paulette had a boy over and they were making out on the couch in the family living room. There were lots of boys, but this one took pictures for a living and had some respect for her. He had unruly hair too and she likes that sort of thing. "Happy? Happiness to die for?" Well, not yet, but she was going about it with some urgency. It was late, after Johnny Carson. Her grandmother Kari, the one with the peep-toed shoes, the one who first played her Edith Piaf, she was there in the house sleeping, and earlier had baked a German chocolate cake from scratch. Paulette and the boy were sitting close in the dark, had fondled each other until they had nowhere else to go, and her grandmother walked in with a big piece of cake on a plate, handed the boy a fork. She had a sexy little nightie on that was quite short, and she did not bother to put on her robe. She'd said when she made the cake that the way to a boy's heart was through his stomach. She was not kidding.

That boy, oh, he was shocked at the way her grandmother sauntered around like she hadn't a single care in the world, like it was she who was the one truly liberated. Well, sometimes the room expands and the door in your head opens up wide and you can breathe fully, Paulette thinks, down to your core. The zipper slides up smooth and easy, catches nothing and the belt surrenders, sometimes. Oh yes, another matter entirely.

Her mother has a star sapphire necklace from India too that is thankfully more lavender than blue, and clip-on earrings to match, Paulette remembers. The earrings will pinch her ears, but perhaps her mother will also let her borrow them for the Troubadour. It has been happening more and more regularly now, this sharing of her mother's belongings. Is it generosity, she wonders, or that she really does not care much for the things that interest Paulette? When she lends something to her girlfriends, she does it to please and to bond, just the way her grandmother does. There was not much pleasing or bonding that she could sense in the way her mother shares. Grasping this makes her feel sorry for herself some, since she used to fake being sick when she was a little girl just to lay on the couch beside her all day. Even gave herself serious asthma. Generosity, it isn't for everybody. Neither is curiosity and attentiveness.

A dyed-platinum blonde with an Aqua Net bouffant, Paulette's mother has a lot that makes her worried, and she says that smoking is just about the only thing that helps her to manage it. Her marriage makes her nervous, for one, keeping it together for the sake of the children. Her kids, for another, since the times they are so feral. She's awfully busy at home while her husband manages a small hospital in the South Bay. He's the chief administrator, and one of those who's almost always working. If only he'd had an heir, someone to toss a ball around in the backyard with. Paulette is their oldest, and the most difficult to control. The youngest girl goes to the grammar school at the end of the block. Paulette and her sister are bused into south L.A. for junior and senior highs—public schools, no longer (un)equal but separate, all of them, even though her mother would have liked private better, considering her respectability, considering her color.

If her mother ever had some of her own ambition to become an actress on the stage, or in Hollywood even, oh, that is behind her now. All that's left is a reel of her performance in *Guys and Dolls*, a bit part at a small theater in the San Gabriel Valley where she was born and raised. Yet, the drama and energy required to play the role of a responsive mother is vast. Here, there, then back again and there again. Her husband makes enough money that she does not have to lose sleep about that. Not about the money. There are plenty of other things to fret over, though. If she'd stop to mull over every little one of them, including the way he doles out the money, the way she has to hide how she spends it, she'd surely run off to a therapist. And her cynical husband, he would be having nothing whatsoever to do with that. Therapists are quacks, he says, and being head honcho of the hospital, well, he ought to know.

"Your mother is so happy," her father was fond of saying, a strained smile spread across his face. "Just look at her." Aqua Net, for days.

An unhoped-for longing suddenly to flee, to travel to India strikes Paulette and she has never thought of that before. Not even when the Beatles made their pilgrimage to Rishikesh, at the foothills of the Himalayas, altering forever attitudes in the West and beyond regarding Indian spirituality and meditation. France, oh yes and the Philippines yes, England and Russia yes, from the novels she had read, Jamaica too, from the music, and Greece, from the ancient sunshine, and Israel of course, but India not even once since her father had told her that women had to enter the Taj Mahal separately from men. It did not sit right with her, even though like most teenagers she listened to *The White Album* over and over again and found the influence of the Maharishi Yogi there to be nearly irresistible. It was not messianic for Paulette, though, not yet, even with that big crush she had on Paul like a million other girls. Some pop culture, it just seemed so easy and trendy, while real attitudes, they seemed not. They were like old wrought iron, real attitudes, had to be forged carefully by hand.

"America treats women here better than 99 percent of the rest of the world," her father had said about his days abroad in the military. "Smile and be happy like your mother."

This daydream of India makes her feel sleepy, the way a half glass of rosé makes her feel sleepy. Those red dots on the foreheads of the Indian women; the gold rings in their pierced noses; the metal bracelets clinking on their wrists; the lovely darkness of their skin beneath those gorgeous colorful silk saris; their naughty Kama Sutra postures and oh-so racy seduction, both carnal and cerebral; their mehndi sun on the palm. She has had Indian food only a couple times, in the home of a colleague of her father's, but the smell of yellow curry powder tinged with turmeric is right on the tip of her mind. Oh, many times she had longed to flee, but no, India was never on the map of her imagination.

She has piano practice which she has to be swayed to do, homework in U.S. history and a short rhythmic poem yet to write for English class, and soon her mother will be here and she'll have to slice up decaying vegetables for salad with ranch dressing at dinner, presided over as it always is by her father. Yet she'd rather now pose before the bathroom mirror in her mother's Kashmiri dress, black as the sky on a moonless night, moving about the universe freely as a bird, a little sparrow, without even so much as a passport.

Eternity is right in front of me, Paulette thinks, tipsy still. They said that in a sermon at her girlfriend's spiffy cathedral and though she did not grasp it at the time, the phrase stayed with her, had lingered like waxy red lipstick on a clean white cup. Eternity is right in front of me, right there, in the dense fog with hardly any visibility ahead or behind, she tells herself, knowing how lucky she is, since there are far worse places she could be. Paulette is looking in close, squinting, straining hard to see.

3.

‒ ‒ ‒ ‒ ‒ ‒ ‒ ‒ ‒ ‒ ‒ ‒ ‒ ‒ ‒ ‒

Sugar and Spikes

The zigzag of ricrac repeats every third of an inch and Paulette can't seem
to get enough of its square dancing rhythm, even though officially she
just hates the twang in country music. She cannot stand to hear it, not by
Charley Pride or Loretta Lynn or even Glen Campbell. Trim on aprons,
shoes, pillowcases and curtains. Yes, that is exactly what she feels like in
life. Like sold-by-the-yard, glued-on, eye-catching trim.

Bad grades, bad attitude, bad mouth. Her father is beside himself about
Nixon, wants to move the family to Australia or New Zealand for its social-
ism. And her future—what to do in the next phase of her sullen existence
during this constitutional crisis, oh it races ahead like the Datsun 240Z.
She runs to grab for it but she's just zigzagging. Out of sheer exhaustion
and some panic, Paulette said fuck at the family dinner table and got that
mouth of hers washed out with surgical soap. Defeated? Why, surely not.

Joan Baez is the clenched fist of her far stronger right hand. Fuck fuck fuck fuck fuck…

Over the summer when Paulette turned 17, against her mother's wishes, but with her grandmother's blessing and support, she began taking the birth control pill and has already gained so much weight that this hyacinth peasant dress with the metallic steel-grey ricrac is the only kind of thing that fits easily over her curvier-than-ever body. It has got some room in it, some flow. It is what she'll wear for her senior class picture, she'd decided, even though it is not black. At least her skin should be clear by then. It was that, and her precociousness, which firmly convinced her grandmother to step in and help. She could not bear to watch Paulette hiding her pimples with layers of medicated flesh-tone cover-up. It nearly broke her heart. And then there was her granddaughter's blossoming sexuality that Paulette's mother just would not condone. "Oh, for Pete's sake," Kari said to her daughter, clicking her tongue. "Don't be so fuddy-duddy."

Paulette had got the light cotton dress with the ricrac at the Salvation Army near Venice Beach for next to nothing and had to wash it several times to get the reek of charity out of it. "A squaw dress," some lady with savage red hair standing close beside her had said. "We used to wear them to school in the '50s. Made in Arizona, usually, and very good quality, kind of middle-class haute couture. Check the label," she told Paulette, putting on her crimson glasses and looking closely at the inside of the garment, showing her where it might be found. "Hmm. These dresses, many by Dolores Gonzales, they were for the frugal, but charming for their flair. The word 'squaw' is originally Algonquin, for 'young woman.'" The lady, she stopped talking and turned away, though she did not disengage.

Chatty, thought Paulette, and kind of chummy. And she noticed the way she touched the fabric with such affection, like an embrace. Most shoppers at Ohrbach's, where she went with her girlfriends who had cars, tossed items around, grabbed at the bottom of the piles and simply yanked, but this lady, she fondled things as though they were beloved heirlooms. "In English, though, the word 'squaw' became derogatory. If you want, you can call it the 'patio dress' instead."

Now there's a person with some kind of peculiar energy, Paulette noted, the same sort of fizzy thing she observed in her grandmother. A cleverness that was neither cold, nor aloof. Spiffy, she'd thought, the way their curiosity went alongside their consideration. Quite different than the simple nosy of most people.

"Have you got some old cowboy boots?" the redhead asked Paulette softly, seriously, searching and sorting through piles of vintage that somebody had just thrown down haphazardly, without regard, without second thoughts.

Who wears cowboy boots anyway? she wondered, imagining Dolly Parton and her "Jolene," and thinking to herself: no way, José. Yet she didn't laugh. It would not have been kind to laugh, and Paulette was that, mostly. She had been laughed at plenty in life, and it always left her a little bit lonelier and a lot more tormented.

"The handmade '40s boots from Texas had beautiful leather inlays. The ones with the short, curved tops would look really nice with that dress." The redhead, she smelled like roses, Paulette noticed, and her voice was soft like roses too. Purple ones, spicy clove. Well, she hardly forgot her. Every time she wore the dress she would think of her, that affection she had for clothes and the tales woven into their history.

She finds when she tries the dress on again at home that the round drawstring neckline and short, puffy elastic sleeves covered in silver criss-cross accentuate her new 36C cup, and the pale charcoal print, repetitive and running vertically, is kind of Islamic in feel. It highlights her dusty blue eyes. The middle is blousy, but nipped-in and shows off her figure 8 shape. The length of the tiered, rockabilly circle skirt falls just inches below her knees and hides in an honest sort of way most all of the uneasiness. *How can anyone call this sort of thing tacky?* she wonders, considering her reflection in the sliding mirror door to her closet.

Play up the slender part of her frame, draw attention away from her hips, she thinks. It is defining her style, this dis-ease and how it triggers her to camouflage her body, though she does not know it yet. Does not grasp that fit goes so well with flare, that her physique was really made for dresses. So she will come to it like a sickness but then be healed by it too. Recovery time is not swift, however, as this is not a broken ankle or a trauma to the head. And red flags flying high and snapping, they very often go unnoticed.

At least in this particular blue dress Paulette feels like somebody. Like somebody Mexican or somebody Italian, harsh and wary and sullen, but nevertheless up for the fiesta like the rising moon. Like somebody Egyptian or Greek, with ancient history and temple walls that could be the oldest on Earth. Somebody stinging and sylphlike, she thinks, soulful, lyrical and rhythmic, like that ruffled gypsy girl with the steamy eyes on her phony ID, the one worth turning around for and staring long and hard at. Hopelessly hopeful as the brittle dahlia edge of joy in high winds, knocking her head against the wall. She'll use fresh lemons squeezed on her unwashed hair and lay outside to activate it, render it even blonder by a few shades, she decides. Approaching fringe, it parts down the middle now. No more bangs. Second glance like full afternoon sun, somebody. Come to it like a sickness, yes indeed.

She's been trying desperately to lose weight, jogging, jump-roping, doing aerobics with disco music and sweatbands, doing anything she can to create gaunt in her over-plump face. She's been thin as a carrot stick for years. But now her hormones have made her body more like the butternut squash. So she will force herself to eat less, refuse rice and potatoes and spaghetti, bread of course too, and if she must, give it secretly to the dog waiting underneath the table. Trying to be smart about it, she quietly pushed the food around her plate, arranged and rearranged it with her fork to seem as though she was eating. She gave away every bit of her packed lunch that was not cucumber or celery, which she swears has got the negative calorie effect. Strange, to cut out almost entirely everything that you imagine makes you fat, which is just about all that you consume. And she and her father were really the only two in the family who ate fresh vegetables, so there were few of those zucchini and broccoli and cauliflower to fill the void.

Like everybody else who fancied being Twiggy, Paulette wanted a new version of herself faster than a diet could bring into being and she did not like at all the pang of hunger. So, rather than starving herself, she'd begun to eat more heartily, and then right afterward, when nobody was paying much attention, she would quietly disappear into the bathroom, lock the door, put the seat up on the toilet, stick her finger down her throat as far as she could and get rid of the food, all of it, and the hunger too. This became a ritual, or something like it, after almost every meal. The senior picture, well, it goes into the class yearbook, and that is forever, she thinks. Set in stone, like a dog footprint in concrete before it can dry. Nothing you can do about it then.

In November she can start eating again and stop the throwing up. It is a worthy goal, she reasons one dreary Saturday afternoon four weeks into the new school year, her last one in high school, searching through the cupboards and the fridge for anything in the kitchen without calories like lettuce that she might keep down. This morning when she'd purged breakfast, the toast with apricot jam and the fried eggs, her heart sped up dangerously and she thought more than once about it. She did not always want to be dead. Not permanently dead, anyway.

There were graham crackers, Fritos, peanuts salted in their shells. There were green apples and watermelon, the kind with seeds, chipped beef, cooked hamburger patties, leftovers of frozen peas from dinner the night before. There were raisins in little red and black boxes. There was matzo. There was Wonder Bread, soft and doughy and white. Everything is so boring, Paulette thinks, feeling worthless, tasteless, helpless, hopeless. Less and less and less, every single day.

Somewhere on Earth, children were starving, but Paulette was nowhere near there. The mother-of- pearl globe of the world sat on the bookshelf, gathering dust. Beside dreary hardcovers on JFK, post-Keynesian economics and John Kenneth Galbraith, it merely took up space, just the way that she did. If only there was a little food for thought beside that Buddig chipped beef. Some tuna, even, some Chicken of the Sea—she might be able to keep that down, become the blonde mermaid with the golden scepter and swim away.

She goes into her shocking-pink-painted room with the blacklight posters covering almost every inch and she lays on her bed to sleep. At least when she is sleeping she can sink herself into serial dreams of her Canadian pen pal, and she does not have to think about food and hunger. And in those reveries with him, she could go entirely out of order, since every single word seemed cut open and bleeding yet sounded like a mandolin and a banjo on the stationery. And spilling her guts, it was a viola. Paulette would sleep day and night if she only could. She would catch that train and take it all the way across America, and then some. So much forward momentum in her imaginings, so much force; so much lethargy in her prissy empire-waistline present. A quick nap, a way free, a portal out.

With matter and energy squeezing, well, it can only implode. That's why destroying things comes so easy to Paulette. Stealing soft-top sports cars from a lot on Centinela. Boy after boy. Drug after drug. Now had she been quite good at something, something like track and field, or swimming maybe, even biology. Had she actually got the part of Christina in *The Princess and the Pea*? Or found an old guitar to strum. Had her voice been halfway decent, that is, the instrument might have carried her tune. Sinking into sleep like a needle into the arm, she makes a run for it.

Her father told her a year or two ago that it was fortunate she was pretty, since her grades in math and science were not up to par. Well, she did not think she was pretty. In fact, she could hardly look at herself sometimes. But when she put on dresses from another era in lovely washed-out colors of pinks and greens and corals that caressed her body in a drape of woman, she took a whiff of some old-world glamour and it was as intoxicating as a red pill or a blue one. She imagined other lives in other languages, in other eras, in other landscapes, tripped far out and away on her rousing hallucinations; she had a cigarette holder and a beauty mark over her lip; hung out in smoky bars drinking lovely Campari soda; made dresses by hand that laced tight up the middle from worn curtains and nightgowns, sold them from an elaborately painted vardo. She even played a violin that people danced by.

Now Paulette's girlfriend Gabby, well, her father said to his daughter something altogether different. "Good luck finding a guy, since you are not at all pretty." Grew her hair out long, put mascara heavy on her lashes, pierced her ears with sparkling rubies and got her Greek nose fixed. Tried to pretty up fast, that one. Didn't matter that she was over-intelligent, optimistic and a comfort to almost everybody who knew her. Low self-esteem is like a cracked tooth. It does not go away and the nagging ache, it curls your toes. Only way to treat that is to kill the nerve.

When she thought of this, Paulette detested fathers and liked herself a little more with that rage inside her. It was something tangible she could bite into. And when she saw her reflection through a Vaseline-covered lens of history, one that blurs the flabby edges and softens the bulging lines, she bit down even harder. She really liked herself in skirts that dragged along in the filth, in poet's blouses with sleeves rolled way up high, in coats made of flower drapery still filled with daylight. Style is a way to explode. Fortunately.

Her mother knocks softly on the door, comes inside the bedroom before Paulette says that it is okay. She does not like to see her daughter so glum but is not too sure what to do about it. It might bother her even more if she actually understood it, or if she cared enough. Bonds, they take some effort in the best of times, and while she loves her daughter, this one in particular, she is spread awfully thin. PTA vice president and church choir pianist, mahjong player, agreeable wife; why vacant teenage girls aggressively seeking to fill themselves in the American wasteland is really way over her head.

Now if only Paulette were actuary material, she muses, like her sister-in-law's daughter, who already passed a few of the rigorous exams and bought her first townhouse on the water in the Marina del Rey. At least she won't be needing a husband, her mother reasons, relieved some when she considers her niece. Paulette's father, now he is demanding and moody himself, volatile actually, and her mother has got that to think about. First and foremost, for the sense of security, she has got to think about that. So far, her other two girls seemed headed in the right direction, getting A's in school, doing their homework and respecting the curfew. They did not throw wild parties weekends when they were out of town. They are her easy chair, one that reclines so she can put her swollen feet up.

"Did you ever wear cowboy boots?" Paulette asks her mother, revived a bit from her slumber and sitting up, leaning against the pillows and thinking what besides a silver mesh choker with matching earrings to put with her blue squaw dress for the yearbook picture. Well, not 'squaw,' she reminds herself, but 'patio.'

Feeling herself in a spot without rhyme or reason, reading the words on the posters, blending into the fluorescent orange of Peter Max thought feathers, facing anywhere at all in the room but the direction of her daughter, she says: "Sorry, dear." Besides Roy Rogers and Dale Evans of the movies, she did not know a thing about authentic chap attire. "I was never very fond of cowboys," she says, turning her nose up on the Wild West and looking away still. Didn't own a pair of denim blue jeans, even.

Paulette reckons that her mother probably liked the boy-next-door types, as she has often told her daughter that she was a "good girl." The '50s had more than their share of them; clean-cut, clean-but... Paulette lays back down and closes her eyes on her fatigue and her hunger, on the silence, on the deep loneliness, on the smell of cigarettes, dreaming of some scuffed-up white cowboy boots with grey stitching, fried chicken and a little buttered corn on the cob. Down the street, choruses of dogs bark at sirens blaring loudly nearby. Next door, beside a swimming pool, a mother prays that her soldier son will come home from the war in Vietnam. On the other side, a black family moves in and the for-sale signs spring up all over the neighborhood. The world is faded blue on so many fronts, and Paulette longs to be dressed properly for it. To look her part.

Before the commonness of sewing machines and metal sergers, ric-rac was used to finish up the edges of fabric—to decorate, construct and reinforce the garment. It was versatile, despite its pioneer sentiment, and gave way to something called the lettuce-like purl stitch, a more advanced decorative varnish made by feed dog gadgets that stretch the fabric while pressing it forward and are all about the timing. Trim. By any other name it still smells like trim all the same, smells like sugar and spice. Sugar and spikes, in Paulette's case.

"Have you even touched the piano yet today?" her mother asks, filling the air with something maternal that she expects will sway things, hoping Paulette will get herself up from the bed and go practice her "Greensleeves." It just might make her feel better, the classical music that is, since it soothes and relaxes her mother when she plays. Her mother rubs her hand me-chanically up and down her daughter's back, her marquise-cut diamond ring throwing rainbow prisms around the room. Paulette, caught up some in the facets of radiance, lays on her bed stiff as a floorboard. She hides the fresh cuts she'd made on her left wrist beneath her pink bedspread, hoping the blood is finally dried up. Her parents don't know and Paulette wants badly to keep it that way. The only one who does see was sworn to secrecy. She would be punished no doubt in some dismal manner, by her parents and others too she was quite sure. Heartlessness, no matter which way she turns, it hardens her up like a gemstone. "Half an hour's more than enough," her mother says, stroking as she does a dust cloth.

Paulette hadn't much passion for the piano, not the way her mother did, but she liked the old English folk song well enough to painstakingly memorize it and play it occasionally for her family. They'd sit quietly on the two-tone beige vinyl couch and make an effort to pay attention, her sisters especially, hands on their laps, knees together, fingers clutched tightly, knuckles reddish. Nobody really listened though.

4.

----- -- -- -- -- -- -- -- -- -- -- -- -- -- -- -- -- -

Top Half of a Heart

Silly perhaps, this choice to study fashion design in New York, except
that the photographer whom Paulette was dating, almost exclusively because she really wanted it that way, thought it was just the thing for her.
And he was quite persuasive, more than her parents, both of whom were
consumed by their own troubles. Her father wanted to climb the world's
mountains with the Sierra Club, since the arteries to his heart seemed to
be near clogged and nature was an anticoagulant. Her mother preferred
to cruise the South Pacific like a blue-blood, leaving the girls behind with
her parents, of course, as harried fathers could not altogether be counted
upon. Wrapped up almost entirely in themselves, they hardly say a kind
word to each other, except during the occasional late afternoons of bridge
when her father politely asks her mother across the card table to please
pass the chocolate-covered almonds. She does it without looking up from

her hand. As candy goes, well, the See's goes, almost all of it before the last trick is played. Oh, he likes his sweets, her father.

"Get away," the photographer says one day when Paulette is listening, "and far," placing a pin of red cherries just off the center of her yellowed-white lace blouse and looking at her sideways, as he often did. It matches her scarlet cords that are on this side of baggy. Smile, he says. Sex, he says. She tilts her face some so that her pimples don't show. Click, click, click.

Surprising herself some and her parents too and delighting to no end her grandparents, she was accepted into the Fashion Institute of Technology, and was hoping to study fabric styling and possibly run off to Europe to learn even more about old-world textiles. There was money for it, her father assured her, so long as she did not waste it, so long as she took it seriously. "Be the best at whatever you do," he often told her, "even if that's collecting trash." She often wondered if he told her sisters the same. They had gone walking with the dog to the local Sav-On for ice creams, 50 cents a scoop. She had rum raisin and her father chocolate. The dog, a German Shepherd of liver and silver, he had vanilla. "Every girl ideally should have a vocation," he'd said off the top of his head, holding the cone up for the animal to lick, drips of ice cream running down his hand. And professions? Why, they were, of course, for boys. Like the tree-lined park they'd float by on the indirect route home, his dime-store wisdom always seemed so child-friendly. Even a swing pushed too high though has its dangers.

Paulette had never lived in a chilly place before, not for more than a weekend, and she had no clothes for it. Not a coat, not a hat, not gloves. She did have a cheesy ski sweater with royal blue and fuchsia snowflakes and klutzy snow boots that she wore winters in Idyllwild, though hardly funky or chic enough to consider where she was headed. Three girls covered up from head to toe in warm generic clothing; brands, sizes, styles, structure, nobody cared so long as it was snug and dry as a bone. This sort of utilitarian fashion psychology had spread over into life. No frills. Well, the socks, if nothing else her mother made sure that those matched each other, so there were some standards. And rules—the color white, for example, oh, even in California it had its own distinct season.

There was a plain wool jacket, grey, with real fur at the collar that her mother wanted to send Paulette off to New York with. Fat chance, though hardly for the right reasons, as nobody around her had a passion for animal rights, or any awareness whatsoever of the mistreatment of them either. It was just homely, that coat, didn't even show off wealth like chinchilla or sable, which was the only reason Paulette could think of to wear it. They argued some about almost everything Paulette wanted to leave behind, settling on nothing more than some silky long underwear of a biscuit tone. Carry the trail of her mother's Chanel No. 5, this, since she was the one who mostly wore them. And her grandmother had some solid cashmere sweaters in pea green and banana yellow that her grandfather no longer used for golf. They could be buttoned up or buttoned down, depending on how you felt.

During the spring sales, her mother took her to May Company, the branch on Pico at Overland in the Westland mini-mall, looking at coats, rows and rows of them, all saying nothing more than the rock-bottom practicality of warmth. Life, not lifestyle. Yet, there was this nifty navy pea with some nylon blended into the wool that called up the seas, and was considered more classic fashion. It had thick black plastic buttons, a "fouled anchor" design imprinted on the shiny surface, a traditional image of an anchor wrapped in a rope, a logo dating back to the British defeat of the Spanish Armada in 1588. She'd go with that, smiling, for the time being. It was certainly not the cheapest on the rack, but her mother very quickly tired of the quarreling. "It will have to last you," she'd finally said, issuing an order that to Paulette sounded almost threatening.

Former classmates, they are traveling here, there, to study medicine and business and law like their parents, the boys at any rate. The girls want to be nurses and teachers, mostly, secretaries, although one, now that women actually could, was going to run the Boston Marathon. But Paulette, who got an A+ on her term paper about Wounded Knee, is a metaphor without a medium, without a map. She might be a missile too, with some guidance, yet there isn't much of that. Only a cold war growing colder, a planet in a space race drifting further and further apart. "What can a person do with philosophy?" her father asked. No, he was not asking. So much for being the best at whatever you do. If life is soup then her father's a fork, sometimes.

"Well, it is art, not cheap fashion," she tells the photographer over and over, reaching up for the creative intelligence of his beloved Man Ray, finally convincing herself. Ray was inspired by mannequins, threads, pins and needles too, she points out. "My little Kiki," the photographer calls her, laughing, quickly taking off her clothes, flicking her nipples lightly with his tongue until her legs just spread themselves apart like feathers on a wing. Click, click, click.

"You'll be gone and I can't stop you," the photographer says when she is near finished filling out the school application, adjusting his camel beret in the rear-view mirror. "It's fate, really; you can make what I can't photograph." That long, thin, sensitive face, pale as the white of old silk lining and just as smooth, why she is having second thoughts. Seriously.

He was 26, the photographer, when he met an actress coming up in the world at some swanky L.A. party and began to cheat on Paulette. He grew secretive and distant, became critical like her father. "Don't you know anything?" Paulette's skin got so bad that she hardly wanted to go out, fearing he would only see that, and her swelling thighs. She drove to his Venice house late at night, and made him keep the lights low. She sat with her arms on the table and her head in her arms, hoping he would not look at her too closely, at the makeup she'd carefully caked on over the red marks and covered up with powder. A face dried so tightly that it might break. Why, she could hardly move it.

He liked old, torn-up skirts and dresses with some wiggle room, and Paulette, she liked them too. It was where they met, inside the frayed, tropical barkcloth and the tattered hems that had seen much better days. He took pictures of her in those dresses, posed her in jackets of black velvet and sequined teal, and on weekends they strolled the boardwalk together arm in arm, ate spinach-filled omelets with yellow cheese in dives beside the murky Venice canals, rode the merry-go-round on the Santa Monica pier. He made her his canvas, put bright purple gloss on her lips and told her that melancholy suited her quite well. "Whatever you say."

The relationship ended finally when Paulette went to his house in the late afternoon, light fading and the fog rolling in, and he and the actress were there naked in his brass bed and they invited her to join them. Paulette wore a black and creamy white cotton dress from the early '50s that looked French and chic with a very fine drape, though must have been unlucky, with vines climbing up the full circle skirt and a sweetheart neckline that tied into a droopy bow at the middle. Vines on barbed wire.

She'd pulled it from a junk basket outside Muskrat on Third Street in

Santa Monica, unable to ignore the pungent smell of urine, just near the doomed Newberry's where she often loved to see her reflection beside the mannequins in the old storefront windows. As mirrors go, this one was kindlier than most. She had friends in the windows, lifeless and frozen as she.

Sleeveless, side zipper, cut small at the waist, the dress seemed to Paulette just the perfect size. She tried it on right there in the shop, did not even close up the curtain. Five bucks it was, and full of tiny holes that she rushed home to sew with a needle and some black thread. With that same needle she sometimes made crosses in her skin, like stitched embroidery. A quick, orderly fix, and then relief, the kind a drunk has making the wall a toilet. Well, not only a drunk. She never means to go for an artery, though, just something red that trickles and can be pissed away.

She could not blame him really, the photographer, since she thought herself an 18-year-old nobody who couldn't even hold her gin. She tried though. At least she was thin, now. At least she was able to keep down most of her food, since she ate almost nothing of substance. Carrots, celery, cottage cheese, the three Cs. The photographer was a vegetarian, ate roots and sprouts and seeds, that sort of thing. And he preferred very young girls. The actress, she had a pixie cut that reminded Paulette of Mia Farrow. Clear skin and ocean-blue eyes on a round white face. A face that was famous. Somebody. Jealousy, oh, it had run her blood biting as a winter storm, a nor'easter. She stared into the future with a blank expression and thought the world horribly cruel. "Oh, you'll get over it," her mother told her. "Plenty of fish in the sea." Seriously?

She began counting the days left in L.A., dying for a bit of fun. It dragged on and on slow and sometimes, often really, she wanted to hear herself scream. Rising expectations, faster than the dam can release the lake water into the river. Building up, threatening to burst. Hold on, hold on, she had to tell herself, packing up to go two weeks early, tailoring a transition, cutting into her wrist, letting the blood go by way of the river. With barely enough calories to support her hormones, she did not have her period for what seemed like months. Her arms were like twigs on a dying tree.

Finally the moment in late summer arrives and she is eager to board the eastbound train in the downtown L.A. station on a Saturday afternoon. She has got an upper berth that promises to be cozy enough, with a garment rack, a fold-down table and fresh towels. And she'd heard the dining car served a terrific consommé that she would invite in, keep down. The ticket was a graduation gift from her grandparents, one she could use to travel the country and arrive back east in time for school to begin come early fall. She would see the backyards of America, the clotheslines and trash heaps and the discarded, dismantled cars. She would see the hopeful sunrises and the weary sunsets, be inside of the locomotive's air horn as it whistles the warning, play Solitaire through it all.

As fate would have it, she is wearing that same unlucky dress she had on when she left the photographer's house, seething in panic for the very last time. Pulled the anchor up and sailed into the strong counterclockwise winds, spiraling hot to cold. Since the dress, without a label, without a size, was most likely home-sewn with some vivacity, from fabric sold only by the panel and not by the yardage. Since the creeping plant border, it was designed exactly for the shape of the dress in the polished-up ebony and ivory of piano keys from the 1930s, before they became plastic. Since Paulette has stopped growing like a weed and is just now on the verge of flowering—well, fate would have it no other way.

Can dresses really be unlucky? she wonders, maybe for the very first time. When she put the thing over her head that morning, she was ready to test it. It hung so playfully that perhaps she'd be fooled by it. Had black sandals with cream stitching on the edges to match, and a necklace of jet that could be wrapped twice around her neck and still hang down long. Only a little yellowed by age, she, the dress, though not impervious to the moisture and body oil, to the wear and tear of the times.

There's a boy in eastern Canada she is hoping to meet up with, one with whom she has been exchanging letters since she was 13. Well, he must be a beautiful young man by now, she imagines, a designer of bridal gowns though secretly a bard. She'd met him in an Alaska campground during a family vacation on one of the longest days she'd ever known. They'd walked together upon the railroad tracks and put pennies down for the trains to flatten. They became pen pals there and then, sent the coins back and forth over the years. One flat penny in crucifixion; five when the eagle spread wings. He refused to call her Paula, as her sisters did, and her mother. It was Paulette, full and grand.

From the same charismatic city as Leonard Cohen, she remembers with a start, wishing that some of it rubbed off on her correspondent. From the same country as Margaret Atwood and Neil Young and Gilles Vigneault, a safe haven for those of consciousness who avoided the U.S. draft, objecting to the war in Vietnam, oh, she found lots of nourishment in his clever, literary style. He was not present, not as the photographer had been present, but he was not exactly absent either. A force, drawing her like a filled-up piggy bank on a rainy day. She is not sure if she is stupid or smart, but it did not seem to matter much. She is on her way from doing nothing, to doing something, learning to trust herself, as it happens.

She waves goodbye to her family and all the fuss over little and big things too and hello to her autonomy. It seems overwhelming, huge, palpable, a lump when she swallows. They'd all just had lunch together at Philippe's, across the street from Union Station and a block over from Olvera Street. That French dip she'd eaten, that messy lamb double-dipped with spicy brown mustard and blue cheese and hints of liberty, it fortified Paulette, had her eyes watering and her whole being thirsty for lemonade. She ate it like she hadn't eaten in years, consumed it heartily, every little bit. It came with no sides of remorse or judgment, no asking for two to become three, no choosing her over she. And she would keep it close by like an amulet, including the perfectly baked apple with cinnamon for dessert. Her father loved it there in the sawdust; it was a family tradition she was fond of, like the occasional Sunday Dodger games and the twice-yearly visits to the zoo, and despite the steeping sovereignty, it made her a little gloomy, knowing she was leaving and it would carry on without her. She hid it, though, the way the horseradish inside that mustard hid itself. Shine it on. She made herself good at that.

Determined and brave, though she hardly sees herself that way, she's driven to become solo, to change directions and run counter to the flow. She'd thrown her friends aside when things became shaky with the photographer, wanting to share none of it when eyebrows got raised. Fortunately, they will come around again, the ones who really matter anyway. Oh well, everybody's got their own trials. No, she did not feel unlucky at all. Just unreal. She wonders if the ones with firmly fixed plans feel just as illusory, just as lost. Schedules and timeclocks and 9-5s and uniforms, it did not seem safe at all to Paulette, while reliability, it sure had its plusses. Her sweaty hand grabs for the railing, and the dress of vines and tiny flowers moves up the steps swinging wildly into the hissing, squealing train with her inside it the way a poem is inside a book of longing.

She finds her place on the left side of the train that is punctual today and nearly always, and peers out the open window to see her mother and father looking sad, the both of them. She prefers to think it is real sadness, rather than something else like duty, or even relief, as she'd heard that some parents were celebrating their own freedom. Her father, why, he never cried. Not even when he left the house and moved into a hotel by the sea. He only came running home when in a salty voice she'd called her mother a bitch, since her mother she wanted him to be the one to handle things. Or so goes that childhood hallucination. Her grandmother is in the arms of her grandfather and the both of them are beaming with pride. Paulette leaving, her going off to develop some knowhow, it has swelled them like a broken ankle that is in the midst of healing. It will only grow back stronger.

Her sisters are blowing kisses, hurling their bodies with exploding laughter and devotion. They looked up to her but she looked down on herself; she did not make being their older sister easy. They had not known a day without her and had no idea how quiet the house would soon become. No more blaring Led Zeppelin, no more Saturday night histrionics about this boy and that, no more hogging the kitchen phone until way past their bedtimes; hogging the TV and the bathroom mirror too. They learned as much from her whispered secrets about hypocrisy, hate and privilege as they did at school, why at times even more, the math and science notwithstanding. "Paula," they squeal, "write us, and send pictures!" Their father tells them both to shush.

"Check you later," she says to her family, her spunky tone carrying across the murmurs of those gathered to say goodbye, waving a hand held high. Long skinny fingers, the kind ideal for the virtuoso piano, even though that too would soon become history, they flutter with anxiety. Her knees shake with it too.

A dry, burning wind comes through the window, so intense that the glass seems undulating and it creates a sort of panic. Paulette's heart pounds fast, up near her throat. She can still taste the horseradish hidden in that mustard. Red-hot and glowing all around like fire, the air, with fear a strong kindling. Sometimes it stops her dead in her tracks, but not today. Today the plant border on her dress magically transforms from cream to green. It will wither in fall, surely, but flourish this summer, wrap around the fences that enclose it and then out and beyond wherever it will. Chills move across her shoulders and down her spine, animate the dress with electricity and it stands out full as a parachute.

One final glance back, she thinks, frantically finding her father in the crowd. His head is bowed into something other than prayer. She can see the sunlight flashing down on the bald spot in the middle of his greying brown hair that, when he needed a haircut, fell in tiny curls. She had hated him, and loved him and hated him again. There was never anything much in between. His teeth were as perfect as his good driving record. Even his curls were just so hereditary. It stings to let go, yet it stings way worse not to.

Two houses, two neighborhoods, two best friends, two dogs, two sisters, two parents, two sets of grandparents, a quite stable and balanced serialized sort of snap, crackle and pop upbringing, and she is leaving it all there at Union Station as though it is a naïve, useless cliché of a cradle. Oh well, she is after the *cric*, *crac* and *croc*, the *piff*, *paff* and *puff*, with a spirit that seems unable to let her rest until she extracts it, the thrust being so forward now. Not even her mother could halt it now, but Christ almighty she would totally like to, hard as it's actually been. Well, not totally. She lights a cigarette, her mother, inhales deep then exhales vehemently upward; smoke signals.

Beside Paulette are passengers standing in the aisle single file; some sway blissfully, obliviously to "Take a Letter, Maria," warbling over the audio; some smile politely as they search around for their seats, not very anxious at all to sit in them though; others look sadly at the floor, crying softly into tissues, and some wave to loved ones outside as the train moves slowly, mournfully, creaking down the rails. It will all look quite different when Paulette returns, will not seem so much like a yawn as it stretches away on both sides into avenues lined with skyscrapers and red brick offices and heavy traffic going in every direction with the blast of a steam trumpet, but this here's surely a five, flat-penny day. Boo-yah! She double-checks her ticket with her near-perfect eyesight and rustles up the folds of her dress behind so that she can finally sit down, like a lady.

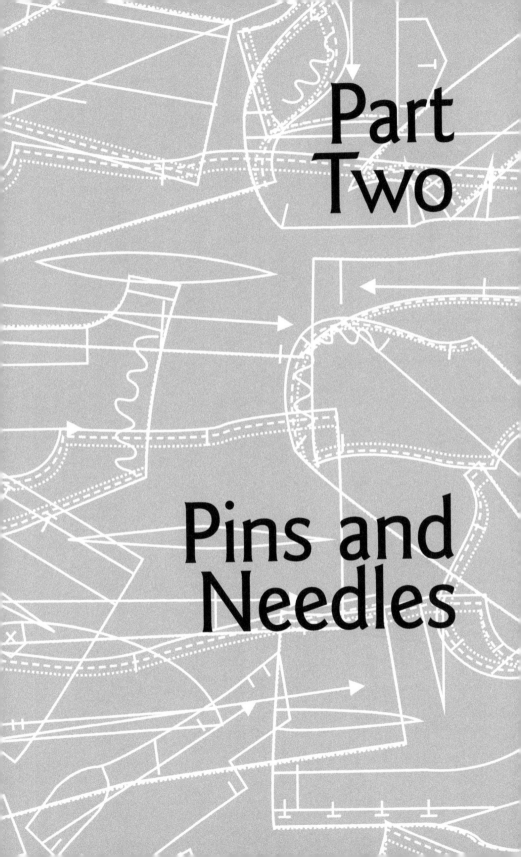

Part Two

Pins and Needles

5.

‑ ‑ ‑ ‑ ‑ ‑ ‑ ‑ ‑ ‑ ‑ ‑ ‑ ‑

‑‑

The Suzie Wong

While examining something of fashion's interdisciplinary history, Paulette quickly finds a haven among the social gypsies of London's Bloomsbury group in the '20s and New York's beats in the '60s. Four decades apart, these daring pioneers threw away the manuals and defiantly challenged the swatches of the status quo. It is the tyranny of bland popular taste—the blatant urge to spend time, money and energy keeping up appearances—that chokes Paulette to the point of exhaustion. It is the Chrysler LeBaron and the Loubella stretch pants and the beige nylon pile carpet and the reproduction Greek artifacts, the Navajo ones too, the ranch houses and the Spanish Colonial Revivals and the Taco Bell on Friday nights of where she'd come from. It seemed to her all so sanitized, so soulless and so senseless. Well, the pageboy and the perming did anyway, though not the punk. If only she'd grown up more authentically in Europe,

Paulette muses; Italy, or Portugal, although she'd still never been.

Yet fabric, well, it is a swathe and drape to cover up tastefully with beauty what is battered and dismal and depressed. What is to Paulette mostly humdrum—veins, flab, pimples, bruises, cellulite, scars. What is New World beige; she'd modify every single bit of it and herself if only she could, especially the aesthetic void, especially her thighs. With its pigment and its fold, the texture and nap of fabric can become multisensory the way perfume oil lingers across time and space and can reek of ancient Rome or even Bulgaria, vanquishing any stink around it and invoking visions, some made up, some genuine. A thousand-year-old tapestry from Guatemala can hide away in its vast layers every whiff of Spanish violence to salvage itself and leave in the withered old indigenous finery merely grace, merely splendor. It is the real mystery on a nude beach, the gauzy layers upon the body before they come off, that cleverly instigate the eyes and the skin and the hair the way a sacred silk thangka instigates the heart. Oh, forget that Gernreich monokini—it's those '40s-style ruched jersey one-piece bathing suits that send such a seductive message, show nothing but expose absolutely everything, yet do it in plum or in periwinkle or in pea. Elasticized shirring binds it all with *ooh la la*. Cloth can be for curves quite the way that blush is for cheeks. One can go without, sure, *au naturel*, Paulette imagines, but she'd look dull and pale by comparison. Even slimy polyester, which had for years been growing in use like weeds, has its charms. Nearly made ironing obsolete, and ironing, how it slows a girl down.

Inspired somewhat by FIT alum Norma Kamali's iconic parachute garments of billowy silk and nylon that drape for days, Paulette tears apart old sweatshirts from the Gap, lays the pieces together as dresses, mixing velvets and brocades full of age with voluminous soft cottons of turquoise, orange and black turned inside out, adjusted to fit with drawstrings. Bedspreads of tropical flowers made in India from Pier 1 mixed with yards of burlap become raggedy jewel-toned saris threaded with elastic at the bust to wear with fishnets and boots and drag in the mud. White T-shirts, a youth size 12, become sexy backdrops of amethyst and khaki tie-dye that she lets go random and edges with crystals. Hems of vintage tablecloth circle skirts mixed with mud cloth get cut with pinking shears and left frayed. Why, she hardly uses any proper sewing skills at all.

She studies with intention Duncan Grant and Vanessa Bell and the cushions and the curtains and rugs that began as play with dogs, as movers' blankets, as maps for underground wartime spies, as artists' canvases. She finds irresistible the bizarre, the theatrical and the glittery, the idea that everything and anything goes, that tolerance, like art, is a way of life, much to the dismay of a few of her stiff-backed FIT teachers who love to keep things proprietary and segregated. Oh, who cares what they think? If she wants to try soaking a gaudy orange print in tea, well, why not? In London they are using Kool-Aid to dye hair. Why not use it on T-shirts too, she thinks, and on tights with holes and runs in them, for after all, isn't college the time and place to indulge this willingness to see what will happen if?

"Paulette, my dear, you are seriously lacking meticulousness," a design teacher is saying, wagging his finger at her the way her father does. "In order to break the conventions, you must first know them from memory. They become force of habit, unconscious, like tying a bow."

While she was not inclined to speak up, she did so when he'd mentioned Elvis Presley and the Beatles wearing Dacron, and the chemistry of dressing with some tolerable discomfort. "It just does not breathe," she'd said, "even if it lives." Wrinkles are verses, she told herself, subject to shrinking and stretching and stains, the marks of existence, imperfect as it may be.

"Those otherworldly oranges in Paul's shirt, well, they have got a very distinct formula, you know," the teacher answered glibly, smirking. "Miracles cannot just happen," he'd assured her and everyone else in the class, shaking his head. "Dig?"

"Well, what about carelessness," she asks, quietly, under her breath, "what about carefree, shouldn't that take precedence over expertise? It is inexhaustible, after all, unlike the controlled precision of a machine." She gets a little dizzy from her fear of being wrong and laughed at. "Doesn't expertise come way later, after innovation? After the free hand?" She focuses her eyes on the ceiling to stop her head from spinning.

"Gad, when you study the Omega Workshops in the early 1900s, you will find that most of the art was not well made," he says, his finger no longer wagging, but with that same threatening sentiment in his voice. "In other words, crap," he says smugly. "Oh, for art's sake, hah!"

Her classmates giggle, though not at her, and raise their mostly plucked eyebrows at this persistent clash between what is serious art and arbitrary high fashion, and what is cheap imitation trendy, though noteworthy nonetheless. Most of the girls in class wear long, straight hair like a uniform. A couple dressed them to one side, often in ponytails. Paulette's shaggy mane was becoming shorter and more spiked by the day. Nothing too androgynous, though.

There is original bohemian style, and then there is the less genuine interpretation, like him, Paulette thinks, looking carefully at her teacher's black wool suit and taut white dress shirt that seems completely lacking originality. Even his black shoes are polished of all their untidy life. She listens to the subtle sound of his accent and thinks that he might be British, or German, but she doesn't dare ask. She tries to decide whether his smile is malicious, or professional, or both. She wonders, what kind of fellow calls a vivacious artistic experiment "crap"?

Outside glass doors that slide onto a small tiled balcony strewn with potted plants, she sees window washers on scaffolding, three of them, 20 floors up a massive high-rise. Rebellious as she is, well, she could never do that. The height is quite beyond her risk-taking abilities. It is worth aspiring to, she tells herself, this fearlessness. The wooden scaffolding has a kind of beauty in its meticulousness. Yes, she imagines, it is good for that. Do what you are told and do it right, to the letter, and those men, they will be safe. Yes, useful for that, she thinks, barely conscious of the lecture on the Cubist and Fauvist influences on textile design. She only perks up when she hears about the Maud linen of the dressmaker that cushions the chair in a painting by Roger Fry.

She pulls at the hand-stitched hem on the mustard silk lining of her heavy cotton dress, a bit shorter than she typically likes, a bit tighter too, remembering all the Brits and Germans she'd met in Montréal when she visited over the summer, after the pen pal became Dylan and Dylan became doubtful. Vastly different than the French and Spanish. It is the slick and perfect finish versus the dust and disorder, the sausages versus the runny Brie. She'd had a German lover there, the first boy she'd ever seen uncircumcised. It shocked her, though she hid it well enough, when she pulled the pulsing thing rock hard from his teeny Speedos, the way it seemed to outgrow its sheath. Tall and blond, he was wildly romantic, in a disinterested way, a tidy boy with a clean-shaven face for whom less was more. And for Paulette, who much prefers the filthy and the unkempt, undefined yet as she is still, less is never more.

With a print of tiny boxes in curved rows colored wine and olive and black and mustard like a visual illusion, the dress was handmade for a '50s woman in the slender and form-fitting '20s style of a Chinese cheongsam. Once upon a time baggy and concealing as the qipao, disguising age and body type, it leaped out high-collared and side-slit and sexy and silky red from the '60s film *The World of Suzie Wong*, starring William Holden. Well, it made Nancy Kwan an international star. Hardly aware of the East-West thing, Paulette wears her cheongsam in the fall with beat-up old chocolate boots and black lace stockings that barely show themselves. Slits, modest ones, are on both sides of the dress. The teacher asks Paulette about the dress from across the classroom, diverting from his discussion of the false rifts between the decorative and fine arts, and she lowers her eyes coyly, fiddles with the hem, trimmed in the same dark red piping of the short cap sleeves and high buttoned neck. "You know popular culture," she says, "how it hijacks everything." The dark wood chair creaks when she shifts her weight. Embarrassing, she thinks, hoping her face is not altogether flushed like a raspberry.

She's gotten a few B's on class assignments, even a couple A's, and it has given her some vertebrae. She'd had just a little to begin with, but it swings to and fro. Guts, grits, gumption—if you could find a way to bottle it as they cleverly did Lemon Up, then everyone under 20 would be buying shinier, brighter. Juice of a real lemon in every cream rinse, babysitting money could not be better spent. If only an A could be as easy as the comb-through, and just as squeaky-clean.

In high school nothing much woke Paulette up except driver's ed, poetry and woodworking, and she barely said a word in her classes, smoking weed on the athletic field with the renegade boys whenever she could. School kept her busy, sure, but engaged her hardly at all. She'd read some unforgettable books, *Lord of the Flies*, *To Kill a Mockingbird* and *Animal Farm*, but that was her fault, not theirs, since many students cheated, scarcely read a page and passed anyway. She took copious notes in colored pens, committed facts to memory using 3-by-5 cards, learned to regurgitate them back, though not that well. More skill than real enthusiasm. She had become an imitator, filled in the blanks, found the missing word, grew into a user, not a creator. Had the answers but without the questions.

Now there is rhythm and movement to most everything, and imagination, a more genuine curve, and she is taking to it with a revivalist zeal. Every muscle in her being is flexed, now, fingered deeply in geometric style, almost to the point of orgasm and she wanted more more more. Vorticism, the Rebel Art Centre, Ezra Pound.

"Since everything has already been done, is ready-made," Paulette goes on, "all the books written, all the art expressed, the songs sung, no new ideas, nothing dynamic really, then we are no more than a band of plunderers." A couple of students nearby grin nervously, boys both, wondering most likely what they are even doing there in the first place, when their parents really wanted them to become accountants, CPAs if you want to know the truth. Oh, how it aches deep to be the keeper of a lyric yet generated, feeling the root of it, the sense of it, way back and strong as the hair in a twisted Navajo chongo. Done, then done again, oblong, like an éclair.

The teacher, left hand on his ashy cheek, he appears to be pondering and he sure seems to know about plenty, is razor-sharp in fact. He slips in and out of lateral notions that design might be traced to what the sofa wears, to that Eastern inspiration where chairs have never been preferred seating, adding some dimension to his perspective, some lighted candles and some chanting music, and this makes Paulette feel a certain fondness for him. Digression can be transformative, in all sorts of ways, like the nude painting that became an abstract mud bath. Wondering if he might be high on something as he speaks so effervescently about the *Ballets Russes*, Paulette sinks deeper into the classroom. His classroom. Odd, how a teacher's vigorous grasp of a subject can mean everything. Pink stripes, velvet scarves, flakes of gold, Max Ernst and Joan Miró collaborating.

"We have to poke around in corners where 'buy me, see me, watch me' is not written all over." In dark corners, he says, frantically pacing. "There are things that insist on being expressed, no matter how strange or difficult it might be. When the Shanghainese let go of the Suzie Wong, after the Communist Revolution, remember, it gave the traditional Chinese women modern, Westernized design options for party or uniform, for high class and low." Fusion, he says, and freedom from male control over female sexuality, "with that revealing slit."

Paulette raises her hand and waves it around but does not wait to be called on, as her teacher is standing by the window peering outside at a couple of planes flying much too closely to each other. "I have seen little girls wear them as Halloween costumes," she says warily, hoping she'd found a dark corner, pulling her dress, a West Hollywood garage-sale find for next to nothing, down further over her knees, fixing the slits closed, first one side, then the other, then back to the first side again. "That is the wholesale importation of the style, and not just the flavor."

When her classmates smile, and her teacher quickly turns around then nods, she no longer hides inside the dress, the small boxes in rows like tiles set so careful, then grouted by a mason at 1/16th of an inch. The tension leaves her body as her legs cross and she leans back calm in the chair. The slits on both sides of the dress open up for some fresh air. Relief feels like that a little, sets her loose.

She wonders if Betsey Johnson does a Suzie Wong for her Alley Cat line. It might be purple with red, she thinks, and long past the knee. Well, not long past. In Chinese silk brocade, with a keyhole at the neck, oh, if it must be current fashion, flavorful and respectful of the past, suited for a night at the bar in the Formosa Café, where Frank Sinatra pined for Ava Gardner over Mongolian beef, well then, simply add some long red glass beads and scruffy motorcycle boots. Well, not simply. Adding wasabi to mashed potatoes only seems effortless.

Living on campus in the dorms, everybody in her life now is just a little bit peculiar, just a little bit marginal, even the teacher, with his love, peace and nature-shagged hair, making the school and its vibe somewhat free-spirited, cool, at least part of the time. There is a lot more jam than medicine, in other words. When she is not cramming for essay tests and paying attention to fashion industry trends that revolve mostly around pricy department stores and the *haute couture*, she is reading Virginia Woolf, listening to Patti Smith and dancing to Lou Reed, getting drunk on whatever older men offer her and having random flings that always seem to turn out sad. The Chelsea Hotel isn't very far away, nor are the hip parties where nobody has a noble thought, and the crazy drugs that promised ecstasy yet delivered a lot less. She's tried them all, even horse shot by a stranger in the vein of her arm just for the warm and happy hell of it. Donut shops open 24 hours all over for the occasional binge-purge, yet.

Her period came back again, though it was only slight spotting at first and she hardly recognized it as blood. In the dorm bathrooms, she sometimes hears a girl heaving and it makes her even more content with what little contentment she actually feels. No crushes, though; pushing 20 now and not even a disappointing one. Honestly, she tells herself, if you can't have a steady boy, well, you might as well have a great dress. Sometimes she wonders if she even likes boys at all, since many of them seem to her like beasts. Yet girls at this age are competitive and cagey and hardly any better. When she speaks to her mother on the phone, the time is filled with small details. How much her sisters eat. What her mother takes for headaches. How many pages in *Dolores*, that skinny book about Jackie O by Jacqueline Susann. And small news items that mean nothing, really, to Paulette. Whose daughter got married. Who's moving to Cheviot Hills. How good-looking that boy actually grew and became, and how much money he inherited. Who started jogging around the neighborhood. Smaller and smaller talk. She wonders if her mother even notices it, the way it feels when she hangs up, as if there was nobody home.

Be it out of style, or in, as in the *Village Voice*, Paulette would like some intimacy, something personal, a way to make herself artful and useful, a bit of joy to come spilling out in the quiver and misregister and flaw of the hand-done, yet she really hasn't any idea how to go about finding it. The printed patterns of what's possible have nearly always been the same, at least for white American girls with a little beauty and a little breeding like her. She would do fine without the brains, her father told her, which was fortunate since her sisters got all those. Trying to find herself, Paulette goes to the alternative press, and to the *New York Times*, the action and reaction to the world and each other, seeking how best to Lemon Up, set one's own agenda, outside of the one she was encultured into. It is what she truly wants to know.

Sure, the rock star counterculture, it had opened things up some, but the dreadlocks of that revolution have lost a bit of their shock value. The peace signs, they were mass-mediated now, and saturated all around her, though nobody really seemed peaceful, least of all her. What shall one do in life to avoid becoming stagnant? Well, her father told her she can become a wife and a mother. If she played her cards right, her mother added, if she was lucky. PTA, mahjong, bridge, perked-coffee circles, cocktails shaken at 5, shopping sales at the Broadway. Such big, ill-fitting shoes to fill, size 8-and-a-half to her 7.

Birkenstocks? Why, they are just plain conventionality, an ersatz symbol of radical churned out in some mill. And for girly girls bent on backlash of that Jesus get-up, even plainer still. Like it or not, though, Paulette seems stuck on the hippie trail, and while she may feel desperately the need to stray, she cannot think to where, since the second-hand clothing she finds so utterly captivating is not merely an anti-consumerist statement.

And Paulette wouldn't want to wear a deliberately offensive DESTROY anything, nor S&M leather, rubber or vinyl, not ever, so why should it become a part of her professional toolbox? Not very soft at all, she notes, even though it is called New Romanticism.

Ripping your fishnets is one thing, even spotting your shirt with red dye to look like blood in the spirit of non-conformity is another, but swastikas, safety pins, razor blades and sharp studded jewelry, not now, not ever. Oh, maybe a diamond stud pierced into the side of her nose, one day, like an Indian girl.

Even as Vivienne Westwood tries so stylistically, so famously to make it so, anarchy, while a protest of privilege and injustice which Paulette is all for, it is not really all that pretty. And for Paulette, pretty bleaches everything like the early afternoon sun, and is just as vital, just as rad, flowers the blooms in the garden and the dandelions as well.

In the midst as she is now of many creative, authentic and honest souls, all seeking to express something new and provocative, to push things, to generate discourse in areas where there had previously been none, Paulette is hardly as lonely as she'd once been in high school, where she was the elective and not the requirement, the African American spoken word and not the English lit. There is music on the NYC streets all around her, jazz and disco, salsa and reggae, and a theatrical vibrancy of humanity that she had never known before in Los Angeles, Venice Beach on weekends being the only clear exception that she could think of.

The boundaries between art and life are blurred some now, with free-dom flowing as never before from one minute to the next, the deli pastrami sandwich and the pickle green are side by side on the very same purple plate, and the skin on her forearms, it is almost healed up, for now at any rate. The scars, they are tiny as jute macramé, and she covers them up with old rhinestone bracelets, five or six on her right hand, two or three on her left, mostly all shiny black, mostly all '40s Weiss. Their quality is so first-rate that the stones remain intact, despite the dozens of years.

She can wear these shorter sleeves again, and proudly take her boxy velvet jacket off to show herself fully. Yet off it goes slowly, carefully, almost ritualistically, since aged velvet smells so splendid and all, so exquisitely civilized, and even with a slight tear in the satin lining and some yellowed water spots, the black wrap has always been a sleek, silky cocoon, the stuff of butterfly dreams, actually.

6.

------- -- -- -- -- -- -- -- -- -- -- -- -- -- --

Dead Stock

Here's the real skinny: vanity sizing in America took the '50s dress size 12,
the perfectly acceptable and nearly enviable 30-25-33, and with a pop-top
of the fingertips, transmuted the metrics into a 6 by the late '70s, the 33-
25-35. At least that is the way some in the know convert the measurement.
Heartless standards for those not built like Marilyn's voluptuous 36-24-37,
at any rate. Paulette tries not to care much about the number or letter on
the ticket and how those labels can cart the lie, so long as there is room for
the swathing. She cared plenty before discovering vintage though, would
not try on an M for the life of her, stretched the S to its very threadbare
and bursting seams. Old clothing figures to have been assembled with it,
that opportunity for the curvy, that natural M, that easy 8, and the new
apparel figures not. Might be that women in the '50s were some 20 pounds
lighter, Paulette thinks, though they did not necessarily wear a smaller

size. Might be that the times were more generous for the females of the male imagination, despite the thrift and frugality, that zero was not the magnitude number used to quantify the size of a woman. Girls back then wore girdles and they wore waist-cinchers and padded bras though, Paulette muses, so when polyester came along in 1951 they could hardly even feel it.

So much deception today, Paulette thinks, so much pressure preaching around her to be thin, the white models who wear XS and the magazines, newspapers and window signs idolizing them, promoting them and their hungry beauty all over the world. Fictionalizing it such that it became a shoe without a sole that just about everybody wanted to wear, including her. Even the designers participate in this charade, relabeling large sizes, making them play smaller. No relation at all to satiety. In the midst of the new fast-food burgers and fries, she is famished nearly all the time, but eats so little again and sometimes feels faint because of it. Though as with certain foods, she forbid herself even a peek into the magazines and stopped staring at the clothing in the windows of the department stores along the streets where she walks, she does not ever forget for a moment that the fashion system expresses beauty as thin. And thin she is not. There is the rounded derrière; there are the puffy cheeks, the jutting thighs. If she eats anything unyielding at all, thin she is naturally not. She is looking for some dead stock, dresses that were designed and unsold in purer days, packed away in basements and attics that do not know this kind of burden, hoping that somehow it might rub off. Light-headed and full of angularities, she is tormented by nothing and everything, depending on the day. Depending on the hour. Her sterling silver seed pearl-studded mood ring that she'd got from an aunt for her high school graduation couldn't even keep up.

One of the keener glass-closeted teachers at FIT got word and pointed

Paulette in the direction of a place in Brooklyn, just off the Nassau Avenue G-train, where everything is arranged and organized by color and delightful to witness, he'd told her. "Well-curated," he'd said, "and primo, just gobs of it." They use vintage clothing pickers who scour the countryside, finding overstocks and seconds that luckily never made it to the sales floors. "Do me a solid, darling, and tell 'em I sent you."

"Gee whiz," she'd said, thanking him, feeling a kind of kindred spirit right there in the dim, narrow hallway. It happened a lot with vintage, a connection that is like moonlight on a dark night. Bar talk is fleeting by comparison. It ends when the glass is empty. Vintage is a more lasting heart-to-heart. Money needn't even change hands when ageless beauty bats its French or British or Spanish eyelashes. Broke as a tatty lamp almost always, but psyched nonetheless, she'd figure something out, find a way to shine. Skip a manicure, a meal, eat Danish cheese, nuts and apples, smoke a few less cigarettes. She'd cut down substantially already; a pack every three days now instead of two.

Paulette takes the train east, then southbound on the teacher's leg-up, walks a few minutes outside in the mid-afternoon cold that's only just bearable. Cigarette in hand, she's wearing massively flared high-waist jeans and a butterscotch button-up cashmere cardigan that had been eaten by moths and then hastily mended. That, layered over a midnight blue leotard, sleeveless with a turtleneck, sans the bra, still. As she prefers not to be so entirely covered and formless, her navy pea coat's thrown over her elbow. Twenty-one now, she just might stop somewhere later in Greenpoint for a beer. Only the one though, since she did not want the empty calories or to spend the moolah. She'd been drinking scotch and gin for years, thanks to a fake ID. That she is finally of age, why, the thrill is gone. But there are other thrills. Being far away from the catwalks and nearer the 5 and 10 Dee & Dee variety is one of them. The idea of a new old thing is another.

It is a riot of hues, Paulette thinks as she enters the shop, attracted right off to the black section on a chock-full rounder that's topped by gobs of purses and shoes, with a pineapple cookie jar in the center. Funny how she wants to stroke with both her hands each garment, its collar and shoulder pads, the nubs of its fabric, its glass buttons, its darts and pintucks. It is therapeutic in a way, like a tonic, and the time just stops like the old watch her grandfather had given her when she left L.A. She has to consciously wind it up, and then rewind or else it is useless, a men's Hamilton. *How did her grandfather ever remember?* she wonders, since she hardly does.

A sales assistant with a helium voice asks her more than once if he might help her find what she is after, but she does not look away from the rack and barely hears a word of it. The music consumes her too. It is AB-BA's "Take a Chance on Me." She runs her hand through her messy hair, now feathered some, and like badass Peggy Lipton, a dirtier, ashier blonde.

"Rumor has it on the streets around FIT that you got some excellent dead stock here?" Paulette finally says to the guy hovering from somewhere just outside her haze. She pulls out a hanger with a sleeveless black and cream rayon print dress on it that looks as solemn as the women's rights movement. It's a bit blousy in the middle, with a thick yet tighter dropped-waistband that gives way to a long, knife-pleated skirt, and with a low Peter Pan collar. At the center of that collar is an Art Deco dress clip with rhinestones. She drops her purse and coat down on the floor and holds the dress up to her in front of the wall mirror.

It is a friendly enough reflection, but there is a matronly flash to the thing so she decides against trying it on. Kind of '20s, she thinks, a straight-line chemise, returning it tenderly to the rack. Stunning diamond print though, she admits, and that shiny clip, a delightful distraction. Yet the '20s, she thinks, too much Depression ideology and the sisterhood that comes along with it. Pushing her way through the gloom and doom inside, she is. "Dead stock, as opposed to livestock," she says, hoping to make him chuckle and herself too.

The sales assistant is tall and lithe, has sulky red hair with a Brylcreem shine, wears a skinny grey tie, ruby Converse high-tops and rolled-up Levi's. He's gay, obviously so, and looking right into her eyes through his green Jackie O glasses with very dense lenses. His long thick eyelashes captivate her, grab her attention, rewind the watch. She knew quite a few of them, a strong out gay community, now that she was studying fashion. Drawn to it just like her, and maybe for some of the same reasons, the flamboyant do-ups, the glamorous powder and paint, the high-camp drama, that craving to self-construct. In high school, had there been even just one groovy guy, well, she might have reached out and been less isolated, might have gone to Ginger Rogers Beach with some drag queens and felt much better about things.

"Rare breeds? Yes, we certainly do," he says warmly, "many with the original tags still hanging from them." He reminds her of someone she'd met once though she can't place it. It gnaws at her. There's his David Bowie edge, she thinks, but it isn't just that. He wanders around the shop, quickly pulling dresses from the various racks as though he'd memorized every single one of them, and flopping each fondly over his arm. "Designers want 'em, for prompting," he tells her. "And the wacky thing is, no two pieces are exactly alike."

She stops perusing the black dresses and suddenly feels the need for a smoke, digging into her purse to find her cigarette case. What he says stuns her, makes her tipsy down to her toes, like a beer. In a world where mass taste and manners make up the seat of power, there is much wearisome sameness. It is the Farrah Fawcett layering of every young girl's hair, the Tupperware parties, the McDonald's arches and the packaged exotic holidays abroad. Here is a place that has almost no duplications. Like craftsmanship, like artist's lofts, like unwired music, it is a concept seriously under threat. At least here in New York City, John Lennon and Andy Warhol stroll the streets.

"Back in a flash," she tells the guy, leaving her coat and purse right there on the floor, and she goes outside, lights up, leans against the red brick wall. It is a kind of mecca, this place, Flora's Flea, named for its owner who came from Texas to be off-off-off-Broadway. Flora was better at costuming than she was at acting, so she created a shop dedicated to those wanting to live outside the capricious, hyped-up fashion cycle. And she is serious about her buy, sell, trade merchandise. Paulette thinks that she is serious about her employees too, since this guy has got about a dozen dresses over his arm, and through the shop window she can see him gently hanging them up one at a time on the wrought-iron hook outside the changing area, where curtains of pink taffeta waft like skirts in a breeze. He twinkles at each and every one. Doing what he loves and loving what he does—the greed of the era is having nothing to do with it.

A mecca of sorts for those like Paulette who cannot sew well enough and without a pattern, nor find such gracefully old fabrics and who are vaguely dissatisfied with a life increasingly characterized by how one consumes. For her, it is quite like a record shop, where inspirations and impulses with tones dally as a burning incense hangs in the air. Permeates the senses, every single one of them, makes everything dance with energy, so much so that it radiates outward toward strangers who might instantly become acquaintances, the interlude being so cozy, so welcoming and all.

Bookstores, art galleries, small cafés in storefronts that brew coffee and tea blended with ethics and empathy, they are her lifeblood, her American dream. And awareness of this surprises her, and for a brief moment comforts her, though she does not want to be defined by blood and dreams either, since becoming tiresome, becoming something that can be assigned, oh, this frightens her more than almost anything. And while she is encouraged to buy everything, everywhere, she does not find much gratification in the ethos of goods and gadgets. Their buzz is brief and from what Paulette has taken in school through her classes, she is nearly hip to it. Very nearly, as the edge of a cliff.

She steps on her cigarette butt, rubs it into the pavement, pushes it off the edge of the curb with her foot into the gutter. She marvels at the effect this place has on her, how it calms her. The candle shop in Idyllwild used to do the same, she thinks, remembering some of the palm wax scents, the flickering cinnamon and the pumpkin and the backwoods cider. For a split second she is quite homesick, and deeply lonely, and ravenous, overwhelmed by it in fact, missing sharply her sisters and her mother, mostly, and her father too, but it goes fast as it came. Stings like a vaccination. Ouch.

Fighting the urge to stop and look closely at the racks of yellows and greens, to caress each and every chic garment, to spend hours that she does not have, not really, she picks up her paraphernalia and then heads straight to the dressing room, passing an open door to the back stockroom area. On the purple doorframe is handwritten vertically in gold: "where the margins fade forever."

Wow, she thinks, remembering the way the Charleston artists painted their houses, with even the floorboards becoming the colors of jewels, stamping themselves and their personalities every which way they could. More ABBA, this time "Thank You for the Music." Must be the whole album, Paulette reasons. Well, she likes it okay, catchy, upbeat and Euro as it is, though some friends sure make fun of her for it. Got quite used to being ridiculed and found it tough to develop herself and frank interests with all that. Some criticize you no matter what you do so you might as well like what you want. Thank you for the music, she mutters under her breath.

Another customer enters the shop, ringing the bell, a dark-skinned girl about her age with finger-wavy hair asking for something in the way of a '40s suit. Padded shoulders, boxy cut, sleeves just below the elbow, a militant, masculine look. "After the war, during, or before?" the guy asks, grinning, showing himself to be quite a scholarly resource. "I'm kinda petite," she answers, "and I have a thing about undyed, so I'd say during." For some rationing was limiting, even depressing, turned things slimmer and more grey, Paulette supposes, and yet for others, a far better measure and cue.

While the guy pulls '40s suits from a lean rounder, the petite girl wanders the area close to Paulette, picks out a dress that she herself had just passed up because she was sure it would not fit. Grey and white lacy print with a touch of black, it was perfect, but for the smaller size. Even had carved Bakelite buttons down the front and on the sleeves. She can wear it, Paulette thinks, smiling at the petite girl in a way that tries to be engaging, but isn't. "Pretty, no?" Paulette says to her, feeling somewhat territorial.

"Do you think it will look good on me?" the girl asks, eyeing the dress every which way. Yes, she did, unfortunately, Paulette thinks but does not say, sighing inward as the girl holds it up in front of her. The whites of the girl's eyes sparkle like pearls when the dress comes close to her body. "Like it was made for you," she sullenly concedes, in honor of that moonshine, walking away. Fifteen pounds thinner, at least, Paulette tells herself, her watch stopping again.

The dead stock the guy picked for Paulette, all sorts of colors and fabrics and styles, dresses ranging in eras from the '20s through the '60s, it hangs at the side of the small room, still, like in a photograph of some other time. She pauses to consider the split pea greens and the buttermilks and the pasty pinks that she cannot possibly take for granted, even if the photograph were in black and white. All are new in the sense that they have never been worn really, never been washed or cleaned and each has a tag on it somewhere making it the real McCoy. A few look smallish, since she is bloated some, would fit that petite girl, make her happy, but most seem as though she could wear them as is.

An oval rag rug of pinks and greens and flowers covers most of the wood floor as icing on a cupcake. When she takes off her boots, she feels it soft and gooey and she snaps out of her funk quick. There's an old chandelier inside with diffused white lights and she can see herself plainly in the near-neutral looking glass with birds and a palm tree in its corner. The pill fixed her hormones, made her skin mostly clear now; the red pock marks from her oily teenage years have now nearly disappeared, even from her T-zone. The imperfections left are covered up almost entirely in Max Factor's ultralucent face makeup. Pale pink as the birds, powdered as she is, and not even close to natural. The only thing breaking out at this moment is her utter sense of anticipation. It wants to spread wings out and fly.

"I bet I know the one you'll choose," the guy says, pushing his glasses up on his nose, close enough to her now that she can feel him breathing and smell his cumin and gardenia aftershave, "but I've been wrong before. So surprise me," he says with a shrug of his shoulders, winking, hanging five dresses inside the room and gradually closing up the curtain. "Name's George in case you need anything." He turns to go ring up that dress and a wool houndstooth suit with a cute little appliqué in the shape of arrows for the other customer.

If only she could buy them all, Paulette muses, looking carefully at the various necklines and the sleeves and the Deco prints the way a guitarist might look at instruments to pluck the very strings of his heart; or in the case of Bonnie Raitt, the strings of her honeyed heart. And yet, this challenge to pick only one, it is to be a honing and refining of her style. It will force her to decide just who she might like to be on the outside, and how that relates to her inside, in a fleeting impulse that can only be seized. Sure, she can try them all on, but why should she? Each shade alters her. Each silhouette too, malleable as she is yet. And honestly to be quicker about it, since she has homework, and sheets to wash, towels too, since she can only afford the one. To find the Gibson, the piece of equipment that can scream and shout.

Black, she senses instantly. It should almost always be rooted in black, like the vinyl of a record roots a song before it flies out over the airwaves and gets sung over and over again. And you can trace it back. Black, as opposed to white or cream or grey or even a beige backdrop, since it is solid and unyielding and predominant and honest as the night is long. Black, it grounds her the way a base coat and top coat on painted fingernails starts and finishes things up with a strengthening sheen. A print with lots of weaker white simply does not have the same sort of protection that lots of bolder black provides. Cracks, chips, breaks, bends back entirely even, manicure and all, on occasion.

Still wondering whom George reminds her of, she unzips the side of an early '40s black and white shirtwaister day dress with thick red lines on it in a slightly heavy puckered cotton. Rice pudding and sugar, she thinks of its texture, remembering the Hindu words from class, *"kheer aur shakkar."* The pucker is for ventilation, she'd learned about the seersucker, to hold the fabric away from the skin, for the heat of being alive. The label inside says Wildman Original, crease resistant, size 12. The price is $23, very reasonable for this part of town.

She notices the beautiful pintucking and the red plaid stripe against the small black-and-white chequered, the way it matches so well at the seams and changes into a diagonal at the pockets and at the collar, the way it pops out almost three-dimensional. And the little black buttons, they are like cut gems laid out in sets of twins. Jet, she supposes, French and faceted. Underneath the arm is the original tag, a yellowed cardboard piece on string pierced into the fabric, but the store and the price have both been lost to age. It looks like it might have come from I. Magnin, yet Paulette is merely guessing. The original Bermuda pink hang tag beside that, also cardboard, is quite discolored, though it still says clearly in black: "Another Wildman Original. Just Ask the Girl Who Wears One."

Ask the girl what? Paulette wonders, curious, noticing the old script lettering of the logo, the flourish to the company's name. She had never once thought to enter the soul of any girl, really, let alone her own. Was she oppressed? Objectified? Subservient? Silly? Stranded? Was she in some manner covered by creases? Did she feel huge? While the men were away at war and the lives of women were expanding outward from the kitchen, while there was Rosie the Riveter and all, Paulette is not too sure just what to ask, if really she could. Society's roles and expectations are inscribed into the design, yet that was the '40s and this here is the end of the '70s. Sure, the World Bank was created and capitalism straightened itself up, and there was now a Head Start, Job Corps, Medicare and Medicaid, feminism, black power, punk and plenty more on the planet and beyond had been vastly transformed in the race for space, but it did not show much in Paulette's house. The Domestic Violence Act made that no longer a private matter; Beverly Johnson even made the front cover of *Vogue* as the first black model, and yet the topics of abuse and race were kept safely outside with a double lock and chain on the massive wooden front doors. Even birth control was taboo there.

Unlike the archetypal Barbie, though, who stayed put in her sports car in the segregated suburbs and blended her cat-eye, Paulette was venturing out some, sensing a bit of the underbelly of society, though not exactly certain where that is just yet. She observes more now than ever the down and out and the ones seemingly with no choice, the ones looking desperately for fixes, the poor, the hopeless, the homeless, the suffering, the slums, the refugees, the people of color, the Indians, the Latinos. She experiences empathy, compassion, cultural dissonance. Barely aware of her privilege, she does not give her whiteness or heterosexuality a second thought. Yet second thoughts were creeping up on her, like black and Mexican gangs on L.A.'s orderly streets.

Paulette studies the seersucker dress as a girl who will masquerade in it. Not for shopping. Not for class. Not for a dark bar, or a dark cloud or a silver-lined temple even. Hardly scandalous though, prudent yet, neat and orderly, she decides, buttoning up the gorgeous beads and buckling it closed tight at her waist with a fallow belt of the same fabric. For some special moment that has not happened, that has still to find its story but surely will, she thinks, hopeful and a bit nostalgic, adjusting the straight and long, elegant line just barely over her rounded 36-inch hips. That it has never been worn to any first day on the job, not stereotyped by any activist nor by any bard, not by any sexpot nor by any internalized misogynist, and not by any housewife either, it is untainted historical text—hers alone to one day animate.

It will need a thin choker of jet beads to match the buttons, she thinks, examining herself sideways in the graceful old mottled flamingo mirror, and earrings that dangle some near the collar when she moves. Without any cleavage at all, defying the gender stereotypes, it has an elongated contour, fits closely from the shoulder on down, goes past her knee where it flows a bit wider at the hem. It can take a cotton slip and nearly-black stockings. It is crisp as a fresh baguette on a late-summer afternoon. Did she need it? Of course she did not, especially since October had come and gone. But bread is life, sometimes.

Abba's "Move On" is playing softly and Paulette finds irresistible the waltz in it, and the lyrics of it, "the restless body and the peaceful soul." Though ankle-straps are a must, and only black patent ones, yet maybe red wedgies, though they'd have to be blue-red and not with any orange, she puts back on her boots for some height so that the dress can thrive. Perk up and hang as alivestock, the way it was meant to with her gladly in it. She calls out happily to George. "Got any water?" she asks him, suddenly dry. Only coffee and a hard-boiled egg yet today, but she is firmly in the midst of working up an appetite.

"With gas, or without," he asks from across the shop where he is helping another young woman find herself a striped sample of the unknown, a yellow, black and blue dress wanting to wake up, or perhaps a hell bunny blouse raring to come around. "Oh, with, please," Paulette answers, thinking it must be an East Coast sort of luxury and basking in it, the fuss she could never imagine finding in a regular L.A. boutique or department store. She needs the sturdy advice of a boy yet and thankfully this one, an unlimited sort, he does not wear a tan or a heavy gold chain. "I could kiss you," she says to him, admiring her mirror image with clear eyes, for a moment. "I don't get many kisses from girls, so I will take it," George says as he moves toward her with a bottle of Pellegrino in his hand. She slides open the curtain, fully expecting that she'll surprise him the way he just did her. Feeling the dress with bumpy sugar yet smooth as milk tight around her hips, she dares not look down at her mood ring.

7.

Avoir Du Chien

"Staying in fashion, making it your essence and your livelihood, it might not be the best use of your brain." There, he said it straight to her face the way she had been yearning for. No interpretations. No missing the obvious. No anonymous testing that identifies your skills, your strengths and weaknesses. The best use of her brain. Why, her father made her feel as though she hadn't one. Such a relief to hear a fellow speak to her intelligence. It grabbed her and left her vulnerable, like a nibble and a gnaw on the back of her neck, from her hairline right on down to her collarbone. But what did he mean by it, she'd wondered in the very center of her left shoulder, this *sine qua non*? Quite the hickey, it was a suck like no other.

Males, well, they just seemed so oblivious to Paulette at near 23, so ill at ease, so lacking in wisdom, so disingenuous, so emotionally unavailable, so unable to read between the lines, the ones under 30 at any rate. They played their games, their roles, seemed frosty and light like salad without the green goddess dressing. Yet the older ones had lots of hang-ups and wanted to take over completely, sway things, thought that women were peppers in need of stuffing. And sometimes life felt so overwhelming that Paulette, floating about the air like grease off a red-hot skillet, would like to give it all. Tell me what to do and I shall do it, she says to nobody in particular. Here are the grains of boiled white rice. Where's the meat?

Fat, thin, then fat again, bloated up blubbery like a swine, and so on. Baggy is not the same as curving. One covers up and obscures the snags and the other shapes, flatters, makes pleasing use of line and form. Hide and seek, she had been doing that for years now. She will finish up school in late May, get her BFA, and be back in L.A. over the summer. It was quite in to be thin, there, everywhere now, yet absolutely no more purging. She was fully committed to that. The Jazzercise craze had spread quite fast from Chicago to Southern California and then to New York. It was rigorous jazz dance mixed with calisthenics and ballet, without critique, in rooms without mirrors, $4 a pop. She felt better about herself, burning calories and energy, seemed stronger and more flexible and way more conscious of rhythm. She learned and practiced the routines with utter sincerity. And dressed in garish-colored leotards with all manner of leg warmers and parachute pants, drenched in perspiration, she made new friends, boogied with them in this deference to disco. Six, seven, eight… Sporty, muscular, fanatic, and just like Jane Fonda, thin again. The nice, neat, only way because really, food for thought and thought for food had been butchering her; and while she was not always certain she wanted to live, she did not want to die.

The man who kissed her forehead wore a large, curled brim hat at a jaunty angle and puffed on a pipe like her grandfather. She met him in a smoky jazz club, The Village Gate, on a Salsa Meets Jazz night when Sonny Stitt and Eddie Palmieri jammed legendary. She liked the conga drummers and he the sax. An assistant professor of sociology at NYU, Paulette spoke up loud enough during a 20-minute break between sets to have a real discussion. When he told her his name was Benjamin and that he was Jewish, she wondered if she'd heard him right. Later, after the music was over and the drinking done, they walked along Bleecker Street in the Village talking about acid rain and the way it had crumbled some of the world's sacred monuments, its churches, spires and crosses. "The ill effects of the bourgeoisie buying effort," he'd said, smoking that pipe. "The Bridge on the River Quaint." Hahaha.

Keep up, Paulette, she'd told herself. Pay attention and for goodness' sake, do keep up. "Impure ideas, tainted air, vanishing vestries," she'd said tentatively, nervous that she might come off sounding foolish, or worse. Beside her teachers, most young men preferred not to talk, at least with her, and she had so little parley practice. Even that defense lawyer she'd seen a few times, he had one thing and one thing only on his mind. Too sultry for your own good, he'd blurted out again and again, like an apology.

"A barbaric force, actually, that very old euphoria finally defacing history, most of it Christian." A slow, deep puff on the pipe that he let drift out his nose, loiter, fill up the entire space between them. "Needless to say, the monuments themselves have become as marketable and ticky-tacky as the very travel guide books which promote them: Michelin, Fodor, Lonely Planet; see the world denatured, dominated..."

While some of her friends' older sisters had made their way around Europe with backpacks on sexual liberty and ten dollars a day, Paulette had seen only a small bit of the world, the America bit mostly, been to the

Big Sur and Death Valley and to the Great Salt Lake, but found reading about it riveting. She discovered Buckminster Fuller and Carl Sagan and the re-visioning of Planet Earth, became quite interested in future studies and some abstract muddy-hued fabrics coming out of Scandinavia that derived inspiration from nature, its plateau, plains and its mountaintops. Transcribing a seedpod materially was to grasp its geometric form rather than the actual object. More than simply charming, fanciful décor, it is meant to reveal the torrents and the gorges dug up amidst solitude and contemplation. Enter Japan into the mix and the unploughed fields and vacuous sky get injected with something quite painterly. Acres away from kitschy, one could even grasp the gusts of wind in them.

Paulette looks over at her reflection through the exhale of her Virginia Slims menthol smoke in one of the shop windows as they slowly wander along, she setting the pace and all. It is not half bad, she thinks calmly, in a slightly surreal way, her reflection. After just two glasses of red wine, well, most everything seems a little trace Joan Miró. Those Spanish, they have such a knack for the unrealistic. "I sometimes think that tombs are the garments of the dead," she says to her reflection, and to his.

"Bring the rich hordes to their knees," the man says, engaging her. "By the way, I love your dress. You are a vision of the steamy tropics. A real getaway," he says, smiling. Hahaha. "Is that fruit there kiwi, or is it lychee?" His finger comes very close to touching the dress, at the waist where it's tightly tied with a fabric belt, but then stops. She can sense it in the nerves on the small of her back, regardless, sense something tender flow from him to her.

"Fresh either way," Paulette says, shrugging her shoulders, watching Benjamin admire her in the window and feeling the swank of her outfit, the height of her peep-toe shoes with velvet bows clipped across them. The fleshy leaf in the fabric is grand like a plume, and gracefully rhythmic, a philodendron. The chartreuse in them lights up her eyes. The orange fruits are prickled some, probably lychee. The high shoulders of the dress' profile and its long, flowing rayon skirt gives her some Hollywood poolside glam, with just a hint of masculinity. A wide, circle skirt of several folds that kicks up and salsas, rhumbas too. The whole thing sweats, jazzes, even on a late-April night and she goes without the tight, black-beaded sweater. Draped over her purse, it's under her arm. She feels it close, though, the scratchy, warm woolen threads of her security blanket. Her verticality in the dress accounts for his interest.

"I really like evocative clothes. They are nifty, no, like your hat?" She tries not to be too self-conscious, not to overthink before she opens up her mouth. He is an academic, after all, from a very good university. While it might take him years to become a full professor, he is on the tenure track. And his discipline, it is full of theories about poverty and social inequality. He must have a very big mind, she thinks. Big feet too, she can see that all right. His boots are scratched and unmannerly, just the way she likes them. Their gracelessness and uneven heel accounts for her interest.

"So you approve of my hat, then?" His deep-set eyes flash rare bottle-green beneath the street neon. Gemstones, both, the man and the city. Faceted, polished, precious, could be beryl, could be garnets like the Tiffany-launched tsavorite. He is tall, willowy, pale-skinned, stubbled, handsome, with slightly imperfect brown hair that comes down his back in dazzling ripples. It is a question, not a statement, and she can feel his waiting. It glitters like the mica of Manhattan's bedrock.

"I do," she answers, right off, fretting over what next to say. Another drink and those frets might leave her. Yet, she is trying hard to learn to negotiate the world on her own, with her cleverness and her sensitivity and her resolve, with her instincts and without the aid of a drink or a drug. She is growing beyond all that utter mindlessness. Oh, but the dress, it holds her up firm, vivid, keeps her steady the way Friday keeps the weekend steady. What next to say will come as surely as Saturday.

Below the hat, the rest of Benjamin is drab grey mixed with some charcoal, and battered, except for the colorful scarves round his neck, which add a bit of the wild herb to him and fragment his ambiguity. "Do you wear it to class, that hat?" she asks, pointing to it. She had been setting out for somewhere else, and suddenly she is here where it seems she should be going.

"But of course, it is a part of me," he says. "My students are often quite amused by it." He tips the brim of his porkpie down, his fingers dashing along its slightly domed crown. Could be worn by a Pachuco or even a Rude Boy—she'd studied both their subcultures in school. "They think it must be inspired by an elegy," he says.

"My grandfather has a whole collection of pipes. Most of them are wooden and fine, some with leather, like yours," she says, pointing toward the bowl and part of the shank of Benjamin's pipe. "He keeps them on his dresser in a solid teak rack, beside his glasses, his comb, wallet and keys." His necessities, she says, remembering her grandfather's kindly voice on the phone a few days back. They spoke often, bi-weekly, the grandparents and she. "Every now and then he let me draw on his pipe," she tells him, recalling when she'd inhaled the smoke once like she did her cigarettes and he'd shouted at her. Burned slow, that bark. Nothing like the bite of her father's, though. No fluffiness whatsoever in that. An elegy, she thinks, hmm.

From the pocket of his wide-leg trousers Benjamin removes an old leather pouch, to show her the tobacco, a tabula rasa for blenders and near sugar-free. He opens it wide so that she can smell the burley leaves, their nutty, chocolaty, slightly bitter aroma that is almost drinkable. He's still searching for the perfect air-cured balance, he tells her, but the pursuit, it is his pleasure and the ritual mighty appealing. "This pipe's from Bulgaria," he says. "It is an old one, but not to me. I only recently broke it in. Still has some ghost to it. Look," he says, pointing to the mottled root-beer stem, "it has some Bakelite on it, like your bracelet."

She touches her thick black bangle. An old carved piece of thermoset plastic that her grandmother gave her, it was heavy enough when she wore it. He seems to notice everything, takes it all in, she thinks, the one percent he can see at any rate. Bakelite, a once-common substance from the '30s with a brittle quality to it, and a hollow, flat sound; that's how you can recognize it, her grandmother once said. Tap, tap, tap, with the knuckles of her fingers, oh, Grandma swore she could hear it.

"It aims aggressively, alchemically, to be anything at all and isn't the least bit pretentious, is it?" Benjamin says, holding up the bangle and her arm too. A black couple walking hand in hand quickly pass by, turn back and look, beam like starlight. Pineapple-style cornrows on her, Afro on him. Like roots, passion is catching and they got it too.

"Hmm," Paulette says, thinking about thermoset and its utilitarian uses, the buttons and boxes, radios and mahjong sets she'd seen in vintage stores, hearing that tap in her head. "Egalitarian, then, maybe?" she asks, paying attention to the bumps and cracks of the sidewalk, the footing from trees of long standing that bulged it up and affected her balance. "Radical, even?"

"Exactly, and in this constant state of resistance." Benjamin looks up at the skyline, and at the moon beyond, which seems to him unnaturally transparent and prismatic. She's an homage to the idea, and her beauty is like vegetation, growing, he finds himself admitting.

Charmed completely, he, she; they stop for the red light, wait there at the corner until it changes. Cars whisk pass; cabs stop to pick up fares. Doors slam, horns honk, laughter swells, sirens blare, trash travels, bottles break, accents mingle, night seeps in and out of open doors and windows like cigarette smoke. The elemental vigor of the city collects what is within it, though Paulette is oblivious. Benjamin is on the outside and is aware of everything on the street, across and down the alley too. He's a native New Yorker. It is what they do.

"Where'd you go to college?" she asks, still waiting in a haze for the "Walk" sign to flash. She is guessing he is not long out of school, wet behind the ears so to speak. A little bit like the French essayist André Breton, this man, when he was young, she thinks, and modest and living on breadcrumbs in Pigalle. *All my life, my heart has yearned for a thing I cannot name.* His words were her liver, her spleen. Smoked a pipe too, her grandfather had told her that. Knees are a little weak, she notices. Shoulders are a little tingly too.

"Boston University," he answers, "I studied Marxian literature on the role of the state in advanced capitalist countries." He draws on the pipe, blows the smoke upward, out of his way. "My profs, they were Cloward and Piven, and Howard Zinn, revisionist historians, challengers of the status quo. Perhaps you've heard about or read something of their work?"

Knowing that she can never learn less, only more, she would look each of them up in the library soon as she had the chance, but she liked the subversive, political action types, identified with their rebelliousness and she tells him so, her heart suddenly racing up around her throat. She had been taught about sweatshops, about the low wages and long hours, crowded workspaces and poor ventilation, and about the picket lines to stop them in her labor class. She came to understand that the substitution of less skilled labor for skilled labor, and high-volume mass production, it has gradually reshaped and transformed the shop traditions and work cultures of craftspeople in American shops, plants and factories. If she were ever to one day become an employer, why, she would almost surely be a reformer.

The light changes and Benjamin leads the way into the green. She wants him to lead. To be led nowhere and somewhere both. "This dress, it was made by a person's hands," she tells him, lifting the hem and showing him the black lace that lines the inside stitching with prosaic prosperity. She imagines some blood in the lush fabric, from the prick of a needle, some teardrops too. "In the late '40s, after the boys came home." All the people assembled at the light walk ahead with the force of a breaking wave. Benjamin and Paulette stay back, like surfers on boards paddling, hoping for a better one.

"Yes, I suspected as much. Frankly, that's what makes it so, umm, so alluring, that it is personal and singular. 'Course, that it is on you; that narrow waist, a trace wider hips." He's thinking out loud. Hahaha. He'd learnt from his mother just exactly what not to say.

Learnt just what to say too. "The French, they call it *avoir du chien*." His smile is a wink, one that aims to please, and Paulette, she blushes hot, darts away from it coyly, slowly. Not fluent in French, not formally or informally, she assumes it vaguely means effortlessly chic. She couldn't be more wrong. "Do all your dresses wield such power?" he asks, tipping his hat, showing her that she has indeed got *some* dog. "A regular backyard barbecue, this one," he says sweetly, a bit nonplussed. Blushes red-orange hot, she.

Paulette found the dress at a thrift shop in old Pasadena for $60 the summer before last, a steal for such an elegant rayon, once considered the new synthetic fabric used exclusively as a cheaper substitute for silk. It had majestic aspirations, rayon, in its imitation of the rare mineral world. No tears at the waist or discoloration beneath the arms and no stains, not a one. A very good metal zipper goes almost all the way down the front and does not get stuck on anything frayed. It was worn as simply and carefully before as Paulette wears it now, for only the third time. When she flicks her cigarette ash, she does so behind the both of them, though without regard to where else it might fly.

Inside the Gate, she never got close to any hands with smokes in them, or with glasses of red wine in them. Rayon is quite dimensionally unstable when wet. It becomes very fragile. The first moment she tried the dress on, she pictured herself in the lobby of an old ritzy hotel. The Biltmore in downtown L.A., perhaps, for its frescoes, murals and crystal chandeliers, for its hand-oiled wood paneling, for its carved marble fountains, for its elegant strangers milling about in the brilliance. Odd, how meeting Benjamin has made her want for L.A., her sisters, her pup, home.

"Have you ever been to California?" she asks, eager to tow him in closer, to reveal something of herself, perhaps even become a bit more exposed, open some to the elements. She had gotten quite sharp at flirting, at turning it into souvenir sex, yet this is not that dallying dead end. There is some spray off the top of this lip, the face of the wave unbroken. Mostly she felt quite alone in her indifference to shoddy, valueless commercialism. He seems good company, unlikely to fold.

"USC has an urban planning program that's notorious. So yeah I've been there, a few times," he answers buoyantly. He takes her elbow and turns his head to look at the street both ways, but she can feel his focus on her still and she is glad for the Beaux Arts, for the concrete and the thick steel. She is 11 stories upright. She gathers her skirt and the silky nude slip beneath, lifts it and all its postwar indulgence as she steps off the curb cautiously so that she does not trip. From her three-inch heels it's touch and go, a long way down and there's dirty water flowing in the gutter. She's already falling, though.

8.

The Teardrop in Paisley

If Paulette feels at times trapped by the scale of her body, its littleness and its plumpness, its closeness to the ground, then her dresses tend to release her. She did not have to occupy a single place or time, a single person. She did not have to become the amplified grown-up to her childhood summary. She could define herself linguistically as any particular archetype she chose, depending on her whim. A '40s cotton dress with a sweetheart neckline and a girly shape in bombshell pink, for example. A color so seductive to her and so very good for highlighting her hair and skin tone and the aura that surrounds her that when mixed with black, it was like slipping into a satiny Leonard Cohen song. Like wearing "Suzanne," when Nina Simone gives her fiery breath. Madonna, mother, mistress. An ancient, earthy pink from the realm of the feminine, with pleats that move out from the waist playful as son. The *boteh jegheh* decoration of the dress' print has been used in Iran since the Sassanid Dynasty. Has its own wavelength entirely, this kind of recycling, its own mystique. Color and cut recombine and conspire to exalt the struggle of identity. History holds it all up high, yet weighs it down too, bending it against strength and resistance into a certain kind of modesty. Suzanne encounters Saffronia and the tea from China miraculously turns to wine; peach wine, from the ripest, juiciest fruit, and seriously potent to say the least.

It almost did not fit, the dress, since she'd put on a few pounds after coming home from school and her fairly ascetic student life in New York. Except for cheap Chinese food and the occasional bowl of chicken noodle soup with matzo balls and kreplach that she'd shared with Benjamin at the deli, every extra dollar went toward buying up vintage. It was her nourishment and thankfully it gave her negative calories. When food again began to consume her, to take over her dreams, to obsess her, she simply went to the sale racks where some things were a bit more worn, and maybe even a little ugly, yet still undiscardable. A kind of diet, you might say. A hunt for treasures too, bygone ones, reincarnated. The world threw down an apple. Not only Venus picked it up.

Since she has been back over a year now, she has often been having her mother's special matzo brei for breakfast. It was comfort food and had gone straight to her middle. And her thighs. And to the tops of her knees too, thickening her all over so that whenever she actually felt good, she looked down at her puffy knees and sank. Made that matzo with bacon fat. Her mother kept a coffee can full of it on the stove, and every time she fried bacon, which she did more than once a week, she added to it. Uses it in her warm bacon salad too, for the dressing, and for French toast. Even puts it in her hot dogs with baked beans.

Laying around wondering just what exactly to do with herself, pulling on her split ends, popping blackheads, plucking ingrown hairs and stragglers on her chin too, staring into space, as her father flippantly called it, well, that did not help Paulette's middle much either and she fretted that she was becoming more and more like a pear. No shape for a girl, a pear, the ads all say; *Body-Do*. This transition from child to adult, this reapportioning of life's bottom and top, this socially sanctioned squashing and this rounding out, it was not going so well. Flowers, even wild ones that nobody really cares about, they need more than sun and rain to bloom, some, oh, a whole lot more. A good pruning, for example, a little remolding of the body-don't.

When she went to zip the Suzanne dress up at the waist, she had to inhale deeply to do so. She had to elongate her torso such that the zipper at the side might curve around, and up, without getting stuck on the threads of fraying cotton. She has got her skin caught in plenty of zippers, and that's why she now wears a girdle, the Concentrate. Well, one of the reasons for it, anyway. It is not the pain of it, but fear that the zipper might break. New ones are never quite as thick and hardy and it spoils something of the magic. Most vintage garments were more carefully assembled: craftsmanship, fabric and details are almost always sturdier. A fanatic? Why yes, though she prefers to be called purist instead. One questions her sanity while the other confirms it.

In truth, it is actually the back of the thing that no longer seems to hold together, just above the waistband, along both sides of the darts at either end of the bodice, and she worries more about the delicate Suzanne dress than she does about how silly she might appear in a disintegrating garment. Fabric that looks like this usually can't be saved, so she will need to get creative, use the stylized paisley floral motif both between and in the striped patterns to keep her protected and resilient like the bowing cypress tree. It is decay-resistant, that tree, a Zoroastrian sign of life and eternity. She had sewn the back of the dress up at least twice before, when there was hardly anything left of the actual cloth to put the needle through. Yet she kept right on sewing.

Walking down Sunset Boulevard with summer coming on strong, toward the fairly new Spago that everyone is raving about, in this beautiful old dress that seems to be falling apart like everything else in her life, she takes a little black cashmere cardigan to cover up the brokenness and tries her best at shallow breathing. Pink lips sink ships, she tells herself over and over, like a mantra.

It is warm and sunny today, with the Santa Anas blowing away the usual sea breeze, devil winds, they call them, and she does not really need the sweater. Inside Tower Records, though, right across the street, the air-conditioning nearly froze her so she threw it over her shoulders. Everyone else looking through the stacks of albums was wearing denim jackets or some manner of them. She stood out in her WWII victory dress, got lots of attention, like always, and she had learned to depend on it the way she did the sharp razor blade that shaved her legs. Some girls went without it but Paulette just simply couldn't.

After listening with little earphones to a song by X and another by the Gun Club, she bought Joni Mitchell's new *Wild Things Run Fast*, thinking that it will satisfy a committed enthusiast, thinking it might help her sort some things out the way music often did. It seemed always to go so perfectly with her staring into space.

When she and Gary meet up later for smoked salmon pizza with crème fraîche, she will have to keep her sweater on, she thinks, keep some of the design and decay on the dress concealed. In Hinduism, kidney-shaped paisley is symbolic of the goddess. She will try her very best to summon up this aspect of herself, even though it might be hidden in the garment's dilapidated decoration. Given that she does not have a good track record with married men, and all. The lioness face on the woman's body is there to worship, yet Maya keeps her very occupied. Illusion, delusion, in this materiality she'll grip it either way. Grip it and hang there blistered for dear life.

They have not communicated much at all, she and Gary, since both finishing up high school, he two years before her, with him having gone off to study in San Francisco to become the captain of a ship, a sailor. He'd traveled to Tahiti and to the British Virgin Islands to practice, and found work on a small Caribbean cruise line, ten months on, two off, with some time for vacations in between. This week is one of those. His wife was at home in Hermosa Beach with their infant son. Paulette is glad not to be the wife, although she has missed Gary, his certain flavor. They'd made love in the desert once, outside on the sandy ground, in the darkness of a new moon, galaxies, star clusters and cosmic gas clouds twinkling all over the night sky like the planetarium at Griffith Park. It was the only time she felt real physical affection for a boy that was not merely lust. In fact, there was almost no lust at all. But what was it then, besides the whole solar system without the glare? He'd worshipped her and she'd sensed it. There were no finger jobs.

When they come face to face on the busy corner just outside the restaurant, Gary grabs her and all the months of Sundays that were silent, pulls her close to his body and holds her tightly in his arms, and the dress, it tears a bit more. She can hear it and feel it both, the giving way of everything that shrouds her. Gasping some, Paulette moves back, protecting both herself and her frail outfit. Everything about him seems flexed, like the moon when it waxes crescent. Cars whisk by when the light changes and the speed of the street lifts them both up. Beside the Marlboro Man billboard, the late afternoon roams the range.

"It's so good to see you," Paulette says, and she really means it, smiling nervously, hiding with her hair the part of her chin that is broken out due to her period. She had spent nearly an hour just concealing the redness and scabbing with tinted drying cream, foundation and then powder. It was a careful process, requiring patience she did not always have. Layers and layers, she would be careful not to crack it with a smile. Gathering full and curry yellow around her face, just above her shoulders, her unruly mane was a good cover. "How long has it been now?" She is figuring five, maybe six years.

He's bashful and looks down, away, appearing young, hopelessly young. They never did go to the prom together. Something brash about being above and beyond all that, the both of them. How much they'd wanted to grow up. How much they wish they hadn't. "Good to see you too," he says, his head bobbing up and down like he too means it, really. He is taller than she recalls, and granitic, not an ounce of fat anywhere. Fixes cars on his off time, he tells her, the muscle kind.

Sidney Poitier's at the bar, and Michael Caine is at a table in the middle of the restaurant, waiting for someone. Or many someones. Angelenos in this part of town are used to seeing stars; no big deal for either Paulette or Gary. "I hear the food's amazing," she says. He'd asked for comfortable and quiet, like the Moustache Café, but mentioned nothing about cuisine. She was hoping the sophistication of it all just might floor him.

"You know, I've never actually seen you eat. Ever. One of your teenage quirks. I hope you can stand to do that with me now," he says, really thinking about it for the first time in years; all those months they went to movies together, not a kernel of buttered popcorn passed her lips. "Junk food was everything to teenage boys," he said, "especially after we'd smoke weed and get the munchies. Three hamburgers at a clip. Then H. Salt fish and chips." He laughs a little, assuming the memory is one they might share, start the ball rolling. He waited for her to laugh too, or even smile, and when she didn't, he realizes it wasn't funny to her, then or now.

She could not eat in front of anyone in high school, especially the boys she was partial to, she tells him. Food, like lung cancer, was cryptic, then, now. Images with rugged cowboys could disguise almost anything. "I didn't want to be the girl with broccoli between her teeth," she tells him, forcing herself to chuckle. Her conviction to rewrite her history is strong, at the moment. "I could eat with boys I did not like much," she says, lying just a little. She was certain he did not know what her grandmother did. Thankfully to him it was just a quirk.

She'll make sure today she cleans her plate, all of it, hoping it will erase her younger self in Gary's mind. Replace it with "Paulette, great girl, great appetite." She will. They sit outside on the patio, Siberia they call it, beneath a canvas awning. Lucky to get in at all, is how it was put. Place is sold-out for months. The ground is covered in sawdust and some of it gets inside Paulette's open-toed wedgies. She kicks a bit of it out, but decides that it might be easier when sitting, since balance is tricky for her. It is early for dinner, which was her idea, a strategy to get in that seemed to work, and the place is somewhat muted yet, as Gary had requested.

Smoked salmon pizza isn't on the menu, but they order it anyway because it is already legend, and another one with artichokes, leeks, red peppers and shiitake mushrooms. Paulette asks for the fresh mint tea. "I'll have the same," Gary says to the waiter. They both take note of his bistro apron and pink satin bowtie, of his raised eyebrows and wide, haughty grin. Place has a reputation for cheap friendliness. She'd read all about it in the L.A. *Weekly*. The many phones in the front room ring constantly, as though nobody answers them.

"So what are you doing now?" he asks, rubbing his bony hands together like he's cold. Sparks fly, of the imaginary sort. His eyes, dark brown and puppy-like, are wide open, like portholes, and his hair is black and shiny as a seal. It curls near his left cheek and looks happy. Time is far kinder to some more than to others, she notes, feeling awkward about the plump of her pudgy cheeks. His face is chiseled some, masculine lines that will only get better with age. A deep bronze in his skin, lathered from the sun, from the salt, from the sea air. It seems applied gracefully like makeup, Paulette thinks. What a little contour two shades darker might iron out.

"Writing fashion ad copy, freelance, for a smallish firm in downtown L.A. Nothing much, really. Still trying to, oh you know, figure it all out. You doing what you'd hoped for yet?" She keeps her head down and her chin hidden from his view, holds her back steady so as not to further stress the fabric of her dress. She'd written a few poems too, but they weren't ready. Well, she had not found her crooked floors yet. Only a few tiny moth-eaten holes, was all. Yet she is almost 25, a quarter-century, and she knows she really ought to be doing something to manage her own affairs. Many of her former classmates were wedded and settled now, some with a kid, or even three. But Paulette did not want to be settled, not ever.

She was not the sort to gossip about old friends, and frankly neither was he, so they catch up quickly. And sometimes her thoughts were not small enough for talk. Sometimes his were too small. What's done is done, and yet here they both are sitting. Not everything that's done is done, obviously. Mistakes might be mended like the seams of one's dress. Less anxious today than most, Paulette is less lonely too. Since graduating college, she had withdrawn some, moping, seeking recognition in herself. Meeting up with Gary, preparing for it with a semi-parasitic awareness, it had relieved some of her alienation. Trolling, oh, the both of them.

The waiter brings two glasses of water with ice and a basket of French bread, nearly throws it on the table. He's in a hurry to get back to the main room, it seems, where all the action is. As celebrity hangouts go, this one is it. "I am really a family man, but haven't got much time for it. I'm at sea a lot. It's better that way, that I'm occupied. Otherwise..." He tears a small piece of bread off and bites into it. Breadcrumbs scatter across the table.

"Otherwise what?" she asks, taking a slice of bread she has no intention of eating, holding it in front of her mouth, her pink grapefruit fingernails digging into its velvety softness. Pale, her nails and toes, next to the pigmented raspberry of her dress. Bread is a no-no, still. She does not feel she deserves it. It must be earned, starved for somehow and used as a reward. Could be for something she is proud of. Could be for when she feels good about herself. She couldn't remember the last time she ate any. Yet the illusion of eating it, that she had down. She breaks a bit of bread off, rests it just off the plate, since she made a vow, and motions Gary to continue.

"Otherwise I might become even more about money, the way that she is." She is the nicest girl he ever met, he tells Paulette, and nice is all you need, right? But boy, does she like those labels. "And she likes dressing me. Can't you tell?" He's wearing Levi's and a Ralph Lauren Polo sailboat print button-up. Short sleeve, seafoam-green water, nautical breezes, whitecaps. A real cult of nature, oh, Paulette could tell all right.

"And piece by piece, I am disappearing into all our trappings. Sound familiar?" He reaches across the table to touch her hand. There's no wedding ring on it. Familiar, she thinks.

"Everybody is all about money these days." She wishes for just a moment that she herself was more about it, or the lack of it. Either way it hardly concerned her. Making a living seemed more about finding oneself than about putting money into California Federal Savings and Loan. Either way it hardly concerned her. So much for the Me Decade and the liberated workingwoman.

Now apartheid in South Africa, why, that concerned her. The Berlin Wall, that too. The revolution in Cuba, oh, that concerned her. The death squads in El Salvador too. The broken heart of the planet is on her shoulders, beside its broken rules, tearing at her twisted teardrop paisley dress. Tearing at her skin, too, though she keeps away from cutting herself. That she does not do this any longer, that her essence rises up above her condition, it makes her feel somewhat accomplished. Many more concerns than actual accomplishments, though, because however does one manifest worry? Beyond thought, beyond language, beyond marching in the streets with picket signs or joining the Peace Corps and heading off to Uganda to dig up wells, what is an appropriate response? Indigo Slims: "It was made to be worn." She moves her hand away from his and sweeps the breadcrumbs up into a neat little pile.

"The people I work with, men mostly, they are much more about survival than money," Gary says, chewing on crust. "Many of them are just content to be making decent wages. Some never see daylight on board the ships.

Labor is pretty much constant. Being a sailor sounds a lot more romantic than it is, really." He cracks a piece of ice from the glass. Phones continue their ringing. It annoys Paulette, but Gary does not seem to notice.

Freedom from grinding drudgery, well, she certainly did have a good deal of that. "I suppose," she says. Having never been on a cruise ship herself, well, she had no idea what went on. Only what she has seen on *The Love Boat* television series. She knows they dump sewage in pristine waters, though. She has paid attention to that. "But some can be cheery on very little, no?" she asks. "A perfect sunrise after the night shift?" Paulette says dreamily, seeing it somehow in her imagination, feeling the intense heat of the bottom ship where one gets seasick and can hardly breathe. "But you are the master who commands the bridge, no?"

Gary cocks his head sideways, gazes into Paulette's bedroom eyes, at the pink and black of her dress and the onyx beads that hang around her neck. He lingers there for a bit too long, and Paulette fears that the small bonfire once between them burns still. It was never out of control, only constant in those fresh years. "I have been wanting a long talk with you, and a long moment without talking," he says. "Still blonde, I see." As if she might not be. As if blondness aged and darkened like fine rum. "You have really grown into your good looks," he says buoyantly, drinking water, drowning in it. She blushes rosy, turns those heavy lids away just as the steaming mint tea arrives.

"Thank you," Paulette says to Gary, and to the waiter with the pink bowtie. The satin in it is dull, glazy as dusk over the Boulevard. Paulette tries hard to relax into the compliment, into the tea, into the waning light. It is a pick-me-up in the material world and as a knick-knack there, Lord knows she could use one. Sadly, she thinks, she had grown into little else.

Well, maybe not yet, he'd say, if she spoke about it. That is what everyone chirpy tells her, so why bother to bring it up. The truth is, nothing had gone as planned, not for him, not for her. Nothing much ever does, though, even for guys like Sidney at the bar in the other room.

Not everything raggedy falls completely apart to worthlessness. *Humata, Hukhta, Huvarshta*, says the Zoroastrian theology right there in the pattern on her back, meaning: good thoughts, good words, good deeds. Hold her to it, it will, to be sure. It chose her this morning, the Suzanne dress, the one Simone certainly made feel better, and not the other way around, suited the day's energies and its limitations. Everything in her closet surrounding it simply paled by comparison. She'd found it in a pile at a swap meet one Sunday in L.A. It was on the ground with some other disappointments, like debris. Not even worthy of a stapled-on tag.

"Hey, you and me, we used to have this song by Boz Scaggs, 'Loan Me a Dime,'" Gary says, "do you remember? It keeps playing over and over in my mind." More to her than meets the eye, always was, always will be, he tells himself, staring across the table at the black beads encircling Paulette's long, thin neck. Sometimes he sucked her so hard there that he thought he might completely swallow her up; occasionally he even supposed he drew blood. That was farther than she'd let other guys go, she told him, by miles. Her cha cha was far less sensitive than her *décolletage*.

Green kryptonite to his Superman, he recollects it all now, plunging into the cloying nature of old passion beside the nouveau pizzas on the table between them smelling darn near holy. Roasted red pepper holy, they both agree. "*I need to call my old time that used to be,*" he recites, enunciating every blue-eyed word. "You can't hear it, can you?" he asks, doubtful, let down some, examining her face for something, anything. His voice is lower in tone than she recalls, and softer. No kinder though because he was always that.

"Read somewhere that Puck uses honey in his crust." She offers him this, rather than lie again. Biting down hard into the pizza, Paulette relents that no, Gary is not the Sandinista rebel fighting for justice in Nicaragua, but sure, he has got her attention and in the here and now, when she is to herself something like stark profanity that nobody else can hear, he will do, since he remembers her so affectionately after all this time, since she has not yet been relegated to the garbage heap of history. Since all men, they will be sailors, like Leonard Cohen sang—seafarers and scavengers; well, Paulette tells herself, not only men.

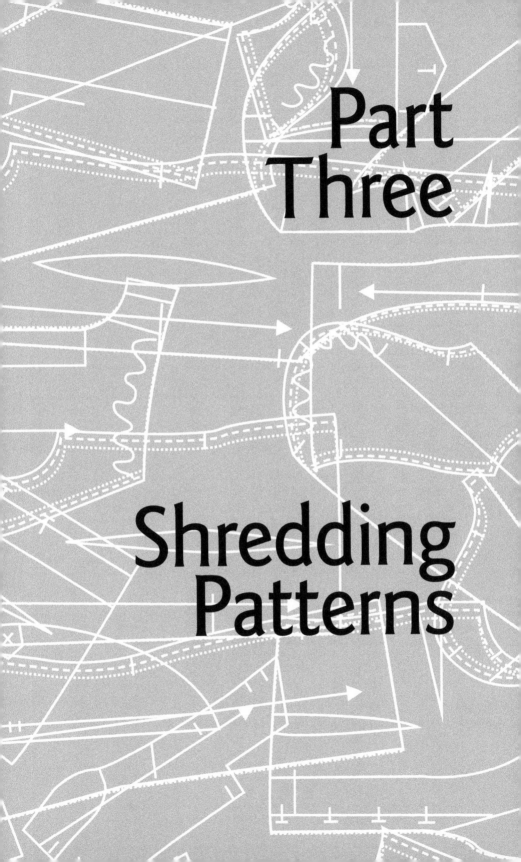

Part Three

Shredding Patterns

9.

‑ ‑ ‑ ‑ ‑ ‑ ‑ ‑ ‑ ‑ ‑ ‑ ‑ ‑ ‑

Heels Over Head

The husband of her beloved grandmother, her mother's father, had an attack of the heart. Paulette is dutifully attending his funeral service. She hates the idea of it since her Jewish grandfather never really wanted one. No casket. No headstone. No *Barukh atah Adonai Eloheinu melekh ha'ol-am, dayan ha-emet*. He'd just wished to be long remembered for what he was, for what he would never be again. A delicate, soft-spoken man with undemanding brown eyes and a shiny bald head for as long as Paulette recollected, he wore starched white shirts with French cuffs that kissed on both edges, drank pulpy orange juice and ate eggs poached from a little cup every morning before he went off to work in downtown Los Angeles, the same corporate rag job for 48 years to which he was never late. Not one day. She ran things, though, her grandmother, and he let her, even after they moved out to Simi Valley and took up golf. Well, him anyway.

He'd had a fairly good life, a long one too, some par 5's, even a couple birdies, died serenely, painlessly in his sleep the night before last, a full clogging of the widowmaker at a few weeks short of the morning he would turn 79. The only way to go, her mother had sworn to Paulette and her sisters and to the girls' aunt, crying hard enough for all of them. Crying like there was no tomorrow. His pipe and his blood pressure medicine sat on the white wooden nightstand beside the *Times*, the newspaper that he'd read faithfully because the world was his burden. Seeing his eyeglasses there smudged with fingerprints on the lenses gave them all a peaceful, melancholic feeling.

As Jews before him for thousands of years, he will have a green burial, shrouded in raw silk with hand-sewn lavender, white sage and rose petals, at Hillside Memorial Park, just off the 405 and right near Dinah's, one of Paulette's favorite restaurants for German pancakes and fried chicken. Linen was a bit cheaper, but her grandmother had wanted only the best and her mother said they'd help if need be. The Olam has four cotton web handles with lowering straps for the pallbearers. In Gan Eden her grandfather will keep the company of Jack Benny, Milton Berle and Moe Howard. These funny guys will have him laughing for perpetuity. Not far from Marina del Rey, the ocean breezes will soothe him too. And to think, his last meal was a juicy steak. A filet charred rare at Morton's in the San Fernando Valley. Like her mother declared, with the prayers and the psalms and the ritual bath, the only way to go. Her mother made it sound like a return-to-earth vacation spot that frankly nobody could argue with.

Paulette has just one fully black respectful dress, since she had never really otherwise needed (or wanted) one, and it hung intentionless at the very back of her closet, covered in plastic the way her mother covered things in plastic she would most likely never wear again. The Peter Pan schoolgirl collar seemed quite young to her, and awfully dull, sexless, if you want to know the truth. With all the complex patterns in the world, with all the beauty and drama of colorful prints, well then why wear only black? She fights back tears she was not expecting as she takes the '50s linen dress out of the closet and scrutinizes it. Appropriate for this time of year, she thinks, when the air is springtime light as the flax fabric. Needs pressing, she tells herself, seeing the way it just hangs there so limply. An undress.

And the waist, it seems quite tiny and inflexible. She might have to skip breakfast and wear a tight girdle to fit into it, and even then, her body had vastly changed since she was a starved teenager when she'd bought the thing cheap at a mid-Wilshire vintage shop. Everyone needs at least one black dress, said her girlfriends shopping for club gear at Judy's in Century City one Saturday afternoon, repeating what they'd read in *Cosmopolitan* and *Vogue*. Must have been peer pressure, she thinks, and the fact that in the Bible, angels wore fine linen; Revelation, chapter 15, verse 6. Her Christian friend Alix sure was on the ball. So much rubble left over from those years, but certainly not this textured yet smooth black dress. Style is so-and-so, forever and ever. Friends come and go, like trends, in one year and out the next.

She ate mindfully, counted the fats, the carbs and the proteins, paired good foods with bad in unison, but nowadays Paulette just couldn't bear to get on a scale, so the only way to know for sure how much she weighed was to judge how her clothes hung on her. Mostly, Paulette does not feel thin enough, or pretty enough, or smart enough, or popular enough, or worthy enough, and she likes the pain and suffering caused by fading away to nothing, thinks that honestly, she deserves it, since she is not much of anything.

Yet when she stands before a kindly mirror, which is only a reflection and not yourself, it all goes in the way of the drape. It defines the sulk of the moment, mostly, the golden cage. Manically up, depressively down, the circle of the wide skirt twirls toward some calm center. Like with a dog, or a cat, or a bird, even, when it hangs just so, a dress that flows elevates her mood with happy hormones. A wagging tail, some days.

Yet just now, the despair of loss, it bewilders Paulette. With the exception of her 93-year-old grandmother on her father's side who left when she was praying to go, and everybody said it was honestly a blessing, nobody she loved with lots of life still left in them had died before. And she loved her grandfather dearly. She loved his cufflinks and his French accent and his pipe. She loved his lap when she was frightfully alone. She loved that he had courage to fight for what was right. And how he loved his wife, it is what often defined him, the way he cut the edges of a grapefruit for her, the way he whipped the cream for her coffee. Touched by the vacancy of the moment and the cynical way it makes her feel, as if she has a headache, or when she is hungry, she takes an Excedrin to diminish it.

Choosing the right dress for a specific occasion is like reading the right book at the perfect moment. If it is apropos, the precise biological urge and emotional impulse, it stays with you, declares to you personally, becomes part of an identity, one's oeuvre, so to speak. Refers itself to you over and over in fitting ways that extend you, highlight passages, turn the pages down dog-eared for reference at some later date. She had never been a mourner before, never revered anyone or anything the way she did her grandfather. Sure, she had gone to temple and to church, with boys, with friends, with family, out of curiosity, out of obligation, boredom even, recited words that sounded like pleas, but that was long before enduring clothes spoke to her, before they called her by her first, last and middle name. Half-hearted simply will not do.

She considers the black dress carefully knowing that it too considers her, pulls the plastic all the way down, rips it and throws it into the empty trashcan. She hopes it is solemn in just the right measure, this traditional regalia of remembrance. It hints that way at least. Oversize black plastic buttons and reinforced, decorative buttonholes, finished with a kind of thick piping-inset, give it some lovely character. Two slit pockets, one on either side of the full, bias-cut skirt, are reinforced in the same manner, with edges rolled in beautiful ways you never see anymore. Unadorned, why yes, she thinks, yet finely sewn to show style in the very stitching, and not the least bit boring the way that some black dresses are, not a uniform that hides you in plain sight the way that some black dresses do. Cloud nine? Cloud six, maybe, since her grandfather was gone gone gone.

When she tries the dress on for her grandmother, who's decided herself to wear midnight blue because that was her husband's favorite color, a wispy wool suit that feels good next to her skin, Paulette hears the widow saying that the collar on it is just too much of nothing and is screaming for a brooch. And so she goes looking in her Oriental mother-of-pearl jewelry box for something vivid and proper for the day. Paulette did not like wearing dress pins at all, thought they were old-fogey, but her grandmother insisted and was in no mood to disagree. Keen to please nobody these days, not even herself, especially not herself, she always had this soft spot for Grandma Kari. Hash out anything, the two of them, well, just about.

"Here," says her grandmother, showing Paulette a pin of blue, green and pink rhinestones in the shape of a butterfly with its wings spread wide. "I got it from Aunt Lilian," she says. "It was her mother's." Aunt Lilian was not the wife of the uncle who molested her and her sisters before she was a decade old. That was the other one. Telling her grandfather about her uncle's wandering fingers put an end to it, fast. Unlike her father, who could not tolerate nor deal with things messy, who liked all the dirt swept under the rug, her grandfather, now he had his head on straight. A flat cap sat on top of it quite nicely. Usually it was a shade like tobacco that went well with his pipe. If his temper was dreadful, well, he controlled it. Bit his pipe right in two, that time.

Framed in charcoal metal and black rhinestones for the body, red ones for the eyes, and diamond-like antennae, the pin is indeed a work of art, feels heavy and substantial, not tinny. "Comfort comes on the wings of a butterfly," her grandmother says, her night-blue eyes deeper from the redness of her lament. "It will be picture-perfect and true at the very same time." Paulette and her grandmother stare at each other, a kind of hand-holding that eases the both of them. They could feel the pulse there on each other's wrist.

The dress, which fits, but only just, lays out on the bed and Paulette pins the brooch on the collar, high up as though the butterfly had flown in from the garden and simply landed there by itself, naturally, a caterpillar at the end of its world. "My best guess," says her grandmother, standing right beside her, "is that this is a Rainbow Butterfly. Moves from the Earth to the sky, dear, and has time enough." The colors of the brooch cast light on everything in the room like stained glass windows in an old church.

"Is that like for-real, Grandma?" Paulette asks, clicking her tongue, thinking that dippy is just not her style, sitting down on the fluffy golden quilt covering her grandparents' king-sized bed. It always did smell of fragrance in this bed, she thinks, a mix of theirs both, Youth Dew and Brut, and it still does. Death did not seem to leave any trace, even though

Paulette searched around the thickly layered bedding for it, something raw to render it bitterer still. She and her mother and sisters haven't left her grandmother alone since her grandfather didn't wake up. Her father would just have to fend for himself, her mother told her. When she'd said it, Paulette could see the matzo crumbs and the watermelon seeds all over the kitchen's mushroom-color tile countertops. She could see the seats up on both toilets in the house too. Some mysteries are so easily solvable.

"Its transformation is very real," her grandmother says, winking. "Ephemeral, masterly, going where it pleases and pleasing where it goes." Tears stream down her pinkish cheeks leaving vague lines in her semi-transparent face powder. She wipes them gently with the back of her hand. It is cracked and blue-veined and gives her real age away. Nobody believed she was not Paulette's own mother, the way the two of them went on and on about violets and purple roses, graceful substances and all the time dressing up to the nines. Peas in a pod, the two of them, since as far back as heavy and light they went. "Elves, spirits of air, they come from the Norwegian mythology. They are represented as small people with wings of a butterfly." Falling into a sort of stupor, her voice becomes inaudible and her fingers clasp at nothingness. "*Sommerfugl*," she murmurs.

How'd her grandmother get so cool, Paulette wonders, shivering some, fixing the pin shut and in place, moving it back and forth to be sure it is locked tight and secure within the dress' fabric. Even if she did not like it all that much, she would never want to lose it. Aged nearly one hundred years, she reckons, the patina dulls the sheen, pales the bright colors of the rhinestones. Its beauty overwhelms her and all the second thoughts she might have of wearing it. She might crumple the pages of that myth, but instead she asks what this butterfly had done to reach its place on her collar?

What had she done? Not much, she admits. Ambition, for work, for money, for travel, for love, for kids, for sex, for something, for anything really, it all seems to elude her. Once, she dreamed of becoming a warrior, had energy, drive, determination, ambition, passion even. Once, but that was a while ago. Now she is lost in a muddle, one that had been dragging on and on. "A bridge somewhere behind, within, the rainbow," her grandmother says, lips trembling, perspiration gathered in drops above them. Dew on a proud daylily, thickly rooted, apricot fudge.

Living in a single cubby-hole with only half a kitchen on a walk-street in Venice Beach and writing ad copy full-time with benefits to elevate butter above margarine, Paulette had far grander plans for herself at 27. Once, there was some real cheese. Not this inauthentic, polished stuff that only passes for it in all its cheesiness. Whitney Houston may be well on her way to becoming a diva, a bigger star than k.d. lang will ever be. And yet, all the beating on a glittery chest will never ring truer than the purity of an easygoing, transparent voice. At least Paulette will not be moved by the swelling orchestras, not by the synthesizer riffs or the electronic drum machines, either. She has not lost her edge completely, at least. That walk-street in Venice near the Rose Café, well, it has got some holdouts. She'd managed that, at least, she tells herself, sometimes.

She puts on her black pantyhose with the reinforced toes, the see-through lacy ones that don't seem to run or get caught on any of her bracelets, no matter what she does to them. The linen of the dress and its shorter sleeves requires a bit of skin showing, a bit of the leg exposed, toe too, otherwise the look at the bottom is too heavy for the springiness of the array. Out of balance somehow, she reasons, like a crooked picture on the wall. Set it right and the world is just so again. She'll wear her grandmother's faux alligator shoes; black pumps, with a platform, a peep-toe and a slingback. It is so pleasant to put on something that isn't covered in yellow smiley faces, she thinks, that isn't neon or velour or jelly.

The stockings smell rank, are in need of washing, so she takes them right off and heads to the bathroom, puts them into a ceramic sink of hot soapy water. She wonders if she ought maybe to go back to school and learn to like herself a bit more. Perhaps she can rekindle some of that flammability of her college years, study political science or sociocultural anthropology. Her grandparents had been speaking seriously to her about it recently, asking her about Benjamin too, since she seemed to them both so wretched and alone yet, so unsettled. "We are worried about you. More school might be the best thing for you," they'd both said, eating canned peaches with syrup from pretty stoneware bowls. "And that dear boy, he seemed so smitten," said her grandfather, putting on his glasses to read her face like the newspaper. "Head over heels, I thought," he'd said, raising his shoulders up high and throwing out his hands to bolster the moment, "the both of you. Poor chap." With all her grandfather had given her to remember, how could she forget? After a few moments of soaking, Paulette opens up the drain, lets the dirty brownish water out and then rinses the hose under the faucet in clear, warm running water.

Paulette's mother steps out from the shower onto the pale green fuzzy bath mat with a tea rose towel wrapped around her body and a white plastic cap covering her bouffant hair. She'd had her hair done up, roots retouched too, and slept with toilet paper wrapped around it; she does not let it get wet, ever. Her deep-set hazel eyes are puffy and bloodshot, betraying her tears, her grief. Her nose is red too. She was very close to her father; still called him Daddy, at 51, still teased him about his Adam's apple jumping up and down his throat. He didn't like her husband much, though, and didn't trouble himself to conceal it.

Seeing her mother that way, so broken, it makes a large and sore lump in Paulette's throat. She keeps swallowing it, but it comes right back. Her hands are clammy too. Even her bones feel cold. Carefully she teases and spritzes her hair, follows Cyndi Lauper's Blue Angel days lead in that hybrid punk way. She has it highlighted and lowlighted every so often, and wears it down past her shoulders somewhat like a tousled bed head. Not a shag, exactly. Not a mullet either. The less she has got to do to it, the better, as far as she's concerned. Some girls are obsessed with their hair. Braid it, bind it, blow it, curl it, clip it, bleach it, dye it, henna it, perm it, rat it up, deep-condition it and straighten it. Paulette stopped brushing and combing the snarls out of it somewhere around the time she turned 19. She keeps an Anti-Frizz Rattail comb, though, and washes it weekly. Changing your name from Cindy to Cyndi is only spelling, like changing your hair color. You can change it back, unlike your life. That does not go back.

Drying herself off, Paulette's mother watches her daughter using hair spray and a smile pierces her grief. "Honey," she says, "a friend of your grandfather's sent over that babka you like from the Beverlywood Bakery, the one with the chocolate chips in it." Unable to see much of herself in the steamed-up mirror, she rubs perfumed lotion that to Paulette reeks of gardenias on her arms and legs, at the back of her neck too. "When I finish here I can make us some more coffee?" Wouldn't think it to look at her, but she can make a great cup of coffee. All the ladies on the street growing up liked hers the best, came 'round for it mornings when the houses emptied out. Black, was how she always drank it. Not Paulette and her grandmother, though. Keen on a little coffee with their cream, the both of them are.

"If I eat anything at all, Mother, I won't be able to fit in the dress, but afterward, maybe," she says, kindness piercing her own grief, remembering how much she adored that cake, choosing her words and her tone carefully and not rolling her eyes, since there is so much sorrow around her and she would not want to cause any more. She has lied quite enough in her life about food, the dinners, lunches and breakfasts she said she ate, but hadn't, the things she simply threw away. And she had attacked herself quite enough for any one lifetime. It might be a real good time to neaten things up, she thinks, to become pure, in her grandfather's honor, simply have a piece of babka with her mother and carry on. If she could only do that, Paulette thinks, feeling guilty about the many calories. Could be 300 in a few bites, even more.

Thoroughly rinsed now, Paulette squeezes the pantyhose of excess water, hangs them up to dry over the empty towel rack. When her mother folds the towel and puts it back, she throws the pantyhose over the shower door, just to the side of the bathmat. "You do want them dry by morning, don't you?" her mother says, not really asking. Always moving and rearranging something, her mother, and nearly always annoyed. Sometimes it makes Paulette feel as though she can never do anything exactly right. Sneers and judgments all over the place, all sorts, from strangers and the flesh and blood.

Last night, her grandmother gave her a pile of her grandfather's starched and ironed handkerchiefs folded just so to pass around at the service. They were paisley, some of them, and beige and grey and pale yellow, a few plain white. Paulette buried her face in them, imagining her grandfather and all the times he gave her his handkerchief for something or other. All her secrets, they were quite safe with him, even the ones she never told the therapist back in New York when she had some anxiety is-sues and could not always function very well. There were no easy A's. She missed her grandfather so much already that she wanted to quickly find a new razor blade and cut herself, let bleed the hopeless feeling gathered up inside her. Instead, she ended the day, since nights, they were her worst time, since it was the darkness that she hated most. She slept like she too was dead. Her mother gave her a couple good swigs of gin to help, gave them to her sisters too. "Do they have to give them back, Grandma," she'd asked, "his handkerchiefs, at the end of the service?"

"What for?" her grandmother had answered. "They will be stained in tears of sadness," she'd said. "But full of memory and fine for keepsakes, don't you think? You could tear yours and hold on to it, keep it rended near your heart. I know your grandfather would be glad about that." Then her grandmother leaned back against the pillows on her grandfather's side of the bed, beside the red roses and purple tulips in a cut glass vase delivered a couple hours earlier, beside her two sleeping granddaughters who often climbed into bed with her and her husband. Her grandmother looked sort of sedate, as though she might be thinking, perhaps even hoping, that her husband was in the bathroom washing up. A couple of gold fillings in her teeth glinted in the lamp's low light. The Torah says that a garment is not you, that it is merely an accessory, like a handkerchief. Yet Paulette had other distinct notions about that.

When Paulette finally closed her eyes on the made-up sofa bed in the other room, her black dress with the remarkable buttonholes, starched and pressed into fine shape by her grandmother, her suit of armor with the brooch on a satin hanger airing out over the door, she imagined her grandfather brushing his teeth. It was a relief, a cup of lemon tea, made her smile as she drifted off to weighty sleep. The world is dreadful, horrifying even, pointless and then all of a sudden it is not. That it was not made her learn to not always trust herself. Her dresses, though, well, at least they were reliable.

The bathroom is small and tidy. Her grandmother always saw to that, everything just so. Standing over the sink the next morning, Paulette stares at herself and her zitty skin in the foggy mirror that like all the other ones in the house will soon be covered up for the *Shiva*, contemplating her chin and her nose in relation to her mother's and her grandmother's, thinking to use the colors of the butterfly pin as a palette for her eyeshadow, the minty green especially. It will make her eyes pop. "Mother, other than the obvious, do you think fathers really matter?" She watches her mother's bereft face fill with sunlight in a room without any windows, the day coming in huge. Even Paulette's slight hands, with her long skinny fingers, feel it. She thinks it is a full-grown question to ask at a time like this. She sees her mother swathe her sorrow for an answer, grabbing hold of something more or less profound. Just as her mother opens her mouth to say a word or two about her daddy, her grandmother opens the bathroom door a crack like it's an envelope and nearly waltzes in with "so sorry for your loss" flowers delivered only a second ago. She sets them down on the tile beside the sink as though it is the exact and only place the flowers should occupy. It's a small arrangement, elegant, low and tightly packed. "A sweet tranquility basket," her grandmother says dryly. And there, on the tip of one of the cut-short, wired-up orange roses, sits a clouded yellow butterfly.

10.

- - - - - - - - - - - - - - - - -

Signature Day Dress

Benjamin telephoned Paulette unexpectedly proposing a three-day ren-
dezvous in Québec City. He knows how she likes Canada, the French part
especially, and he'd missed her deeply, wanted to see her vibrant smile, to
listen and watch as she revealed her innermost thoughts, to be close to
her again. She was his summer storm and he had not seen one in a while,
that thunder, that lightning, that warm rain wetting the potted pothos
on his tiny concrete balcony with a big view of the city. It's true they were
comrades; as lovers they were respectful of each other's differences, touched
one another tenderly, came close, but not too. The stream, it flows a distance before the water falls. They encountered one another somewhere
in the mist.

For Paulette, Benjamin was as regular and reliable as church bells come
Sunday. When she heard them, she always stopped what she was doing

to listen. And she always smiled someplace near her heart, as though she really were one of the faithful. He answered her letters faster than she could write new ones, and he used Florentine paper that seemed fused and ancient and held a whiff of something peppery, like incense. He gave her puzzles to solve, and when she finished solving them, she always somehow felt better about herself. She stored his letters in her drawers full of panties, slips and bras, his longhand as characteristic as his hat. They kept her company, sometimes.

As she had grown, so did her penchant for Benjamin. The others, they were distractions, dalliances, derivations. Benjamin, he was like a carnation, whose sweet petals are one of the secret ingredients used to make the centuries-old French liquor Chartreuse. When she was younger she did not care much for carnations. Some of them sucked up just too much blue for her pink taste. Lucky for the both of them everything evolves, even closely guarded secrets that are 110 proof.

"It's still warm enough," he'd said with some mustered-up enthusiasm on the phone. He did not have to be back to the university until just after Labor Day. "You won't shiver," he'd promised, knowing how much she struggled with the cold, how awkward she was in it, fearful even, the way her body trembled, and how it hurt her chest to breathe in deep. And the way he saw it, deep was the only way to go. "Will you tear yourself away?"

She remembered the Château Frontenac from when she had visited eastern Canada as a child, but her family had never stayed there. The high-priced rooms were too old and too small for the five of them, the place loaded with tourists, she recalled her father saying about the grand old hotel on the banks of the St. Lawrence River. It haunted her imagination, though, stained it like clerestory glass. Haunted her sensibility too, the Place Royal and the

Citadelle, like a Wilkie Collins novel, like *The Woman in White*. They walked up the old cobblestone streets and photographed its iconic façade, one that held some clandestineness about the allied strategies for WWII. They drank coffee and hot chocolate at outdoor cafés, though not as often as Paulette would have liked. They took the old funicular from Haute-Ville to Basse-Ville, after lots of family pressure on her father, and against his better judgment. Gothic, it went with her mood when she was a teenager. And never left her.

"We can meet there for tea next Friday afternoon," Benjamin probed, hoping. He'd actually called ahead, checked to be sure of a vacancy; called Air Canada too for flight schedules and pricing. He'd thought first of going straight to California, but it did not seem half as romantic. They both had such regular lives, one on the East Coast and the other out West, and he was sure she was breaking it off, but gradually. Well, she did quite a few things gradually. It was something he very much liked about her.

Love. Benjamin had spoken about it once, and only once, when the pitch was tuned up. You must not talk about that, Paulette had said. Don't worry about love, she'd told him, just before graduating college, something she had little faith in ever actually doing. Find herself and what she was meant for, first things first. When he touched her hand she would always quiver like she was cold, like love was a coat with an animal smell that put her off. There was that questioning life-force, Benjamin reminded himself when close to losing his nerve, that intelligent, free-thinking, sexy personality, and there's that body, a state of flesh that could neither be grasped nor forsaken. Yeah, sure, while he remained cautious, he was hoping. Stood beside a blue light that looked like an altar, hoping.

Well, it sure was about time, Paulette's mother had said over steaming coffee, leaning back relieved some into the red booth at Pann's, a genuine

'50s diner near LAX where the two of them have been meeting on and off now for years. Good milkshakes. Good fruit pies. Good mix of patrons in a city all too often segregated by ethnicity, race and class. After all, Paulette was 28 now and should be getting on with things. She herself had three children by the time she was Paulette's age, she told her daughter all too often, and like most mothers she was anxious for her eldest to find someone, simmer down. She wanted her to be happy the way the split pea soup was with the broken soda crackers. Seemed to her they were made for each other.

"Did he send you the plane ticket?" her mother had asked, lighting up a cigarette. "He offered," Paulette answered, putting hers out in the same ashtray her mother was using. "But I said that it was okay, and thanked him, that I could buy my own." She did not want a sugar daddy, she told her mother. She'd met a man in Athens once, a purely physical thing, and another in Berlin. Bought her own tickets, she had, both instances, though she did not tell her mother. And if she had, would her mother have spoken up, offered her two cents about it? Paulette thought not. And would Paulette have listened anyway? Her mother thought not. They shared cigarettes, though, brittle bones and the curve of the nostrils.

Her family had gotten to know Benjamin a bit when they visited Paulette in New York for various parents' weekends. He was an awfully good host, taking them out for authentic Italian food in Little Italy, and to the Queens Center for Art and Culture to see the "Panorama of the City of New York." Commissioned by Robert Moses for the 1964 World's Fair, it was built by a team of one hundred people and included 895,000 individual structures, every single building in all five boroughs. The architectural model, it sure impressed Paulette's father; impressed Benjamin and Paulette too.

To keep her sisters quiet, her mother crossed her heart and promised a visit to Bloomingdale's on Lexington Avenue just as soon as they were finished. It was only the second most popular tourist attraction, after the Statue of Liberty, which they saw on the very first day there. "And the hottest souvenir is just about anything inscribed with the Bloomie's logo," Paulette whispered to her sisters. Well, they simply could not wait. Benjamin bought them both a "little brown bag." He'd insisted, filled them up with pencils, erasers and tiny bronze models of the Brooklyn Bridge and the Empire State Building. Silver skyline snow globes too. Being close to his family, he just took it for granted that Paulette was close to hers.

Air Canada charged Paulette's credit card and even though her father could not sleep nights owing money to banks and other lenders, she'd pay it off over time, years, if she needed to. That's what she had after all, time, her life laid out in front of her, opening up like petals of a flower to the butterflies, bats and bees. Moments, hours, days, weeks, months, years, they had stretched themselves beside her, though not exactly friends. The fashion trends of the postwar '40s seemed a bit formal, had just too much shoulder padding, too much austere pencil skirting for this softer, private moment with Benjamin. It was the tight, fitted costume and if she were to get to know this man better underneath, she would need more space, more casualization. Fancy going to a Renaissance hotel in Québec City looking so plucked, the Venus flytrap, for example.

As housedresses went, the comfy ones women wore to look fresh and cute while cooking and waxing floors, the one Paulette finally chose for tea with Benjamin, it has a dimensional yellow tulip that's really a pocket. It practically jumped out of the closet and into her hands, like it was blooming in solid roots, the Dutch bulb fine and rare. Unlike '40s and '50s housedresses with umbrellas, or ones with hat boxes, or candy wrappers, this was not a dress with a luminous appliqué. The Venice Beach shopkeeper told Paulette the flower shape had to be carefully restored after shipping had flattened it. It was the only one like it on Abbot Kinney Boulevard. On Melrose too, the shopkeeper had promised.

The label said Lee Wentley by Wentworth, so it was not hand-sewn, though the shopkeeper would have sworn differently. She would put her grandfather's torn handkerchief hidden inside the pocket, keep the tulip certain and well-formed, Paulette thought as the cashier carefully wrapped the dress up in bright pink tissue. It was not cheap and she could not really afford it, yet when it came to clothing of this sort there was just no logic to it. Drama could not be translated to a price. You just sort of take it on faith, is what she tells herself anyway. The curtain rises and there you are.

It is so playful, she thinks, trying the dress on in her bedroom, leaving the curtains open for the pure daylight, fluffing up the ruffled neckline, closing the four sunshine-yellow carved Bakelite buttons so that the dress wraps around and stays put. It falls below her knee, toward the middle of her fleshy calf. She'd worn it just once, to a jazz club in Redondo Beach on a lazy Sunday afternoon, where it did not always stay put. Though it is well-made in wispy cotton with plenty of fabric, she would need a large safety pin to ensure it did not open up when she walked in a breeze. And she is planning for a breeze, off the mighty Gulf of St. Lawrence, gateway to the Great Lakes, dreaming of one in fact. The winds of September that folk singers always warned sailors about.

The cap sleeves of the dress are ruffled too, sewn with bright yellow piping to match the tulip. The stem of the tulip runs down the length of the dress to the hem and is the green of emerald on a black background with yellow and white and green polka dots and orange buds that almost seem to smile. It is quite feminine, and cheerful, like an apron, she thinks, magical even, and will go perfectly with black ankle-strap shoes with a small wedge heel that will be good on the wooden boardwalk. The Dufferin Terrace, she ponders, lingering there so beautifully beside the water. Planks built atop archeological ruins, open dawn to dusk, full of musicians and mimes, admission free. Had a pulse all its own, blood and bones too.

Maybe jet beads in a choker around her neck, she thinks, standing before a mirror that does not frown back, not this time, oh, and matching earrings that dangle some. And an onyx purse of old faux leather that has a gather to it, and is big, like a gypsy's. Oh, so much to consider, to plan for, she ponders. And how to do all this without looking silly, as though she were going to play a role in a dated musical on Broadway? Indeed this is quite a concern for those who wear vintage.

While miniskirts and colorful oversized sweaters bloused over big, gaudy, low-slung belts define the epoch, Paulette will pack a small duffel with her baggy, high-waist blue jeans and some short, dollar blouses that she found in baskets at swap meets here and there. One black shirt has Pepto-Bismol pink measuring tapes across the bodice, buttons up the back, and another has brown surfboards in a repeat pattern on a purple background. Both are boxy and dart-fitted, from the '40s and of good cotton. And an old cotton amethyst Japanese kimono robe, she will fold that up too, shove that in there too. Rescues, every piece she will bring, or almost, destined for junkyards and piles of rubbish. The people of Québec City will speak mostly Canadian French there, she thinks. And she will speak back to them with these glorious old fabrics, hope they will understand the way they do the Parisians. Well, it's true, she muses, in the age of upbeat and danceable, style like this is a Romance tongue quite on its own.

She had pretty much decided to return to school, to attend UCLA, and she was hoping she could swing it, do a master's program in philosophy or sociology or political science, study something that may well help her maneuver better in the world. She wanted to pursue design too, but approach it more theoretically, so that what comes out artistically might be fresher and more substantial. Graduate school was not necessarily the path to a job, but to an expanded consciousness, a way to turn cryptic into constructive. Michael Jackson as pop culture construct. Fundamentalist revolution as response to global, godless capitalism. Unsustainable development characterizing contemporary Western civilization. Small is beautiful. That is what Paulette is telling herself, that the future must carry on only with the truth of the present and the past. And she is wearing that past, showing off its bias cuts and its revealing hemlines the way Frida Kahlo showed off blood-red dahlias in her hair. Turning its shabbiness around into swanky, this primeval impulse to adorn herself, recycling it somehow. It is what she wants to talk about with Benjamin. Going off-grid without going anywhere, is what she wants to go on about with Benjamin. And he will grasp it all, she is sure of that, because he is an interdisciplinary thinker in a mass of specialists, a Renaissance chap, like the very castle Frontenac.

How thrilling it is to have such a prophetic man pursuing her, and after so many years, she thinks, rummaging through her tie-dye T-shirts, trying to decide which one to pack, the black and white one or the greens with the royal blues. Mostly men promised things they had no intention of delivering. She hardly ever knew where she stood so much of the time. She could not bear to be alone, but always felt lonely and insecure, as though she mattered so little, as if she might disappear and nobody would even miss her. Such low self-esteem for a girl who gets quite a lot of notice. This was the crux of her eating troubles. In therapy, in life, she has been working it through.

Victorian women, she had learned from studying the Bloomsbury group, had such little control over their lives, and invalidism was a consequence. As women's rights became an issue, as women became more active, nurturing frailty was translated into hysteria quite like designers translated sizes. Paulette's new Santa Monica therapist just told her that she wasn't hysterical, and that she was getting even less so every day as her internal dilemmas disappeared. You can't blame Twiggy and Jean Shrimpton for their regard any more than you can blame Jayne Mansfield for her rejection. Can't even blame the 14th-century Catholic girls who emulated St. Catherine of Sienna, depriving themselves of food to become holy. Fasting and vomiting, like foot-binding in China, like female circumcision in Africa, it is all about the proviso of being powerless girls, Paulette has figured out, and hardly a fad. She wasn't sad as much as she was hopeless, mostly. Sad you can get over. Grey days can end. She ponders all of this as she wings her way to another country, to meet a man who knows her longer and better than most. But not everything. Not like her grandfather knew.

There are hundreds of people in the graceful lobby of the old hotel, as vast as a city street, and finding her way to Le Champlain, Frontenac's main dining room overlooking the river, proves a bit chaotic. There is a forest of polished mahogany and gorgeous old woolen carpets, worn and plush on marble floors, chandeliers, beamed ceilings, attentive bell captains with suitcases piled up high on racks, elegantly suited men, women in high heels and hats, children scurrying about. Paulette moves slowly among the crowd, savoring the moment, feeling as if she is in a trance, making sure her wraparound dress does not fly open, although she bought herself a pretty black slip should it chance to happen. It was a big splurge, of Swiss lace and silk, brand new from Robinson's on Wilshire Boulevard in Beverly Hills. She has a charge account with Robinson's and even though she hardly ever bought anything first-hand, when she did, it was mostly there. She drove her silvery beat-up old Mustang into the parking lot with such joy, not a care in the world. Investments of soft goods, it's like being in gold or in the stock market.

"*Mademoiselle*," says a very chic woman in a short, tight black skirt with deep purple lips and a French twist in her hair, "your dress, it is so elegant, such good style." She scrutinizes Paulette, as though she would like to touch her, as if her eyes are hands that might like to fondle the whole of her, and she mumbles something in French that Paulette does not understand, but imagines that it is kind. Seems kind to her anyway, from the tone, from the texture. When Paulette thanks her in her very best French, the woman lowers her eyelids and waves as she turns and walks away. For one who requires a boost in confidence, who thrives on it like sugar, this was it, an éclair or cream puff, and Paulette walks quicker now, her posture straighter, her visage even more composed as the *pâté à choux*.

She can spot him now down the corridor, leaning against the lighted bar inside the restaurant, waiting for her. It has been nearly two years since she has seen him last, but they have spoken on the phone so often, especially since her grandfather's death, that it feels like just last month. And she knows him from his fine face, bonier than she remembers. And his hair, it is fuller and longer, almost down his back. The last time she left New York in the bitter cold, he screamed for her and she simply walked on, avoiding his green gaze. It was too cold for long goodbyes, she said, but not to him. And anyway her tears would freeze her eyelashes. And she didn't want to lose not a single one of them, no sirree.

When at last he sets eyes on her, Benjamin smiles, bows, twists his fingers nervously, reaches out for her arm with his long, thin hands. His starched linen shirt is indigo with cuffs rolled near the elbow. "Hullo. Wonderful to finally have you near," he says, drawing Paulette close, kissing her cheek, then her eyelid. Through large windows and thin curtains she catches a glimpse of the inky St. Lawrence, bathed in afternoon sunlight. Both it and the kisses leave her flushed, sweating like hell. Her heart turns over and she grabs for it. He makes a little speech about waiting so long for this and that and she wonders if it will stop jumping around like a fish in a bowl and stay put.

Following the tall, black-suited host to a table, Paulette gathers up her dress to sit down and as she does, the lace slip peeks out over the bare of her thigh. She is glad that she shaved up high this morning, since she decided not to wear stockings. This was informal, after all. And the black lace panties, French cut, they too were new. Not that informal. "I left my bag with the bell captain," she tells Benjamin quietly.

"I am sure it is quite safe. We will fetch it on the way up to the room," he says, shyly. Two nights with a woman he honors, it is so rare for him. Affairs take oomph and his was worn-out, dulled, like the brown leather on his belt. Busy teaching and preoccupied with writing a book about social position and the effects of television on desire and consumption, he feels dreadfully out of practice. Dating gets boring and old, the same things said, the same derbies played. He would rather not and say he did to everyone who nags him about being way over 30 now and single, still.

"How was your flight?" he asks, adjusting himself and his polished-up belt in the chair so that he can cross his long legs and still face her. Pictures just don't do her neck justice, he thinks to himself, arched and regal, like an afghan's. A hunter of ibex, and leopard, in the olden times. Woof, woof.

"Uneventful, thank goodness. And not that long. Dozed for a bit. I only read half a novella."

"Yeah, which one?"

"*The Turn of the Screw*, by Henry James," she tells him. "He wrote like an Impressionist painter. It is one of the scariest books I have ever read. Did you ever—?"

"William James, but never Henry," he says, trying not to look into her eyes just yet. They are very intense, spellbindingly so. And he would like to be, not merely have. "Should I?"

"It moved so fast I hardly knew where I was," she tells him. "And I am not one for ghost stories. Too wonderful is often just that, a dead giveaway. Creepy though, the way this gothic tale goes so well with this place," she says, drawing him near, almost drugging him. "A too-perfect backdrop," she says, looking around at the majestic walls, letting them close in on her gloominess. "How was your flight?"

He'd got to JFK early to have a drink, he tells her, looking down at his feet. He'd actually gone and sat at a bar, something he almost never does alone. To make a show of going through the motions, each jigger a bet on the outcome, a cause and its effect. Noisy as they are, bars, almost always, his reserve is mostly out of place. Today is endowed with absolute opacity. He drank to that.

Paulette's hair hangs down her shoulders, curly and streaked yellow blonde, cut only last week with a razor blade to give it some wild edge, some dimension. She teased it and sprayed it near stiff. She runs her hand through it then picks up the crystal glass that has just been filled with icy water. Her skin is near flawless these days, from the pill, which she takes most faithfully, even though it does pump her up with hormones that at times leave her feeling a bit like a cow. Better that though than bad skin, she reasons. For years she had to work the angle of her face when she sat close to a guy so that her pimples would not be the focus. It was consuming, to say the least, remembering the nights when broken out, she did not want to go out, when she could not bear to have someone see her, when she could not even look at herself in the mirror. Having spotless skin gives her more confidence in her personal exhibition. She can be as bold as she likes, can look Benjamin in the face without even flinching. She is fortified, like the high stone walls that once protected the old city of Québec, that stand there mighty, still.

"Lemon, mademoiselle?" asks the waiter, bending in low, slowing things. "Or lime?" His fitted white gloves are clean and tidy as the moment.

"Why yes," she says, "lime," returning the glass to the table, wiping away her lipstick mark from its rim with the corner of her linen napkin. "Thank you." Her nails are a berry red, that lipstick too. Benjamin likes it and takes note of it, how it all seems to go easily together with the ritzy place, how against the dark background of her dress, it glows with otherworldly fire. He's not quite sure however about the way she makes a fetish of the past, though it surely fascinates him. She is a spectacle in a society of them, yet hardly inauthentic, from what he could tell anyway. And he had deliberated her for years now. Hmm, he thinks. The curtain rises and here she is.

The waiter uses sterling silver tongs to gently place a lime wedge into her glass. "And for you, sir?" he asks Benjamin, turning his gaze. "Sure,"

Benjamin answers, feeling happier, lighter than he has in months. He yearned for Paulette far more than he expected to. "Lime also. *Je vous remercie.*" His precise accent raises the waiter's brows. "*Ma blonde?*" he asks Benjamin, standing still, assuming an answer. Dropping a lime plunk into Benjamin's glass, he moves away from the table serenely. How many mercy buckets he'd heard mangled in his days.

The dining room expands, recedes, expands, recedes, almost breathes. Both of them take to it like mouth-to-mouth. The voids between them fade gradually with the daylight of Friday, the weekend presenting itself wide open and foreboding. "In '53, Hitchcock filmed *I Confess* here," Benjamin tells Paulette, uncrossing his legs and encountering her. "It was based on a French play from 1902, *Our Two Consciences*," he says. "Took some 12 writers over eight years to complete." A favorite among the French New Wave, he tells her, explaining why it is that he knows what he does, the little details that may seem to her occasionally annoying and pompous, shifting his weight from side to side in the chair as if to better balance himself.

Her posture is so plumb at the moment that it makes him reflect upon his own slouch. No longer anxious and altogether ventilated, bringing her into some French theory where he might consider her even more fully, like the priest in the film noir is considered even more fully, he grabs her hand across the table and he impatiently kisses it. "When in Rome—ehh, Québec City," he says, grinning like the orange flowers on Paulette's old housedress.

11.

- - - - - - - - - - - - - -

So Raspberry Beret

Paulette gave her entire weekend to the Research Library at UCLA, tackling six linguistics problems on the physical nature of speech sounds that seemed way too much like the math she dreaded, and her dizzying computational homework is due in class this morning. She did not wash her sheets, or exercise, or go to any gatherings. She ate only what could be cut up and consumed quickly—carrot sticks, cheese, dry Italian salami, bowls of cereal with nuts and dried fruit, leftover pizza that she did not even bother to heat. She stood in the kitchen over the sink and chewed it up hurriedly for what it gave to her mental energy, since that is where she found her greatest appetite. Pepperoni or not, taste just wasn't a factor. She even left her bed unmade, which was a real no-no.

And she all but ignored her other two grad classes, both of which had massive readings she did not even get to. Sucks, Germanically speaking, since she has research questions about the power of sticky consonants she cannot pretend to answer. Yet, finally, finally it sunk in that children could not possibly learn a language passively through imitation only, since they often say ungrammatical things like "mama ball," and "I drawed," that nobody taught them. Sometimes a class asks for everything and if you don't give to it, it will not give to you. Reciprocity might well be a social construct, but it seems to work quite nicely on so many levels, she tells herself. Of course, "aha" learning is way more than merely responding to a gesture with a reciprocal action. In fact, the best of it has got nothing automatic in its nature at all.

Certain hypotheses might have got their toes firm in the door to Paulette's perception, yet it is Valentine's Day and she does not really want to sit inside and listen to another monotone lecture about Noam Chomsky and his radical language acquisition device, or about the unconscious rules for sound patterning found in the mind/brain. She is weary of cuneiforms and Amharic script, tired of reading data and taking highlighted study notes, of burying herself in nitpicking science, wants rather to sit on the grass under a tree outside on the quad and ponder poems by Sylvia Plath: "Why can't I try on different lives, like dresses, to see which one fits me and is most becoming?"

It was the typewritten note on the windshield of her car in her Venice parking spot that started the restlessness of it all, that triggered something altruistic—the single, thorny red rose beside the folded white paper beneath the wiper blade at dawn this morning that grabbed her heart and twisted it, like propaganda. In the absence of any quid pro quo, it persuaded her to take a step without feet.

She simply could not bring herself to put on red today, since everyone in the city would be doing that, not even oxblood with purple and brown.

Scarlet and black lace, pink satin hearts, crimson velvet curtains, it was the sappy jargon she could not bear, that corny which shot an arrow right through it all, killing it dead. But something told her she just had to wear romance, to assert it as though it were her point of view, some way, somehow. Love gone runny, like the Dali clock, oh, she is a softy for it actually.

"Every beautiful woman should have a secret admirer," the note read. "Happy Valentine's Day from yours." She thought she was still in bed asleep, had to read it twice and twice more again before it filtered through, and even then she was not exactly sure what it meant, since she did not feel all that beautiful. In fact, she felt quite the opposite so much of the time. Saddlebags and heavy legs, everything clinging to her thighs like the stupid fanny packs so trendy nowadays. Those shiny spandex leggings, those straight-leg stonewashed she could never wear the way Jamie Lee Curtis wears them.

She was like a too-large print on one of her dresses, swamped, and always fussy, never off-the-cuff. She joined the Spin Centre in Santa Monica and three times a week goes off to class to ride a stationary bike. It's meditative fitness worth every penny. And due to her near-starvation, all through the day she must now graze saltine crackers, dried fruit, flavored yogurt, keep her low blood sugar elevated and stable. She considers it brain food, since sometimes she goes dizzy and hazy and anxious without it. Dumb, ugly and undeserving, so much of the time. And the word "woman," it had a certain ring to it which when she thought of herself, she did not hear. Not ever.

If she were still seeing Benjamin and he was not, as he always is and surely always will be, in New York City, why, she might have guessed it was from him. Without a doubt, oh, it is indeed his way. But how could it be

Benjamin? The last she had heard from him left her so uninspired, since it was a waste of time to contradict him, since like her father he knew just about everything, and she had actually been quite depressed about it, not going out with anyone at all for months. Québec had brought them closer, but the distance had wrenched them apart.

He was quite occupied and had forgotten her, it seemed. Every time she called there was some excuse, and the letters, they had slowed down to almost nothing. Doing linguistics puzzles in classical Nahuatl, Agta, Tajik and Sanskrit, while it passed the time and kept her logic flowing like a *wer*, it sometimes made her feel even worse. Sadness seems much heavier than scholarship, like rocks at the bottom of that Luzon creek. It is mostly more captivating too. She had worn it like a cloak over everything in her life.

Well, she got inside her car and locked all the doors, looked suspiciously in the rear-view as she quickly sped off down Rose Avenue toward the freeway. She felt somehow exposed, wide open, and while it frightened her, she rather liked it. Made her pulse beat hard and fast with some kind of strange new rhythm that had Middle Eastern finger cymbals, violin and harmonica, one that touched her humanity and her hips too, like the bellydance.

At almost 30, with lots of men and several carelessly woven relationships behind her, one in particular that she was perhaps still gambling on, that inner bond solid yet, this was fresh and new and peculiar, did not have broken purple hollyhocks to it, not a single one. It made her feel alive and sexy and vulnerable, and she had put all that pretext away some time ago in exchange for some boring, but serious study. It did not go well with cultural discourses and dialectics, half-heartedness, not the way her jean jacket went so nicely with most all her vintage.

She simply had no clue who might've left the words and the flower on her car. Why, it could have been anybody. The hot guy from the video store who only looked like a beggar; his Wayfarers gave him away. The rakish one from upstairs, though she suspected he was gay. The painter from across the alley whose sash window was almost always open, rain or shine. Played a lot of Madonna, that one, a lot of Tears for Fears. Hip and talented, he could be one of those edgy Bohemian gentlemen in ripped jeans, when he liked. Yes, of course, she thinks, it might easily be him, since he knew quite well how to chat her up. The cool guy with the Gumby, why, she had seen him staring at her the way some men do. Yet honestly, it seemed soooo Benjamin. But then they were not really talking much at all these days, and anyway, Benjamin would never use a proxy, Paulette decides, and he preferred handwriting to typing almost always. Cursive engages the brain and helps to distinguish the literate, he liked to say.

The mid-'50s dress she had chosen to wear is a flirty, feminine silhouette, perfect for covering up the nakedness she just felt so sharply. When she'd fetched it from her wooden armoire, unfinished still and packed to the point of near-madness, why, she must have known something enchanting was about to happen. It seemed so funky and seductive, flamboyant even, so distinctly "Raspberry Beret." In the 'out' door, you could say. So red, she'd thought when she put it on, without much red in it at all.

Its fabric is opaque brushed cotton, in a blackish, pale grey and ballet-slipper-pink painterly print, reminiscent of water gushing from a fountain, one in which a bird might even be drinking. A meticulous double stitch is employed on the bodice and at the waist to achieve a quilted effect. The cascading, pintucked skirt is unusual for this time period, lending a sense of passion and movement to the overall surging look. It is kind of timeless, she thinks, the dress; might have started out life as a Victorian ball gown worn with a corset, cut down, then cut again, signaling a lane change to get herself onto the already crowded Santa Monica Freeway, an heirloom really, like love hand-washed and starched countless times, its true colors faded sweetly into their quiet glory and simply more exquisite because of it. She keeps it on a green knitted hanger among her better dresses, though she does not wear it often. It needed lots of punch and she did not always have it, that thing that had to be summoned up for style to flow and resonate. The birds must be bathing in the fountain for her to slip it on. Bought for a song on a Third Street sidewalk, one near Beverly, a shop with racks of old polka dots and new moonbeams. Moody, it is, like the affectionate morning and not practical, not exactly. Well, some of the playlists on *Morning Becomes Eclectic* are not exactly practical either, she thinks, yet she likes to listen anyway. The freeway moves east slowly but it moves. No better no worse, the 405 going north. KCRW, it almost nullifies the traffic. Throbbing love tunes today, of course: Champaign, Foreigner, Diana Ross and Lionel Richie, Gregory Isaacs and his "Night Nurse."

With about an hour to spare on her grandfather's watch, Paulette gets herself coffee with steamed milk in a plastic foam cup near UCLA's parking Lot 4 and heads now toward the general direction of class. The air is brisk and she needs her jean jacket yet. Short and tight and fairly beat-up, it covers little of the dress, allowing the skirt to pour out widespread all over the campus walkway and beyond. Her black lace-up shoes and grey fishnet stockings move straight ahead, in that well-read sort of way, but the ruffled skirt goes in the opposite direction like the uppercase left curve J. It moves to the mysterious flower and note in her backpack with its own awareness. She walks defiantly, her head up, not feeling the slightest bit bewildered. Never perfectly sure of what she says or does, she is quite sure of this, pure matter endowed with meaning, this rose by another name. Oh, perfectly. She lights a cigarette and blows smoke into the invigorating day, punctuating it; an ellipsis, perhaps, following psychedelic pop.

"Paulette, isn't it?" The Persian man smiles with some intimacy that comes and goes, the way French comes and goes from English. They have a class together and he likes her politics, what he knows of them anyway, he says. Yeah sure, she says, wondering what her politics actually are. He walks beside her slowly, almost brushing up against her, letting her set the pace and falling a bit behind so that she must stop occasionally to check, see if he is there. He asks her for a cigarette and she gives him one, even lights it for him.

When he speaks about the fundamentalist revolution in the Middle East, the emptiness of the gold faucets and the diamond-studded Rolls-Royces the oil money buys, about Pan-Islamic forces and Arab nationalism, Paulette listens as one who is hasty to learn. "Iran hasn't launched a war of aggression against another nation in two hundred years. War is not our nature, despite what Iraq imposed." She can hear him inhale the cigarette, holding it between the tips of his left thumb and forefinger, like a joint. Kind of macho, she thinks, and distinctly cool.

"You seem open," he says, when he finds that she is listening. The way he talks about Iran's holy defense and every subject under the sun, including the *Qur'an*, that Islamic terrorism is really a contradiction in terms, and that all the teachings of Islam are based directly or indirectly on the principle of peace, oh, he gets a strong hold of her. From the land of lyrical poets, he declares, Rumi, Sadi and Hafiz, where in the realm of love, monastery and mosque are quite the same. Says to be careful not to mistake him, or them, for Arabs, and calls himself Saje, though he admits that is not his real name.

"What's your real name?" Paulette asks, staring at the tops of the leafless trees, imagining them fully green again, fluttering in the draught. Though nothing at all like New York, she can't bear the winter, even here in a city of perennials and pleasant temperatures. It is often gloomy, and while she can relate to it the way a caramel filling relates to its hard candy shell, it is just not her color palette. Not her erogenous zone either, not like a hot, blue day rising jerkily, winding her up like a spinning top. The Persian man moves ahead very straight with his broad chest well out. His round brown eyes dart rapidly from one side of the walkway to the other, and then behind and in front, past the students and the classrooms. "It's in Farsi," he tells her, his face tense and strained with amusement. "So Saje is good."

They come upon another classmate and stop for a moment to chat about how awfully difficult the homework was, compare answers and to finish their cigarettes. Saje throws his on the ground and steps on it, rubs it with his combat boots. Paulette puts hers out but keeps the butt in between her fingers until she can find a trashcan. The Earth is not an ashtray, she says quietly, under her breath, disappointed. He's only smart about some things, she thinks, remembering when he told the class that truth will almost always be taken to the gallows. Well, not just some things, she admits.

A long-necked woman with pale skin, virgin eyebrows and short black wavy hair who seems intelligent but absent-minded walks up and says: "Happy Valentine's Day. Does everybody have fabulously romantic plans with their honeys?" She stands back, looking at Paulette up and down for an answer, framing her in imaginary mahogany, wood that lives and breathes

350 years. "Your dress," she notes, sensing something, smiling seductively, "it kind of tells the story, you know, makes your decree known, like those, um, ancient Babylonian kings."

"The story," Paulette says slowly, playfully. "Oh really. Is my biography in parentheses?"

"They were Persian actually, five thousand years ago," Saje tells them, not missing the opportunity to illuminate his rich culture, to show his dignity, the entire ocean in his drop.

Paulette laughs out loud, shrieks really, feeling her secret admirer at her back, down the backs of her thighs. She takes up the ruffle of her dress in her fingers and swishes it from side to side, moving the energy around nervously, letting the air cool a bit beneath her skirt. Somebody was actually aware of her. Well, it made everything inside her squirm the way an idea-in-form does.

"No plans and no honey," she answers soberly, remembering then forgetting Benjamin, thinking this is neither good nor bad, but something else vagabond and not really a nuisance at all, something tucked away that nobody, not even she, could decipher. She needn't worry if her skin is clear, or if her eyes are well shadowed, or if her stomach is flat or if her legs are shaved up high enough. She needn't wonder if she is being used or if she is the one using, or if she is saying or doing the right things. She needn't doubt if she is thin enough, or smart enough, or choice enough. She needn't stew over an ogle elsewhere. Apathy, it sure has some big advantages. "How about you?"

The girl pulls down her tight red turtleneck, raises her shoulders, tilts her face to show off her beauty spot and says rather boldly: "After work." She moves her sensible eyes from Paulette to Saje and then back again.

"Long after," she says, winking. Just then a tribe of stocky house sparrows sets off abruptly from the trees across the half-cloudy sky and chirps sharply. Saje seems hardly amused. He would prefer not to see women in their late twenties behave in this rabidly American way.

Plucky, Paulette thinks. She has to work tonight herself on a presentation for an ad campaign that has a Friday deadline; otherwise she might call up to that open sash window. She had thought about it many times, on her way to the beach mostly, when she had an hour or so to fantasize. If it weren't for being so deeply attached to Benjamin on and off over the years, well, she might've, if the sun were strong enough. She could use a little plucky herself, she admits, admiring the deep bluish red of the girl's T-neck that might be cashmere, and the bravado of her push-up bra that might be black lace. *Was that all padding in it or just a bit?* she wonders, having been herself a boy toy on occasion. When she was 18 she might've gone up those stairs, walked in the door, been all over him on the floor, let him have what he wanted because that was what she wanted. She has since learned to tame her eroticism, but particles emerge from it naturally sometimes like long-lasting bubbles from champagne, the kind that's corked and caged and laid to rest for years.

"Have you ever had Persian food?" Saje asks nobody in particular, his eyes still darting. There is muscle in his strong body and in his voice. Both seem carefully toned. He seems much taller to Paulette than he actually is.

"I have tried Lebanese, Moroccan, Israeli. Hmm. Not sure if I have ever tasted Persian before," Paulette answers, "since baklava's origin is claimed by both Turkey and Greece." The girl with sensible eyes says she has heard there is a lot of rice. Piles of it, she says as though it were a bad thing. Another classmate with pale black skin adds that the rice is mostly burnt, crispy. "I heard it sizzle and crackle in a pan once." The whites of his eyes shine pearlescent like shell buttons. A foodie, Paulette thinks.

"*Tahdig*," Saje explains, looking now at the group of students assembled around him. "The word actually means 'bottom of the pot.' Bright gold layers are meant to resemble the desert." Paulette giggles at Saje's manner, and at the curls of his brown hair that haphazardly fall down his shoulders. Too young for that bald spot in the middle of his head, though, she thinks, smiling still. The black guy, he must get around. Sure got some swag. Might be Haitian, she reasons, from the upright of his stand, from the lilt of his French accent, from the fine cut of his smooth red and yellow cotton shirt. An African pattern, she guesses, wax block. Nigerian, or hollandais Dutch, perhaps? Fashion school had left her analyzing clothes just the way Sherlock Holmes did crime. She couldn't ignore it even if she'd wanted to. And authenticity, well, she was all over that too.

There are some decent Persian restaurants in Westwood, Saje says. After class they might wander down Westwood Boulevard and pick one that isn't too busy. "We can share the rice, have it with some sour cherries to honor this grand day of passion." He spots a thrill in his classmates' faces and it beckons him on. Men had authority in his Iranian household. In America, his personal power is for the birds.

"Hmm," Saje says, more relaxed at the moment than before, "truthfully, it's actually such a fickle dish. I know the best place for it, ahh yes, Shamshiri. It's the *crème de la crème*. I can even reveal to you some wisdom from the story of David, the prophet of Love, who was believed to have 99 wives and yet still, still he yearned for another…"

Saje's sidelong glance slides warmly over Paulette. Quite the charmer, she thinks, reading him right to left, wondering why she has never actually spoken privately with him before, thinking that her denim jacket will just have to come off now the way a shell comes off a French macaron, or a boiled egg. The sky is cloudless and the sun shines like a yellow sapphire upon the faceted moment. Maybe later she would telephone Benjamin, find out if he is in L.A., plunge right into Valentine's Day without any props whatsoever, nothing red at all. Since a rose is a rose is a rose.

"*Ouah*, I am in," says the Haitian. "Me too," says the plucky one. Paulette raises her hand high, the butt still between her fingers, moves her wrist like a windshield wiper in a tropical downpour, then she picks up her backpack and feels the weightiness of true romance, the thing, not the word, alive in her now, bubbling up, acting up, consuming both her and her beautiful old dress with its double stitching and all the opposing forces that come together to heave and wrench and wither and tear at the very ancient fabric of it, 100 percent. Birds of a feather, they saunter off to class, hollow as a sweet puff of air, broken as a yolk, starved lovers, linguistically speaking from way far back in the mouth, devouring every disobedient narrative, every sassy root, oh yes, the whole lot of them.

12.

- - - - - - - - - - - - - - -

- -

Floral Print Wiggle

When Benjamin asks Paulette to a family gathering in New York, she is both baffled and curious. His clan from across the seas, Israel, Holland, England, they convene yearly just to stay connected. It is late summer there, like here, and she thinks it should be warm still. Cold bites, even when it is wrapped up in a cozy proposition. The details of the thing don't matter that much to Paulette, but the invitation, oh it matters plenty. More than she aims to admit.

Her UCLA summer school class in future studies wrapped up the week before last and work grinds on slowly. She has several books on food security to read for fall and concepts to ponder, but she can take some time, a respite from the tedious routine of a life she has yet to define in some way other than vague. Such is the fate of the ones who follow no clear paths to speech therapy or even activist lawyer. *To be, not to be, to be what?* is the real question, almost always now. Everyone on the planet must be of some use, one way or the other, Paulette thinks. Now that her weight is fairly constant and her skin is clear, glowing even, almost always. Get one's ducks in a row. And honestly, to see Benjamin shine among his family may sort out some feelings, both his and hers.

She received Benjamin's fiery letter last Friday, took a kitchen knife to the sealed wax quickly to breach the thing and, not thinking too much at all, called him up right away. A stroke of luck found him between appointments and classes and answering his own office phone. He seemed honestly delighted that she'd come. Surprised, even. "My family asks about you," Benjamin says, matter-of-factly. Paulette can't help but wonder what he tells them of her, of their relationship, if you can call it that? "I sure miss New York," she says, revealing nothing of her excitement. "Then it's settled," Benjamin declares, giving her nothing at all to read between lines.

He would send her the ticket right away. She would not object, not this time, and Benjamin would not argue about it either way. Truth told, Benjamin did not struggle much with money or the power he wields with it, and Paulette, she did. *Finding balance is key to everything girl*, she thinks. Stridency, well, it just didn't suit her. It didn't fit, the way tight jeans just didn't.

She made an appointment to have her nails done and her toes too, since the chances were quite good that she'd be showing them in platform sandals. She has acrylics, a woman from South Korea who painstakingly filed and buffed and filled in every three weeks or so. It was an indulgence, yes, but one she did not feel the slightest bit guilty about. Hands are important, for they say hello, goodbye, clap, pray, heal, hurt, hold, play, close, open. They hold the cigarette to her lips and her heart to her sleeve. Dance too, says her Asian manicurist from underneath her mask. "Nails are simply the hand's sparkling jewels," she says each time Paulette struggles to pick the perfect color to suit her mood. And Benjamin, oh, he liked them red, mostly.

Blue-red? Orange-red? He doesn't much care. And red lips too, matte, particularly, for it did not smear. He paid attention to such things. Energy red. Tango red. Action red. Chinese good-luck red. Indian-wedding-dress red. Vamp. Red alert. Ruby. When it comes to cosmetics, Paulette did not know one brand from the next, not like some of her fussy girlfriends who bought expensively, but she did get color. It was always a very hot topic at her agency, carrying a great deal of clout in the design and underlying strategy of an ad campaign. And in fact, she herself was very much affected by pigment. Too much red made her agitated. Too little and she was ma-nipulative. Not like green, the color of the heart chakra. Why, she could never get enough of that. It is a verb to her, the way red is to Benjamin, a state of being that did not matter about what specifically; taste, smell, feel, keep, become. Complementary colors then, she, he, both primaries like in the mottled begonia with leaves the shape of angel wings.

It had been several weeks since she had last heard from Benjamin, but she did not stop mulling him over in her mind. She assumed he had let go of her, that their romance had abruptly simmered, that Québec was just a postcard holiday to collect and look back upon. She had prepared herself for that anyway, imagining all along that he was just too good to be true. But in fact he was giving her exactly what she needed, the space and distance to focus on her life, her future and her academic work. She became consumed by school, just as he suspected that she would. Well, he began calling again occasionally with all kinds of up-and-doings and truthful things and she missed him all right, at times even longed to see him, sometimes desperately, but there was simply nowhere else to turn. When she spoke with him she always had this sense of utter futility, a muted auburn kind of feel, the sort that comes just before winter, that cools one's heels. The temperature drops and the days grow shorter, the trees turn brown and it only goes that way. No surprises. Nothing like a violet-red sky in the clear blue morning.

Yet she is 30 now, just, and that biological clock has gone off ticking like a time bomb as it does for many young women in the Western world. She hardly heard it, though she knows it's there, something irrational and fertile in her stock that she simply can't ignore. And quite honestly, she was growing weary of casual dating. Saje, oh, he was fresh and light and fun to go out with, had lots of energy and fearlessness and he taught her about poetic Persian everything. Burned up the bottoms of most all her skillets cooking too. He was majestic but just not paternal enough.

And there was a charming Lebanese chap, Farez, tucked away where nobody could see. His black hair and black eyes and lashes weren't the only things in his bag of tricks. When she was close beside him in the library, it was a fuzzy, shadowy world. Foreign students from the Middle East, both, neither of whom seemed bewildered by life, considering. Twice Paulette had to talk without guilt about her longing for liberty. With Benjamin that has been altogether left unsaid.

Over the phone Benjamin spoke of an afternoon party in some showy garden restaurant around Central Park. "You'll be right at home and divine in the greenhouse," he told her. "Hot too," he promised, snickering. And so Paulette chooses a close-fitting flowery sheath, mid-calf length with generous side slits, a dress that her mother picked up at some Beverly Hills estate sale. She was helping a friend who reupholstered slipcovers for hotel couches and chairs and she discovered some dresses among the folded-up, stacked textiles. It was one of several at the bottom of a colorful basket that had caught her mother's eye, and she just picked it up and tossed it on the counter. "My eldest daughter loves these old schmattes," she'd told the man at the table collecting money, shaking her head back and forth like she was apologizing for something. "Better than lots of the new schlock," he said, bagging the dress politely in brown paper. No apology necessary.

An old worn garment was something like a fortune cookie to Paulette, could always be made to apply. Having it resonate more specifically, though, as if it were her kismet, now that was something else, and her mother was frankly mystified over it. For the life of her she could not imagine what Paulette saw in the stuff. The man charged her $15 and her mother thought even that was high. She might have considered another one were it cheaper. With three girls, spoiling one always seemed out of the question. Luckily the other two were not particularly partial to Chinese food. They preferred pot roast and potatoes, like their father. Clothing as covering the way brown gravy does, dripped sparingly across the meat as an accompaniment, now for her mother that was better yet. The packaged kind, without lumps.

Though not fully in bloom herself, yet quite gutsy to dig up something if only just her own wellspring, when Paulette tried on the sexy '60s cocktail dress, the lush coral and claret in the roses seemed to brighten things the way glaze on fired bisque brightens things. The mirror all but blushed back at her mere outline, brought to life more fully by the sparkling shroud. The bold silk print, woven with gold lamé threads, is an actual impressionist watercolor painting of plump roses and foliage in various greens, mold and chartreuse. It was adapted to become a printed textile the way a snapshot of a masterpiece is modified to become a poster. Paulette thought of the fabric designer at Maxan, the dress label stitched into the syrupy pink satin lining, alone in his New York City office, yes, surely his, the door open to the buzzing and the bustling, inspired simply by shadow and light, and perhaps by the wild abandon of the rose itself. Oh, to be one so able to look artfully at the dimensional world and reimagine it into flat, repeating patterns, she thought, wondering if Maxan was still in the business and if the women working there are doing more now than fetching coffee and answering phones. Since women with their thinner skin can feel the prick of the thorns.

The lovely curled petals of the rose seem suggestions by a chiseled brush, rather than painstaking details, which suits Paulette just fine. While even less content now just to be pretty and yet hardly even cognizant of it, she still goes more for the easy-going of Renoir than she does for the careful, tormented Cézanne. It will linger nicely among the wine and the finger food and the pleasure, she thought, the straight line of the dress' cut rendering her thin and statuesque, elegant even, with just the perfect quota of red. Oh, it would wink all right, the way it moved around the curve of her derrière like a question mark.

And her grandmother had raspberry sandals with block heels that she didn't wear any longer, strappy with an open toe to balance out the sleevelessness. The concealed pocket at the right hip, it is a good place in the dress to hide one hand at least. The other will simply have to manage the party and Benjamin on its own.

Paulette's hair had turned dark at the base and it made her unhappy, like miasma settling low over her crown chakra. She was a genuine blonde who needed to stay that way, for emotional reasons, though she was hardly brazen. Some girls could afford the muddy, but she needed golden. Her grandmother had got her using that violet shampoo between visits to the beauty shop and it kept her spirits up some, kept her purpose clear. Since her stylist had just come down with hepatitis, she called her girlfriend, one with some salon experience, to do a few highlights, the parts and the zig-zaggy zone beyond. It was something closer to yellow at any rate. When and if her hairdresser came back to the beauty shop, she would have him tone it all down for her. Frizz and split ends can always be stylishly twisted. Her little sister taught her to do a French braid recently, and sometimes she used that to curl the ends. At least the dim was somewhat lifted up and she could reinvent herself yet again, snubbing the appetites and the comebacks and the mass trends willfully the way she always had. Yes, glazed pottery was simply perkier and more reflective. She could not know yet that burnished clay, without the millimeter of glass, has a sincere glow from within.

Like Benjamin, Paulette was a creation of her own making. He was far less self-conscious about it though, and far less insecure, content with his own perceptible roughness. Both of them were subject to anxiety and depression, however, and while smugly indie, quite miserably lonely. Figuring yourself out, and stepping firmly into it, now that was funky business, as was trying to forge new ideas that were not already taken. Neither of them had much use for trendiness, no matter how pervasive, unless still in the organic stage, the way reggae was once, the way rock was too before it was hijacked and sanitized and whitened. Neither would be caught dead tying a sweater around the neck, though both had ripped jeans like the Ramones, naturally ripped, of course. Both seemed to grasp that style is not wholly about the features and qualities you were born with, or without. And while it was not handed down, it certainly had to be picked up.

No, it is not even about money, Paulette had come to understand, although that, like being good-looking or hot, well, that certainly helps. Money, or perhaps the lack of it, turns curtains into barkcloth jackets and Indian bedspreads into maxi dresses. Look at the African women; poverty has never been their excuse. A creative life provides an infinite wardrobe of leaves and nuts and feathers and shoots and furs and mud. That is how the late-'40s poodle skirt was born, when opera singer Juli Lynne Charlot ran clean out of money, but needed a fashionable new holiday look and wanted to start a conversation. Since she could not sew, she fetched herself some felt from her mother's factory, and the circle skirt, well, it did not need seams. Restrictions, limitations, accidents, the tragedy of war, such is the providence of one who is quite resourceful and inspired. Money goes one way and art another way. Both meet up at a fork in the road where icons linger like flowers just waiting to be grasped. Fashion school taught Paulette way more than she ever imagined it would.

Benjamin always wore skinny ties, black ones mostly. He found the shape rather artful and proper for his slim chest size, even when they were quite yesterday's news. He also liked that they came out of global wartime rationing and referenced the democratization of style. Since one had to be clothed, might as well find a way to do it up differently, to march fashion forward like a soldier who would refuse to pick up a gun. The one he chose for the family party is slightly crimson, with a gleam to it, and he knotted it asymmetrically. It went quite well with some old carmine suspenders that once belonged to his grandfather. Snap, the thumb and middle finger.

When Benjamin first tried those suspenders on for Paulette, shortly after they were tucked in to the space they'd share for a few days, she thought they were just perfect, feeling nostalgia for her own grandfather. She pulled at them friskily, grazed his chest, his heart. "I'm happy you are here," he said to her, grabbing her hand. "Bend my ear, Baby," she said, smiling, kissing his cheek, leaving bright red lipstick on it that she wipes away with her fingers. That ruddy lipstick, it went well with those suspenders too.

His people, all 40 of them, arrived in New York City five days before Paulette, and had found a comfortable place in their past, present and future. The drama receded into the couches, chairs and beds of all the sterile rented rooms. The hotel maids came each morning to change the towels and sheets, washed clean of the odds and ends that had cluttered up and separated their lives. Amsterdam rejected apartheid and accommodated the African National Congress, the general Zionist consensus in Israel was shattered, and England was deep in its Morrissey phase. Unlike most families, they tackled one thing at a time, so that when Paulette sits down at the table in Central Park beside Benjamin's banker uncle from Tel Aviv, who is smoking a long, graceful Cuban cigar, it is only the softly fused girl in the mysterious dress that he beholds.

"Em, I would have pegged you for lotus flowers," he says, staring at the florid dress and Paulette in it, clearly moved and grinning, his upper lip, cheeks and chin covered in designer stubble, "or star of Bethlehem."

For a financier, he sure seems to be quite familiar with his flowers, Paulette thinks. She hardly knows what to say, but feels a bit like springtime, in full sun. She hopes, prays it will last, that sun. Dieting for the week she is empty, lightheaded too. This, with that, makes a sort of elixir that has got her drunk. Two glasses of wine is her limit and she'd reached it an hour ago.

"Benjamin tells me that you are, em, studying language and power," he says, lisping some, puffing on that cigar. It is quite aromatic, piquant even, and pleasant, makes her like the man even more. A real paradox, since bankers are the zealots of austerity, economic, moral and otherwise. And saving has never been Paulette's way to salvation. She wonders what else Benjamin has told him about her. That she is here for him, sure, but for what? Theater, affection, a floret on his arm? She decides it doesn't really matter, that she is just exactly where she wants to be.

"Yes," she says, looking over agreeably at Benjamin, who is across the room with his glamorous mother, she in an ensemble of avocado and ochre hues, the skirt a librarian length, her Ferragamo sandals olive-green velvety suede, "among other things, verbing, making a doing-word out of a thing-word, without the doing. A table is a thing that does not act, and yet, the word 'tabled' distorts that meaning, gives it movement like that smoke you blow out from the cigar."

"Em. Don't verbs get nouned?" he asks, with some irony in his voice. He is darkly good-looking, wearing a black suede yarmulke and a wide-shouldered Armani power suit, a foreign prince in an ancient fairy tale. Flags flying, bewitching, well-fixed—a collision with Paulette's principles, head-on.

Paulette's sweaty hand sinks into that one pocket and her heart pounds hard and steady. Nominalization is not party banter; failure isn't the same as failing, not even close. The verb is quite buoyant yet, while the noun is over and done with, washed up, end of story. This is not the first time that she is quite serious and the man, he only wants to play. Benjamin does it too, and she has sauntered away from him red-faced before, plenty. She must tell herself to go on, plead, even though her head spins dizzy.

She pulls her hand out from the pocket and continues, turning her body away, but keeping her eyes steady on the face of the Israeli. She is hoping that Benjamin will come to her rescue, as he has done from time to time. He seems not to get thrown off the way she does by mischief. He does not doubt himself, not the way she does herself. It must be a man thing, she thinks.

"This stuff, it has grim implications," she tells him, feeling her hands sweaty. "Actors are removed from their actions; feelings are turned into actions that are wiped clean of those feelings. 'Bombing kills dozens.'" She makes quote marks with both her hands, the damp on them shines like the gold threads of her dress under the low chandelier lights that seem like small moons above. "Who dropped the bomb that killed so many? It is unclear when newspapers print such headlines. It conceals and reduces our sense of what is truly involved." She grabs for a glass of ice water on the table and drinks, thinking that it is just something to do with more theater to it than gasps. Her groomed nails strike Venetian red against the ivory tablecloth. Bombs away, she thinks.

"Sounds political," he says, leaning back against the chair. He reaches for an ashtray in the middle of the table and taps the cigar, a Cohiba, in it. Then he rotates it before he puffs again.

"It can be," she says very calmly, "and should be. Defending language for the sake of democracy, allowing for ethics and humanity. There is always someone responsible, and that responsibility is never irrelevant. I am looking at the various ways in which language can be used as an instrument of manipulation, as propaganda. I suppose that is intensely political." She wants to mention Hitler, but thinks better of it.

"International law obliges the state of Israel to respect the Palestinian language, and yet, em, many Jewish Israelis are not comfortable hearing Arabic and so it is discouraged. One can be fired for speaking his mother tongue. Language is an important indicator of marginalization. I respect what you are studying. What do you think you will do, em, when you are finished?" He looks sharply at the cigar, to make sure the light on the foot is evenly distributed. He puts the lit end toward his mouth and blows gently until it is all orange-red and glowing hypnotically.

This query, well, it sends Paulette into a sort of panic, and again woozy, she looks away from the flame and about the room for Benjamin. Not that he can help very much with this kind of smoky moment, as she won't make a man her answer, not parasitically speaking, and not in the way her mother did and her grandmother did and her great-grandmother did, branding love and family the ceiling and not just the floor. For Paulette, it would be madness. For the others it might have been too.

What did they all do with their persistent mental energy? Let it go to rot, she supposes, imagining Benjamin as a part-time job with little pay, an excuse for doing nothing further with her life. We expect so much more out of men. They fight the wars and ride the rockets into deep space. Funny how Paulette's favorite professors in grad school are young women still working on their PhDs, yet even they teach the works of men, for the most part. Paulette rocks backwards and forwards in the chair and the wood creaks some. It is her soap opera condition and her soapbox essence both that reverberate.

"Write maybe, I suppose, or teach, not too sure," she mumbles, shrugging her shoulders against the agitation, the sense that she is failing, staring down at the moss-green cluster of foliage and the flecks of golden in her '60s-era dress, wishing it would hold her like a trellis in a *plein-air* planter box; that she too could start a singular, unclassifiable conversation, the way Dior did with a hammer on the mannequin to shape his manifesto after the Second World War. Shocked by its indecent sensuality, by its vulgarity, the wide skirts, the slender waists, the blossoming bosoms, why, it started a revolution, turning the page of unmotivated fashion from gloom and gravity to humanized happiness. Even made the cover of *Time* magazine in 1947.

"Not sure if I will ever be finished," Paulette says mournfully, looking for dialogue to justify herself and her curious studies, a way to pin down its run-of-the-mill utility. It gets stuck in the awkward silence that is cold as the glass of water, which she would break with that hammer if only she had one, and let go all of her raw sexuality into the warmth of the tablecloth. Ice distinguishable, though no longer visible on a table she very much wishes would move. Living in estrangement is hardly a gimmick and it does not escape the demands of pragmatism. Doing what is natural is not necessarily doing what is profitable. Benjamin knows this better than most. The princely banker puffs on the cigar, says that "sometimes you don't want the book to end." She does not look at him, nor at Benjamin, who walks toward them hoping to modify the moment somehow. Everything he didn't hear is in Paulette's face. Springtime in Paris came and went, along with the arc of Paulette's inventiveness, that petal plucked from the daisy and in the squall, nowhere to be found. The frivolous Renoir sun, oh, it did not last.

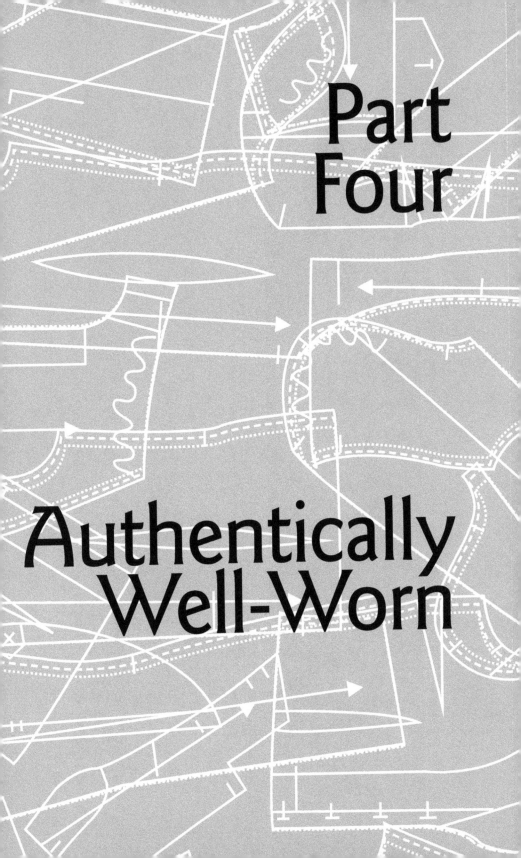

Part Four

Authentically Well-Worn

13.

Fish Net

Paulette quite liked being the victim of fate: Benjamin in New York, she in L.A. While she craves an intimate, steady relationship and what that means in terms of companionship, she prefers to complain about imperfect things rather than to actually fix them. Unlike holes that she'll rush with needle and thread to mend. It seemed more genuine to her, there being no middle, no strategy, and that was crucial. To leave the romance to itself, raw and unpredictable, faithless as fashion.

Yet now that Benjamin is coming into town with a proposition, since he called it that very thing, Paulette is hardly prepared for it. Well, being happy is already-seen, already-felt, a light illusion anyway. Life is cream in the fits and starts, in the broken-down dreams that make you want to slash into your skin, the stuff of heavy cream. She is somewhat addicted to it, that which makes her long to tear things up, even though she'd altogether stopped crucifying her body. She'd known it was risky always, somewhere deep in her consciousness, yet sometimes there is no clear logic to behaviors right and wrong. Like starving oneself, and smoking cigarettes, and having sex with strangers. It has the ring of drama to it, is the kind of thing like *Lolita* that is performed in various ways all over the world. Style, now that kept her from straying very wide of the mark. It too had a stage all its own.

Just as Plato established that word-meaning mapping was innate in humans, Paulette thought that style must be too. The syntax of it, the phonology of it, the morphology and the semantics of it, the tools of language as dress and dressing as act, Paulette thought them quintessential to civilization.

Some just never evolve very much, wear their Levi's solely as frustration, their sweatshirt as lethargy, period. It is quite like growing an expanded vocabulary, like acquiring another idiom even, or reading music. Imagine stopping only at the blues, or trying to read classical without knowing some German, some French? To grasp melodies, basslines, chords, is akin to grasping collars or necklines as an art form. If only it too had a system of staff notations, all could improvise.

Paulette had taken to wearing black again, days and days of it, using it as a phoneme to build upon, as a sign. Representing the world through dark dressing, disrupting it and its excesses if she could, urgently. Suited her just fine, again. Oh, it suited Benjamin too.

Even though her sisters said that everything she wore had begun to look the same, well, if not quite the same, then similar: four pairs of black shoes, three black purses, two old cashmere sweaters, seven skirts in varying lengths, fabrics and shapes, including one pencil, three blouses, no, four. If she could buy an item new and Missoni, it would be a plunging black pullover with scalloped edges, sleeveless, in the shape of a Fellini movie star. Kohl eyeliner smudged, darkish roots, stockings of torn lace, a deep V in the back and in the front. When one sees beyond the very point of collars, to connect the arm with the torso of the body, to their articulating of the cleavage and the chin, even the lips, cheeks and eyes. A turtleneck can violate a shirt and tie. A Mandarin calls up China and India and the military. Then there's the horseshoe, the crew, the halter, the boat. Similar, all this black, well yes, but only if kill and kiss are similar.

Her sisters never went near it, wouldn't touch black with a ten-foot pole, the ones used by riverboat men to fend off wharfs. Navy blues, browns, forest greens, solids mostly in up-to-the-minute lines from the thoroughly middle-America Broadway, which now has about 35 percent of the L.A. market share. They wore standard English to Paulette's tony French, were influenced by Disney films and she by the foreign ones that ran slow and wide.

Their mother is another story entirely. Her perfectly curled and teased, bleached salt-and-pepper hair and colored sequin embellishments, they come right straight out of *Dynasty*. When you dissect drama, it has a range more than one serial meaning. Well, Hayley Mills could never play *Betty Blue*, nor could Béatrice Dalle star in *The Parent Trap*. Style is about survival, Paulette often thinks, oh, about survival of distinction, and then some.

Poles are not just for holding things at bay; they are for dancing, for vaulting, for reeling them in too. The time comes when the twenties are over, decidedly so, and one can no longer pass for it or sink into it or hide behind it, and the future, that begins to seem scary, the options no longer limitless.

Benjamin had gone through it with some harshness. Building an academic career while you are still young is essential. Your best years, it is thought. Paulette was about to finish her master's degree and she wanted really to avoid a job in the university. Though she did want to explore the world's ideas with some depth, doing so in an institution of higher learning that granted degrees seemed much too confining. That publish-or-perish attitude prevailed, and yet Benjamin had made his way just fine, established a fine reputation for himself. His book about the nullifying effects of television is a highbrow work of art, used as a textbook in social literacy departments across the country and around the world. He was beginning to make an outline for his next project, about the nature of photography, its irreducible truth, its significance and its consequences to advertising. A scholar of implied meanings in much the same tradition as French philosopher Roland Barthes, this hotshot Benjamin, and he is a teacher with the highest of ratings from his own bookish students.

That and his cool black ties, anything but voluble, sure, he was a catch all right. A fine one.

Never trust anyone over 30, she'd thought at one time. Well, Benjamin thought the same way. Everybody young did. There were songs about it and posters too, aimed at the ones pulling the strings, the ones buying and selling everything. Paulette's father was almost 30 times two, and her mother was now quite close to that herself. Was she old? She never asked her mother that. And her father, he was happy to look forward to collecting Social Security, since he had paid in plenty. And that pension too, he could take it after 28 years at the hospital and he was nearly there. They were planning an African safari, and getting ready for it—vaccines, cameras, duffel bags and cotton clothing the color of khaki. Benjamin's parents were in Israel for much of the year. His father plays the cello there in an amateur string quartet. From stable, middle-class backgrounds the pair of them, Paulette and Benjamin. It seemed to matter little though when you roll the dice.

Benjamin was far too established to leave NYU, Paulette felt strongly, and his family was rooted there in Manhattan, but she would try to remain open, even though she could not possibly live in the cold, not ever. She'd learned that while at school, trying to stay warm and cute with a jacket she did not like to button closed. It was just something she knew for certain about herself, the way others who liked rain, or wind, or darkness just knew about themselves. Some coveted the changing seasons and others the months of fall. But Benjamin seemed unconcerned with the weather, no matter where he was. Those sorts of layers never seemed to worry him much. Preoccupied with many heady things, he was, just not that. Different strokes for different folks. She'd even begun doing salutations to it, the sun, taking up Vinyasa to honor and harness it.

Despite the fact that the moon had not been full for days, things felt operatic, mythical, though Paulette did not know why exactly. Benjamin coming to L.A. to see her so suddenly in the middle of the semester, his light, celebratory mood like whipped cream, it seemed anacoluthic, somehow lacking in sequence.

She picked a bewitched dress for the evening, one of thick Mexican cotton from the late '50s, a canvas for happy fish making bubbles embroidered by hand in bright, tropical colors on a wide circle skirt that was anything but black. Though she knew well how to swim, and had been before to Hawaii with her parents, to Oahu and to Kauai where she had learned to snorkel, had dived off a Greek sea cliff, she had never been deep beneath the water, not scuba diving nor in a submarine even. These fish were of dreams the same way that Benjamin was, with sequins for eyes.

While she paid dearly for the dress during one of her fits of retail therapy, about $100 at a shop on Melrose in L.A. that provided wardrobe to the film studios, she knew it was worthy and not just of this moment. The shop's owner told her it was sewn by hand, most likely the hand of an aunt, but one who knew what she was doing with lining, backings and the like, for a fantasy cruise upon the vast oceans, temporarily borrowing certain forms of privileged life the way her mother had. When she'd got it home from the splurge, the contradiction amused her far more than it does now.

With cap sleeves that caress the well-formed biceps of her upper arm, the neckline is sweetheart, and below some gathers at the bust that seemed quite good for the curve of her still-firm breasts and tiny waist, the dress seems more a caricature of her inside than it is a portrait. Peppermint pink and kelp green and mango orange and sunset red, each fish on the very full skirt has scales of contrasting woolen yarns; each is swimming for something, heading somewhere. Fish, like people in their right milieu, they seem always headed somewhere. It was what she longed for, to know that magnetic pull to someone, to somewhere, to something.

Benjamin's whole being seemed frisky when she met him at LAX. More sunshine than swagger, she thought. She found it both alluring and alarming, wondering what he could possibly have up his sleeve. She had her suspicions, but they were not trustworthy like the truth. The truth was somewhere, though, oh, she was sure of that. It was in the way he picked his suitcase up and threw it in the trunk of her old Mustang. The baggage seemed light as a shadow.

She sent Benjamin to stroll the boardwalk in Venice Beach while she dressed, as she did not want him hovering over her, staring at his watch. It was always lively there, a circus that never closes its doors, of anthropological interest to him with all the vendors and performers, the break-dancers and the weightlifters and the buskers and the magicians and the jugglers and the jesters. Plenty of baseness, true, but always approaching theater. Beach burgers and sausage and fresh lemonade, churros and pizza and popcorn too, with fairly clean public bathrooms beside a path meant for bikers and roller-skaters in bikinis. Guerrilla theater, yet with high rents, the cops in excess and an utter lack of parking spaces, the fiction has got its friction.

Primping, now that was her own business, not his. He mostly preferred her *au naturel*, oh, but he liked to watch the alchemy of all the tubes and the pots of this and that, the brushes for lips, for eyes, for cheeks, for bronzing and for highlighting and for contouring. It was like watching the overripe colorist Willem de Kooning transform an "ordinary" canvas, Benjamin often thought, anxious for the final result, but aware of the prolific process he'd come to call Operation Paulette. He even had some light-hearted '40s songs for it. "Moonlight becomes you, it goes with your hair. You certainly know the right thing to wear," he sometimes sings inaudibly, his pitch perfect, amusing himself. On occasion he wanted nothing to do with it at all, the curious, relative inactivity of dressing up, and he was impatient and ambivalent to the warm mist and the sweet aromas and the softened lights that created such a homogeneous, doll effect. Sometimes it reminded him too much of his mother and he never liked to confuse the two. Most women he knew did not even come close, though. "Moonlight becomes you, I'm thrilled at the sight. And I could get so romantic tonight."

They were going off to Chinois, a Vietnamese fusion restaurant on Main Street owned by Wolfgang Puck and his interior designer wife. Benjamin loved the catfish in ginger sauce and had suggested it, a special dinner with chopsticks, had phoned ahead, asked that a quiet table near the wall of purple orchids be reserved. It is a voguish spot, and they would walk the few blocks there from Paulette's apartment, pass by the boutiques and vintage shops, despite her three-inch wedges of black patent leather. The ankle straps would keep her steady, she'd thought, buckling and fastening them. Her toenails were painted a sort of muddy pink and they matched her fingernails and her lipstick. She sprayed a little Coco on her wrists and at the back of her neck, sprayed the air with it then moved quickly through the mist. They spread things very far, Benjamin and Paulette, much farther than the direct route from here to there.

Wandering, watching, worrying only just a fraction, hoping to cause a ripple in the water, Benjamin got the strange notion to have something tattooed temporarily on his forearm. There were shops and artists all over the boardwalk where he might have it done. Not the marriage question exactly, he thinks, but rather the one about making a whole relationship of the various parts of their romance. As a speech sound that when put together with other hums and vibrations forms a word, each bit of their liaison carried meaning, like the body movements that showed attitude and emotion, the clothes they both wore that expressed point of view, even the suntans on their skins and the flavor of their lost breaths.

What word, or phrase, or sentence, or image to transmit this sense? Benjamin wonders, like a semiotician looking at codes, opening up books of tatts piled in front of one of the shops that drew him in blaring music by R.E.M. It is "Gardening at Night," an obscure song with maddening lyrics he was constantly deciphering. Sometimes it was about moonlighting marijuana, and other times it was a metaphor for pissing. So underrated, he thinks.

Letters from various alphabets in many scripts and flourishes fill copious plastic-covered pages that turn quite easily. He sits down on a wooden bench with a thin red, black and yellow pillow on it, thumbs through designs and tries to conjure something with a simple, salient meaning—a needle with a spool of thread. It was this kind of thing that he has got with Paulette, this correlation that unites them, their specific chemistry, he thinks. Sewcialists, he tells himself, laughing.

Perusing slowly through page after page of Celtic, tribal and golden goddess designs, of suns and stars and zodiac signs, he comes upon a group of vividly colored vintage flowers—poppies, roses, lilacs, forget-me-nots in white and blue, cherry and apple blossoms, morning glories. They look like some of her dresses, he thinks, aged quite nicely and softly faded. They also resemble a bit the bricolage of their connection, which has an antique quality to it, and has been on and off now for nearly a decade. Mostly on, he decides, and never fully off, not for him anyway, with a history and a geography, a travelogue, a schema, even a literature. He has sent her numerous bouquets over the years; and she has sent some to him too, lilies, mostly, but sunflowers also. And that yellow tulip on her dress, oh, he cannot forget that. Passionified flowers, Benjamin thinks, grinning, pleased with himself. Hahaha. They will carry the message fully as a sign-image in the habit of Lévi-Strauss.

Guaranteed to last 24 hours at least, he is told. Benjamin sits there arranging the flowers and foliage in his mind so that he can instruct the one who will apply them. Ever thought about permanent ones, the real thing? somebody asked him. The boss, Benjamin assumes, from the erectness of his posture and his loosely crossed arms. "Sure," he answers, his dark gaze focusing on nobody in particular. He remembers seeing the word "love" on several of the pages and found it just so anonymous. So much of the world is sentimentalized, all these uplifting signifiers that signify nothing, he thinks but does not say outside the classroom. Scratching "love" on your physique is mostly just an alibi for one's humanity. "If I can find something that isn't empty," he says, hoping not to be offensive in a place with a reverence for permanently stained skin, remembering the Maoris of New Zealand and their doubling faces.

With the doors wedged open to the boardwalk, sunlight floods the whole of the room. The lady behind the counter with a tattooed snake running up her shoulder to the back of her neck, she grins, points to a black chair at a station near the front of the shop. The most public of places, he thinks, for the most private of pipedreams. "Linda's ready for you," she says above the din. He can see the sand beyond the boardwalk, a three-mile stretch of beach flanked by palm trees. He would grab a towel, quickly head down to it, bake himself to oblivion.

"Straight men don't usually do flowers," Linda says dryly as Benjamin relaxes into her chair. "Oh really," he says, taking off his old Omega wrist-watch and putting it in the pocket of his jeans, baggy and JNCO. "Well, this one does," he says, listening to the big ideas, big themes and big sounds of U2, of which he is not really a fan. Sincerity is best when it does not aim for success, goes Benjamin's motto. He rolls up his left sleeve and rotates his arm, showing her the best place for what he has in mind, this cartography of sorts. When he tells her what that is, what he hopes the flowers will do, Linda can barely contain herself. "Can I give you a glass of champagne?" she offers Benjamin.

Getting drunk was never Paulette's intention, not this evening or any other, not anymore. It was, however, a consequence. She wanted only just to calm herself, was all, to find again her innocence, while she waited for

Benjamin to return, that vulnerability that made her so utterly charming. Not that she found herself charming. Not that she found herself much of anything. The dress, it felt so heavy, so consequential, and the atmosphere so carbonated, like a red punch loaded with Seven-Up and overflowing bubbles. It might be joy, but she couldn't be sure of that either, since she felt it so little. She understood more why people jumped off balconies. The half-full bottle of wine, it was opened and in the middle of the dining room table decorating the space. Before she put on her lipstick, she had a full glass of it, a merlot that made her dizzy and somewhat converted. When she walks down Main Street, she thinks, washing out the stemmed glass and putting it into the black plastic drainer, she will need to have Benjamin's arm. A lifeline, she muses, in that haze.

Since she notices nearly everything, Benjamin unrolls his leafy green sleeve so that Paulette won't see the artistry performed by Linda at Evolution Tattoo, not just yet. He puts his watch back on but does not button his cuffs. He likes them folded back without any precision. He walks up the wide wooden steps to #4, knocks. The small dog belonging to the gay couple upstairs yaps and the boys look down out the window and wave. Benjamin smiles, nods. They are not friends exactly but something close to it. He is a bit anxious, jittery, and highly conscious of the old tourmaline ring deep in his pocket, yellow, for self-esteem. His mother and father both helped him find it.

The first thing he sees when she opens the door is the dress, falling off her shoulder, and he is struck down to his knees by its beauty on her, stunned by the expansive skirt and the folklore of the embroidery and the way the whole of it all drapes on her body. He had seen the dress on the hanger but it did not strike him as sultry until it was on her, worn with such reverie, the red of its underside hem kicked up, a mannequin come to life, to afterlife. Others might be erased by such a dress, he thinks, worn by it, but not Paulette. Her hair is pulled up half the way and teased, held somewhat in place with a black velvet band and neater than usual. Blonder than usual too, he notes. Her lips are the pink of Caribbean flamingoes, moist and sparkling and full. He wanted to kiss them but held himself back, did not wish to spoil anything.

"Spectacular," he says with one raised eyebrow. For this there was not enough bubbly on Earth.

It was the pin-up girl who winked, pulled her sleeve back up on her shoulder and asked if he might please fasten the '50s Weiss necklace she was holding in place at her neck. She turns just slightly and lets go of the thing into his balmy fingers, feels the sparks of his élan as they move through her arms, down her spine and up to the very top of her head. It was a crowning moment for the both of them. Love? Not precisely, though near enough and complicated enough, highly contagious, lusty and long-lived, just like the raisin-colored rhinestones fitted so well on the old necklace.

"There," Benjamin says, breathing Paulette and her Coco in like a creature scenting its mate, "hooked."

Exhaling deeply his genuineness, Benjamin delicately starts a conversation he intended to have a bit later at the restaurant. "If I can land a teaching gig at UCLA, then maybe," he says, not finishing the thought, the question only in his eyes. They are warm and honest, transparent, those eyes, and always have been. She did not understand what that meant until she faced her innermost sense of solitude. There were better-looking men, sure, but none smarter or more constant. And he would not try to make her happy, she thought. Happiness, that was up to her.

"Maybe what?" she asks, nearly desperate, yet doing her best not to supply that cheesiness, ready-made. Would she ever be anything more than woman, with its circumstance and its cargo, with its ditzy stereotypes that threaten no one, that disturb nothing? Benjamin lent her the poise to expect so. Prepared or not, something indeed was happening. Chill, Paulette tells herself, staring down at her shoes with their beeswax sheen and the linoleum floor beneath them to keep herself calm.

"I have a meeting scheduled with the faculty of the linguistics department, the chair and the dean, for the day after tomorrow," Benjamin tells her, showing only his poker face. He hadn't shaved in three days on purpose, since he knew she loved his beard when it rubbed reddish on her thighs. He rolls up his one sleeve so that she might grasp the flowers, then turns up the other.

"Oh, well, so that is why you came here, then?" she asks in a careful voice, her high hopes breaking through the window of the building's seventh floor and hitting the street below with a thud. More wine, she thinks, eyeing the corked bottle back on the table. The air in the dining room is cold and sobering. She knows some of the scholars he'll be interviewing with and is trying hard to be delighted for him, thrilled for him, and to pick herself up and become again the vamp in the stiff black dress. It is what she believes a man like this wants, some of the time anyway.

Get real, Paulette tells herself. At least they will be living in the same city again, she reasons, trying to make the best of her disappointment. She stares down at the green fish on her dress, its jagged edges, its open mouth. For food, she supposed; for survival.

"You know Paris 1900," Benjamin says after some silence that both seem to require, his scrutiny upon her, all around her like the bitter air.

She wants badly to call her mother, tell her things are not as they'd seemed, and to cry. She wonders if she ought to change her shoes so that she might be able to walk entirely on her own.

"Paris 1900?" she asks sheepishly, drawing a blank.

Wine, whine, homophones, they sound alike but have got way different meanings and are commonly confused, the way Paulette is. And Benjamin, he is one of those who always means much more than he says. It was nearly 5; the early springtime sun would be setting very soon and the vanishing light might shift things. There was never a rush before this day, Benjamin thinks, feeling the pressure to intersect pressing and clear-cut. Nothing sew-sew about it.

"Yeah, Paris 1900. I've been daydreaming about it lately, that radical storefront on Main Street with the lifelike '30s mannequins who stare," he says naughtily, "the one that stocks Victorian and Edwardian wedding gowns. We've stopped to admire the romantic stuff in that window many times, but the place's often closed. On our way to Chinois, let's dawdle some and be more observant of the open hours, shall we?" Bit by bit he sets thread to eye.

Tacking on tag questions is such a gender thing, passive-aggressive, she remembers from a recent lecture. Men make commands, express their power, though not Benjamin. For him, language is dynamic and competent only if it invites all the factors that cause it to be certain.

He extends his arm unnaturally so, rolls back his cuff and smiles wide as the net that is Paulette's skirt. Then suddenly she sees the colored flowers arranged and tattooed there on his skin, endowed and energetic and mystical as her grandfather's old handkerchief. She gathers them up quickly into her wanton bouquet dream, those flowers with leaf, beside her a pocket of soothing warmth like she has not known before. If she were snorkeling she would stay right here where the chill of the titanic ocean does not touch her at all. Not even a finger or a toe. Moot, mute, tread water for as long as she possibly could, she thinks, holding onto her old black fish dress for dear life, nearly ready to let go.

14.

-- -- -- -- -- -- -- -- -- -- -- -- -- -- -- -- --

As Is

Croix de bois, croix de fer, she was just never going to wear white and Benjamin didn't seem to stress about it at all, not one way or the other. Her mother did, of course. She herself had claimed reams of it, lace and satin and taut tulle, all of it tea-length and snow white. Paulette felt that was simply routine and also aesthetically lame. Her mother's bridal gown was boxed up and otherwise tucked away in the attic, awaiting its role in sealing another bond, or pending its musty decay, its only proof of former glory in a marriage photo or two strategically placed on the coffee table. Even to her mother that seemed like eons ago. Anyway, Paulette had already worn her mother's wedding dress. It was on Halloween, back when being a bride was frilly and fun and ladylike, a costume having absolutely nothing to do with the boundary or bounty of forever. In fact, back then forever was completely veiled, dragged along the floor, got dirty, skanky even, and caused her to trip over it in those skinny heels of white satin that her mother had so happily let her borrow. She was done with them anyway. "Good and done," she'd said.

A lasting, sovereign, creative relationship, one with some soul to it, one with friendship and gentleness and some flexibility to it, one with more than bacon and eggs and buttered white toast and her share of his paycheck to it, what did her mother know of that? It was simply beyond what a virginal white dress could carry, even a lovely yellowed one with an hourglass silhouette from the early '50s.

Paulette sees marriage with Benjamin as a more peculiar bond, dangerously outside the realm of the fairy tale and the frozen peas, and for her that requires color. Brown, pink, red, orange, black, or even a magenta and grey floral print, she was open like a cut seam to just about anything with some shade and tint and age to it, though nothing garish like the deathrocker goth new wave. While she totally loved Boy George and Bananarama and Sisters of Mercy, their brave walking-dead club garb seemed more appropriate for fantasies and hallucinations and for crisis than it did for weddings of the sort she was having. And if she dressed herself up like a vampire for her nuptials and put a bihawk on Benjamin she was fairly certain that her father would kill them both. Toward the more refined ruffles of Duran Duran then, Paulette dreamt of maybe something in silk velvet in a shade near enough teal, akin to sea glass gnarled and tumbled in the ocean for years.

She'd asked her mother to come along and shop with her, thought it was something special and cool that mothers and daughters did in such a genuine moment as this. She suggested they go to some vintage places on La Brea near Melrose Avenue, and maybe later head down to Santa Monica. "Why not visit some bridal shops in Beverly Hills first?" her mother pleaded, "get some ideas for bridesmaid dresses, see what traditional brides tend to wear. We can have lunch after at Ships on La Cienega. I know how thrilled you are by the hard-boiled eggs and Thousand Island dressing in the chef salad there."

"But why, Mother? I'd never ask anybody to wear one of those homogenized, polyester pastel things, not even my sisters." She wore one of those in fluorescent tangerine once, with a garland of orange flowers fairylike around her head. Even got her shoes dyed to match at Leeds. High-heel pumps with bows at the toes. The wife-to-be asked that she paint her fingers and toenails a silvery, iridescent white, and that each bridesmaid wear orange sherbet lip gloss. It was an old friend from high school so she'd reluctantly agreed. But when she put the dress on and stood looking like the other girls, peach ice cream cones posed for photos beside the bride and groom, with her carroty blush and matching posy, something wrapped around her neck tight and choked her until she could barely breathe. If she could, she'd have ripped the apricot satin ribbon around the empire waist, shredded it to bits, and cut the marshmallow puff right out of those sheer sleeves. What to look upon? What to look away from? Times the edges of each get vague. The push-up bra of nude lace, it only helped a tiny bit. She felt worthless, invisible, expunged, but she would not let her chest sink. The bra was a La Perla, satin-trimmed, second-hand, a shameless shrug.

"Who cares what normal brides wear, Mother?" she went on. "I am absolutely never going to be one, no matter how hard I try. And why would I even want to be?" She says this without thinking, and then when she thinks about it she surprises herself. At a certain point in her late twenties, she thought about giving up on 'perhaps,' since the tangerine 'shoulds,' they were everywhere, and she was nowhere. Not coming, not going.

"Well dear, I never imagined there was anything wrong with being normal," her mother answers with a bit of a clip, clearly annoyed that her daughter seems almost always to be outside the conventions. "It isn't a disease, you know. You might try it one day." Her mother ran her red-painted fingernails through her again-platinum hair, exposing dark roots that the week after next she would have pulled through a cap and highlighted. Clicked her tongue too, and went looking inside her purse for the pack of Virginia Slims. With all the information out now to the public on smoking and lung cancer, Paulette wonders just whose existence is really taboo.

"You may even find being normal pleasant," her mother declares politely.

On thin ice, boy, Paulette thinks but does not say, wishing her mother knew that the only way she could manage to live in the wannabe modern world was to intentionally lower its standards in the muddy and matted hues of handmade garments that somebody had long ago thrown away. She wished that she herself fathomed what it all meant, the inhale and exhale of it. Some people needed alcohol and drugs to take them out of their skins, to forget, and some they needed God. To be happier in hers, to remember, Paulette needed the Salvation Army. It was like rescuing some abandoned treasure fashioned by all that time holds, its freshness and its deaths, its indecency and its mercy, worthy in some currency other than money. It dragged her up, inspired her, touched her the way a Bergman film with loads of bloody, gritty metaphors did. She could feel those moving right through her spine, that beauty, that beast, transforming her the way time did tangerine fluff. A rush. Fireworks. And gloom of the slick and the empty and the glow-in-the-dark mass at Mervyn's would kick them down again. Oh, to stay where jade is merely jargon.

Everyone has their sins, she reasoned, ways of casting off the world's spell. While she had stopped cutting and bleeding herself, stopped binging, kept her food down and quit cigarettes, most everyone she knew in fact was an addict of one kind of another. Well, not Benjamin. He smoked a wooden pipe because he liked it, because the smoke wrote calligraphy in the sky, because he could trace its roots back to the Native Americans, but he could give it up at any time. And he managed to live without credit cards even though he had a couple of them in case of emergencies. Addictions, weaknesses, flotsam and jetsam, tears, the world's sure full of it, and he used it all for his intellectual work, for what meanings are revealed, for what biases. He would never become a drunk and Paulette liked that about him, his fierce independence and his unyielding strength. Cross his heart and hope to die. Stick a needle in his eye.

That he was wicked smart, resourceful, funny and quietly handsome too, in a mesmerizing sort of way, well, that did not hurt either. He had found his own base current, the thing that turns him on, and Paulette was becoming closer to calculating hers. In her longing to be liberated, to find her equation to solve the way Gaudi was all about God's architecture, the way Michelangelo was all about Adam, the way Isadora Duncan was all about dancing up the ancient Greeks, he had become one of her true cornerstones. Not many women just the other side of 30 could boast about that. It wasn't a Bimmer, after all, nor was it a huge expense account. It wasn't even a big diamond cocktail ring, and yet, to Paulette, it sure felt that way. Two carats with morganite and rose gold, anyway, and she was beginning to wear it proud.

Holding her breath passing through Beverly Hills as they made their way to La Brea, Paulette felt the impact of a tiny victory and was thankful to find a parking space right in front of the shop. She suspects bridal couture in Beverly Hills comes with valet parking and champagne, but she couldn't care less. They feed the meter, enough coins for a couple hours, and enter a vintage shop famous to designers hunting out inspiration. "Might be some after-Christmas sales," her mother says, staring at the mannequins covered with white plastic bags in the display windows. And the way she says it echoes back nearly 30 years. Stinks, like bitter aloe on sunburnt skin.

Purse strings, oh, they can and often do last forever. Her marriage to Benjamin, and her master's degree, likely to come in May, they will be the sharp silver blades of the scissors to cut them. Then she might choose to live as a French girl with five good dresses. The kind that never go on sale.

Just past the brightly colored racks of fluky swap-meet finds and pro-pitious estate sales, there, on a dressform that at first glance looks to be a size 8, in the middle of what had once been a Malibu Tile warehouse and is awash with intricate color inlays still, is a dress that whispers sweetly to her. In fact, it almost sings, a love song by Joan Baez, "Wings of Fantasy." *"Wandering through the corridors, in an ancient violet evening gown..."*

A lavender crochet thing in a stylized rosette pattern, rows and rows of hooked needlework, it's woven of nylon metallic threads, and is swanky and yet innocent too, flowing out of the hips and down to the ankle in a sweltering bias sort of drape. She examines the heavy weight of the fabric and the nude net tulle lining beneath for rips and tears. *"And there I stood a modern Madame Bovary..."*

Little imperfections, well, they certainly add grace, dignity, she tells herself, smiling inside and out, fit to bust, even. At first glance, with the feminine scoop neckline and cap sleeves, she pictures a long strand of chunky purple-black pearls, the kind that Kenneth Jay Lane made, wrapped double, and plum shoes with ankle straps and a peep-toe. She arranges her cascade bouquet of black, lilac and ivory calla lily and her bridesmaids in garden-print '50s dresses with wide circle skirts.

A small brownish stain there at the waist of the dress is hardly noticeable, though a mark of its love, she thinks, and so she turns quickly to show her mother, who frowns and moves away before she can say a word. It is not so much that she doesn't pay attention; it is that she doesn't even pretend to. She wonders what blood runs in her veins, since surely it could not be her mother's. And then she thinks sharply that perhaps this is the source of her deepest loneliness. It is not the first time she has felt this quarantine. It is like remembering the moment your ears got pierced, that staple gun going right through your lobe. Grit your teeth hard without even trying to.

Disappointment stiffens up her body, suits it like heavy armor, one she knows. She'd heard a few endearing stories about girls bridal-dress shopping with their moms and how the event might bind them. Fibs, she tells herself, real whoppers. She goes to find the side zipper on the dress, despite her mother's frown, or maybe even because of it, she isn't sure, and the salesgirl, quickly excusing herself from another customer, comes running fast.

"Oh please, please let me help you," she shouts out, joyful, over the moon that a patron sees what she does. She'd put it on the mannequin just that morning before she opened up the shop, hoping to catch the right somebody's eye. It is for the cheery new wife in the first act of an Ibsen play, perhaps, she'd thought. Charms the bees right from the hive and into open windows and doors, stingers first. She did not herself shrink from sordidness. In fact, it came with the territory of vintage, she often thought.

"The hemline is a bit uneven, which kind of sucks," the salesgirl explains, carefully taking the dress off the model and handing it over to Paulette. "The 50 years have stretched it out. But that too can be enchanting. A little social science with your allure?"

She holds the dress up in the small space between them as a trophy the two might share, though for what she was not too sure. In places like this, only a little coaxing is necessary, as here, for the most part, is a world of believers.

Oh yes, Paulette agrees, caressing the skirt tenderly, putting her hand flush against the loosely woven fabric, seeing her chocolatey plum painted fingernails through it and considering what bra and slip she might wear, since it will show through and might affect the muddiness of the lavender color. It is like chewed grape gumballs, Dubble Bubble, gnawed on for hours. Too much white beneath will lighten it the way saliva does bubble gum; too much pink will spoil the perfect tone. And she'd had quite enough pink to last an entire lifetime. In fact, before the age of five it was the tincture of choice for the girls in her household. That and other stereotypes about guns and dolls, and about boys being boys. This was the part of old-fashioned she had to stare down, become foul-mouthed about.

The hangtag pierced into the underarm says: "As is," meaning the garment is flawed in some way. The salesgirl says that designers often buy damaged items and tear them apart, study the pieces, so it really does not matter. "They are examining specifically the shape, line, flow." Being looked at, looking at oneself, it did not enter the reckoning. Armholes where arms never poke out of sleeves.

"I want to wear it for my wedding?" she tells the salesgirl, no, actually, she's asking, trying to see herself in the dress in her mind, reflecting and being reflected. "A Sunday afternoon, at sunset, in a vine-covered court-yard up the coast."

"How lovely," she answers softly, grinning, folding and fondling old cashmere sweaters on top of a rack, keeping her fingers busy while her mind wanders where there are breaking waves, wet sand on the shore at Malibu. "Lucky girl."

"My mother doesn't think so," Paulette tells her quietly, not wanting to start anything. She sees her mother gazing at some bowling shirts in the front of the store and is glad there is something that holds her interest. Her mother does bowl, father too. They belong to a couples' league at some lanes in Hawthorne. They both have trophies and blisters on their swinging hands because of it. Has Paulette never been tempted? Not once asked, as her parents were greedy with their own lives, so no. She sure likes those rayon shirts, though, and the old bowling bags in beat-up leather. Even the vinyls in speedboat sparkle. She lays the dress over an old pink-striped chintz chair inside the dimly lit dressing room. She could be sad in this light, have a sudden change in mood, the winter blues. In truth, the leaves are already starting to turn.

"Well, put it on and she might," the salesgirl tells her, noting the fantasies she'd thought up when she put the dress on the form and steamed it in place: a prom, an awards banquet, an anniversary party, a maid of honor, a bride. This of course is one of the psychic perks of her job—that she can call it right, and she is feeling quite good about it, quite rewarded. The shop, and its merchandise, well, it is not for everybody. And it shouldn't be.

Cheap trends occur when pop culture plucks out style and brings it to the fickle streets, turning leather pink and feathers blue and ripping holes in shirts, tearing pants. Vintage resists that, remains elevated and timeless, neither in nor out, the wheat, while the chaff blows away.

Some people see some old tiles and they swoon from their beat-up beauty. Others see the cracks and think they are worthless and just ugly.

Change them, they insist, as they are broken. And brokenness can be beautiful the way a metal garden chair rusted red-orange on bright yellow is beautiful. To each her own, the salesgirl considers, quite generously.

Six days a week and Fridays till 10, every hour on her swollen feet. Paid the bills, only just. Yet 40 percent off the merchandise, some of it grabbed up fanatically and stowed away before it even makes the sales floor. And her boyfriend, he so loves to see her in those elegant rayon pajamas, the tailored ones from the '40s with those beguiling folktale prints. Another benefit and a reason to honestly smile when all the others fade. Seventh heaven, well yes, on occasion.

Paulette pulls shut the barkcloth curtain and carefully puts on the dress. She does not want face makeup on it, or lipstick, and the fabric is so delicate, almost like a light coat of dust gathering for years. To catch her ring or her watch on a crocheted thread might spoil the whole thing, disturb all the atoms that so perfectly bond. Stains can pretty much be ignored, lived with, so to speak, but broken threads are another story. Pull on those and they just keep on growing. Holes, they got a life of their own. Persist, as the fragments, the fleck and the speck.

She inhales deep and holds her breath there, elongates her posture from her very core, sucks in and lets the dress make its descent over her hips, lay itself down elegantly over the good girl in her and the bad one too, the way it was intended, altered anew. It is arguably a bit snug, and seems quite young and virtuous. But it zips up all the way. And with a few pounds shed it will fit even better, she thinks, turning around to see the way the back hangs, holding her body erect and straight up like a rooted tree, a palm, an endangered Foxtail. The metallic silver in the matte purple brings out the jadeite of her eye, pops it right out, and the flushed undertone of her skin too. Even in this old mirror with the low, sulky light, there is indeed a beam, a grey, dusty one. It shines like summer sunlight through a heavy coastal fog.

The $150 price is reasonable too, she notes, considering the wedding's budget of about $4,000, with the average being $6,000, says *Brides* magazine. Yes, of course she peruses those, a kind of guilty pleasure if there ever was one. What betrothed doesn't? Some girls spend hundreds on a full-length designer gown. Why, some into the tens of thousands. Benjamin, he would pooh-pooh that, even become astonished by it. "You wear it just once. And so many are hungry and suffering on this planet. How can $10,000 ever be justified?"

It can't be, she would say to him, to this rhetorical question, one of many he so often laconically asked, to which there were never any good or reasonable answers. Thus, a humble old dress that somebody just wore to pieces and threw into the ages, ravaged by hands careless and hurried, rescued from the trash heap of antiquity to subsist once again. Take up arms, again.

Saved, the dress, for the "*lady in distress*," by some old-world notion of posterity. Not behind glass or entombed or locked up in a vault. Not boxed away either. Protected, though, by something honest, nonetheless, and recollecting something about simplicity and style and a stitched sweetness that for so many reasons got lost. Like a sacred language no longer commonly spoken, yet not forgotten and somehow cherished, if by just a few. Biblical Hebrew, for example, is not quite living yet not really dead either. Quite outside the vernaculars of world commerce, though, the English, the Chinese, the Spanish and the French.

If only her grandmother were still here, she muses, since she treasured Benjamin and all, feeling a dreadful ache in her throat that never seems to dull very much. Sharp for years now, in fact, two and three-quarters to be precise. It was Kari's rhinestone-studded peacock purses, after all, ones without strings, which became their lingua franca. She missed her sometimes the way one misses a best friend who moves far away, to another country. You call and you write and you promise to visit. But you never do. Esperanto, the most widely-used constructed international language, translates as "one who hopes." Kari and Paulette both spoke that hope fluently. For a month of Sundays now it had been catching on.

Revived in an instant, still standing straight as the Foxtail, by that fondness, by that sense of *familio*, she gathers up her long, teased yellow hair into a loose ponytail at the top of her head, the way she will wear it for her wedding, though curled some, with a silk ribbon in eggplant or silver or mulberry and with some rhinestone bobby pins, and she turns to the side to glance at her profile, see herself the way Benjamin might, breaking through all the boundaries, those physical and metaphysical both. He adored her contour, the ghost of the girl prowling in it. He loved to watch the way her skirts moved, with the decency, with the decadence of a tango. More and more she had become transfixed by that, able to embrace the flattering of her figure, her necessary yet unnecessary waist.

She will leave her Venice fourplex when Benjamin starts UCLA come fall and together they will forge a new life. They are discussing Mar Vista or Culver City, both places kind of à la *mode* and not yet gentrified. Her thesis on interlinguistics will be one of just seven to be presented by the department later this year. The fog, oh, it is lifting. The '80s, they are lifting too.

Yearning to somewhere find a black orchid lipstick that Lou Reed was such a big fan of, the kind that Biba once made for rosebud lips and heroin chic, she's preening in this old gown of a pearly, mallow flower hue that moves so graciously between red and blue. Stoked to become Benjamin's wife, shifting to and fro before her reflection, splitting those atoms, she calls out "Mother" in the edgy tone of a vanished child.

The salesgirl pulls back the curtain a touch, peeks inside before she is indeed invited and covers her wide-open mouth and nose with her hand, her eyes lit up and flashing with that nuclear energy. "Oh my, that dress, that dress," she blurts out, just the way her grandmother often did, as though she were a medium for understanding something slang.

Strange, Paulette thinks, *stranga*, in that dialect that transcends nationality, still breathing shallowly so that the rosettes will not rupture too, so that the veins of the dress will continue to swaddle her physique and enliven her, gasping a bit in the humidity of the tiny dressing room that's now oddly charged to the max and expanding, hearing the clear voice she's always known right deep in her fast-beating heart. Oh, but for gravity, she thinks, calling out again "Mother," this time loud enough to be caught.

15.

Trousseau

When Paulette's father had smugly said Benjamin's linguistic profession was intellectual garbage, she felt it was the same as telling his oldest daughter that what she had been studying for several years now and for which she was about to get an advanced degree was a flat-out waste of time and energy.

He seemed relieved she'd be married, though, since he believed that was what young women should be doing. Their fate, he often said. Peeved to have to ask him for the money to foot the wedding bill, she did so over dinner with her family. In between bites of rare roast beef that her mother made special, her father simply said "I'll take care of it." He called his broker the next day. "Barbie money well spent," he told his wife, several months before the 1991 Mattel stock split, a 5 for 4, that would make him even more comfortable, and he would do the same for the other two girls when their times came. At least one of them will become a nurse, he uttered, more than once. "Now that's traditional woman's work," he liked to say, as though the way things were for women wobbling as wife and mother and part-time wage earner suited him just fine. That they make just 70 percent or less of what men make did not concern him in the least. Debris, is how he regarded Paulette's ruminating, in other words. It did not escape her that for years she had lived with her father's hurtfully hurled words and that soon she would marry a man for whom words were everything and they were never hurled.

And when in a moment of ease few and far between, drinking beer with her family only days before the wedding, Paulette eagerly asked her father if he didn't admire his new son-in-law-to-be, the fact that he was a professor and all. Since they were both professionals well regarded in their fields and all. Her father snickered and set his beer down carelessly on the table, spilling it a bit on the laminated pine, said the man frankly seems a bit gay. "And all that gobbledygook he goes on and on about, placing history on top of nature, weighing it down. That nature is itself historical bit, it really bugs me. Try telling that to the Sierra Club."

And with that he raised his beer bottle up. "Cheers," he'd said, chuckling and spilling a bit more. Her mother rushed over with a wet dishcloth to clean the little mess up, hoping to wipe away some of the awkwardness too, it seemed. It was the first time in a while Paulette had seen her mother flushed and she thought it might be devotion, or something like it. From across the room, her sisters were certain allies. It was their vivid eye-roll.

Nevertheless her father's tart truth turned Paulette's honeymoon packing inside out, squeezed it of all its foam and fiber. She was so proud of Benjamin, of herself, of this uncommon scholarly passion between them, this diamond and silk, fur and feathers, the rarest of all substances. And she wanted, no, in fact the truth is she needed her father to be proud too. He'd graduated from USC, after all, the top of his class, 1951. You'd think he'd understand the significance of drawn-out discourse. It was like having the hiccups she just could not seem to get rid of, this need of hers to please him. "Whatever! Dad," she often said of his indifference, clicking her tongue as it ate her up inside, wondering why she even bothered in the first place.

How to let it go, she gasped, *at least for now?* shutting her battered old suitcase tight before it was full, before she was actually ready with all she might require, before her father's diss tucked itself in, digging at her brand new knot. The suitcase itself, once her mother's, was already grimy enough. Scratches all over its beige vulcanized fiber, it had her mother's initials embossed with gold and brown lettering into it: MG. Its original metal hinges clicked closed, like a door.

Some marriages were similar to Lucite, a cheap, synthetic plastic, useful, common, converted from silica matter to glasslike object more quickly than time modifies love. She and Benjamin were aiming for a more organic substance, one just as transparent but far less brittle. Huhpp. Huhpp, it came with such force to the bottom of Paulette's throat, a humiliation reaching way back, a fury, a sense of her own unreliability, her own worthlessness.

Sure, she had met some goals, finally knew roughly what she hoped to become, having at last transformed discipline and rigor into something if not inspiration. She had a bit more control over her base behaviors and her airs. The practicality of it all however, why, that still baffled her. Huhpp, almost a spasm. She held her breath long as she possibly could but it did not seem to help much, that force near her ribcage volcanic inside her.

Two cotton sundresses from the '50s were still hanging in her closet, both of them hand-washed and steamed into their curvy shape, their metal zippers pulled straight up at the back. She had not yet worn either, as this was her trousseau. She planned to wear one of them when she arrived in Puerto Rico, and the other she would save for the time there when she is to meet the daughter of the Borinquen poet Luis Palés Matos, a valued friend of Benjamin's. They had been introduced once at a conference on Afro-Antillean literature at NYU and as academics of pluralism and historicity, both civilized and skeptical, they remained in contact, each studying the avant-garde literary circles of Paris, Rome, Madrid, Havana and San Juan and various aspects of the myths of daily life.

Which dress for which moment, though, she simply could not yet decide. Both were considered cruise wear in lush exotic prints, sold to tourists at hot-weather resorts mostly, definitely not high fashion in their prime, yet in their abbreviated essence in Jackie Kennedy vogue nonetheless. Both were from the family-oriented decade when women's behavior and social norms seemed in total agreement. Paulette had bone peep-toe sandals to match them, with a wooden wedge heel that she could wear on the old blue cobblestones, a sturdy and flat three inches to keep her standing tall, with a tooled Mexican purse in sandy beige leather, and creamy, curdled white acrylic jewelry, necklace, earrings and bracelet of midcentury Hollywood glam.

The two dresses were both found on Montana Avenue near the beach in Santa Monica, at different times, in different shops, and only one of them for a song. The other, it was paid for in huffs and puffs and lots of interest on the credit card. After she and Benjamin became engaged both were packed away in a chest that was her grandmother's, along with thrift-shop linens and dull sterling silver that promised to polish up okay. Smelled a tinge like cedar, as did everything else inside there.

The nut-brownish one with a sweetheart bust and nipped waist looks Polynesian tribal, with a Royal Hawaiian tag that suggests it might have been worn on a tropical honeymoon. That tickles Paulette and she thinks it may be just the thing to wear on her first night married to Benjamin, the dress with the right DNA. The print is tapa, with a pineapple trim. As lines and curves erupt, it has both masculine and feminine energy, is well balanced in that earthy way, she thinks, standing over her shut suitcase, holding breath in her lungs for what seems like an eternity. The other is more girly, with deep red and bright yellow pineapples amid stylized leaves on a grey background. It has boning in the shabby muslin bodice, like corsetry to hold the garment's structure, and the fold-over collar is kind of coquettish. It speaks to the daylight the way the other dress does to the tropical night. Both skirts are unlined and lavish wide circles, giving them mysterious and ambiguous flow and a very full sweep. Either can be kicked up in the lyrical Latin breezes. Salsa, soca, merengue, rumba, oh, for the dancing and the music and the saturated nights she could hardly wait. The coqui would be far shriller than her father.

Exhilarated and shamed, content and not so much with her melodramatic tendencies, a renegade in retrograde, in either dress she is the crushed ice in the piña colada at the posh old El San Juan Hotel. Her nails and toes will be the metallic silver moonlight color left over from the wedding. If she is mindful it will last the entire eight-night *hony moone*, as the ancient Brits used to say of their voyages to the French Riviera or the seaside towns in Italy. Perhaps one day she will become the strained pineapple juice, the main fresh ingredient and the one that, along with cream of coconut, dominates. To be the white rum, as is Benjamin, the real agent of change, sweet and subtle and not overpowering, even that would do. Better still, the blender or shaker. For a frothy piña colada is merely a Staten Island Ferry without that smoothing action. As if. Huhpp.

When Paulette breathes again, finally, after listening to Jennifer Warnes sing beautifully Leonard Cohen's *Famous Blue Raincoat*—Jenny sings Lenny and that torn Burberry coat, those unrealized dreams, loud, over and over—Benjamin phones to say that he will be taking his parents to Griffith Park, to the observatory to have some tea and see some stars.

"Darling," he says sweetly, "won't you come with us? My parents are pleading. You know *The Phantom Empire* series was filmed right there."

She wants to, badly, loves Los Feliz and the building's art deco façade, loves the green of the area and the vast expanse of the old city, its glorious views and those copper-plated domes where the moon, Mars, the eclipses, they all have had their shows, but she is simply not up to it and she tells him so. She has got most everything for the wedding done, but feels the pressure so intensely and wants only to go over the lists, review them more carefully to be awfully sure she has not missed anything. And then there are her hiccups, which just won't quit. Nerves have not been this raw in ages. Huhpp, huhpp, huhpp.

She can't tell Benjamin what her father has said, doesn't even want to go there, and yet, she cannot be alone with it either. Not and ponder and plan and prepare and pack and preen just the way a bride ought to. It has kept her immobile as a dress form far longer than should have been possible.

"You straight?" he asks, expecting that she'll say if she isn't. Long ago the silly games ended before they began. Well, not so long ago. And they did still manage a round of Jacks, occasionally. Rock-paper-scissors decided always who went first. Gung-ho about Scrabble too, the both of them; only Benjamin is bloodthirsty though. "Why play if you don't care to win?" he always asks.

It is the wedding, now just hours away, but it is much more than that. She holds the phone receiver beneath her chin and stares at herself in the mirror on the door of her closet. Benjamin put it up for her a couple years back, took a hammer and some hooks and did a lovely job, and when she looked at him in it as he worked with the leveler to be sure the thing was perfectly straight, she saw what she thought might be a kindred spirit. He was linear and forceful, a woodpecker to her heart. Into this metamorphic moment that would so soon occur, her father asserted himself. Of course, this was not the first time. Those hiccups, they came frequently.

Most of her friends left their parents behind years ago, along with the judgment and harshness, and the expectations. Some went to talk therapy for it, learning how to separate and yet co-exist simultaneously. Not Benjamin. His mother and father were two of his best and closest companions. His admiration for them was an eye-opener, that, and a prompt. Nobody she knew called their parents "friends." Most related strictly out of duty and burden. Sometimes she is puzzled by the affection Benjamin and his parents share, and she's nearly always envious. Forget Norman Rockwell's sentimental view of things, she knows from her own talk therapy that Benjamin's family is how it ought to be.

Wanting desperately a part in some of that, Paulette takes a deep breath then answers Benjamin in the only way she knows how. "He hates me. I can do nothing right." She vents her torment in the safest place she knows. She unfurls emotion, not food; cuts into truth, not her wrist. Starved for acceptance, for understanding, for attention, she spews.

"I am worthless. Frivolous. Blonde!" She turns away from the mirror so as not to witness her awkward nothingness and tries hard not to cry into the phone. She did that entirely too much lately.

Her sundresses, they hang there in the unknown, shell, substance, shape. They will lead and she will follow. It is her last month in Venice and this too makes her heartsore. A few weeks ago she gave her landlord notice, invited him and his boyfriend to the wedding. They will not be the only gay couple attending. Her father would just have to get over it.

"He thinks my ideas of the world stupid." She does not say that some of those ideas her father called daft were his, were Benjamin's. Why start a mêlée nobody should win? No need to insult Benjamin the way her father had.

Silence, for a beat or two, and deep breathing in and out to consider what next, then Benjamin, he says: "My sweet, you are anything but that. You have emerged with all and everything, like a butterfly. I figure you between the abstract and the concrete, fluttering. Please, please don't continue to let him stifle you. Blame it on his low EQ." His voice soothes her like a second drink. "My father, he is nuts about you, and of course, so am I. But my mother is even nutsier. You know that, don't you? And your father does not hate you, Paulette. He just does not comprehend you." Dark rum, neat, Bacardi 8, its bat logo atop red on the bottle, a sign of good luck.

She tries to excuse her father's patriarchal chivalry, point the finger at his widowed-mother upbringing, the Depression and discrimination against Jews. But the masculine world inhabits a big territory. Vast. And the male gaze is all-consuming and restrictive from day one. She inhales Benjamin's wisdom and exhales a small bit of hurt.

"I am thinking about the honeymoon," she says brightly, staring at the dresses, hoping that a change in topic might lighten things up. The vivid fabrics are like maps to worlds she has never been to, where colors are deep and rich yet soft as memory, hiding the stains, the stories of swelter, where strokes and lines suggest roads with no beginnings or ends, and where miles, they are measured in faraway time zones. In this present era of bling-bling and cha-ching, the well-worn duet of dresses is indeed leading, yet which of them is first? One does have to lead; it is nature, after all, yet which leads, is at the top of the totem, and why, that is history. His.

"Me too," he says softly into the receiver. "If you won't come with us, then enjoy your last hours alone. Stretch them out. Soar. Very soon you'll be mine, and I will unreservedly be yours. You will boost your circumstance and depart from it, as wine from water. The weather, it's dry, thirsty. We are fermenting beside the god of time. Hahaha. My parents, they both say hello and welcome you into our love-driven family." He breathes obscurity tenderly into the phone like one who is satisfied to shake and shatter dogma, like one who is uncomfortable in the agentic state, acting according to his own conscience. And that's his basic perspective. Even his snoring sounds like exotic utterances in a language she does not yet know. Since linguistics actively cooperates with poetics, acoustics and psychology and is regarded as the most humanistic of all the sciences, sometimes his vagueness acts like verse and offers Paulette an altogether original way of understanding.

Love-driven, unreservedly, she thinks, her heart pumping loud enough for Benjamin to hear. Hmm. The hiccups they stop, for now. She is not quite sure what he means by all of that, but oh my, she likes very much the sound of it, his words out of the blue in her ears. Dreams of a life with this man drown out her father's negativity, for the time being.

A new second name for Paulette, if she wants it, a new identity, a new purpose, a shared home, an essay, a poem, or three, some individuality, a child, no two, which they both confessed early on in their courtship to wanting, someday, though not simply because women by their very nature were created to give men babies. And a dog, they both wanted one of those, like yesterday. He was set on a Jack Russell and no, she wasn't arguing, even though she preferred a rescue puppy.

Over and over again, she had given up too much, or nothing, or next to nothing. Yet Benjamin has changed his entire life for her, dug up his buried roots and all. He knew what he wanted and it was her, the full manifestation of his wild mind, his unruly heart. Very soon they would both be rearranged, woven together as a plait, stronger for the entwine. Scored, why yes indeed, the both of them will benefit from this budding combination. And Paulette, she can hardly believe her destiny. All the years she might have lost him when she was finding herself. If men make everything exist, like civilization, if by their very history they determine and limit the panorama, at least Benjamin can help Paulette to clear society's conscience by exposing its soft spot and shelter of women who actually go in for the sanctioned roles. A little liberation mixed with a little enlightenment, too.

"Say hello back," she tells him. "Have some fun. You know, you're headed to one of the coolest rank-and-file spots in L.A. And tell your parents that during World War II, the planetarium was used to train pilots in celestial navigation. And a while later, Apollo astronauts." She does not want to let him go. That everything seems in place to alter things between them makes her panicky and her hands tremble, stomach aches.

"Some reality mixed with fantasy," Benjamin says. "It's so L.A." His own expectation of the place comes from the intuitive language of comics, "from the vintage Underground. Rip Off Press, First Edition, 1979, that huge telescopic blue eye. Zippy the Pinhead in his red polka-dot muumuu. A colleague of mine at NYU, she did her dissertation on his pinpointed behavior. Hahaha. 'Are we having fun yet?'" Benjamin says enthusiastically of his own anxiousness, signing off.

When Paulette hangs up the receiver, she takes the dresses both over to the bed, lays them out side by side, overlapping some like fresh flowers in a vase. The coverlet is solid purple, the perfect backdrop to showcase them. The late-afternoon light in the room is dim so she turns the lamp on, asks herself which one Benjamin would prefer. While she dressed carefully much of the time, used her body as composition most days, it was nearly always for herself, with her own mood in mind, a way to air her own inimitable style. On some days, better ones, when the mirror didn't frown back, when the light was just right and time of the month too, she felt quite sure that was where her real beauty came from, from that sort of daring she had to express herself and all the variety that she is inside, the inner drama manifest outward as creative act. Sexy, silly, sedate, sane, surreal, superstitious, spellbound, surprising, spirited, shaky, shrewd, sappy even, but no, no, no, never stupid.

Oh, it was galling, and worse, a dead end, the way she had been made to feel stupid, like cut stems after a week. Rotting, you toss them away and wash the vase out with dish soap but the unforgettable stink stays put.

Boost her circumstance, she wonders, saying it over and over inside her head, searching around the room for evidence of what Benjamin means, stretching as he always does. There is unfinished furniture she never got around to painting, and art unframed, rugs laid, covering up dusty wood floors, a bamboo chair with a torn cushion she'd meant to have reupholstered, books of philosophy and culture studies dog-eared and scattered, several unread, a yoga mat unrolled. Boxes packed with bubble wrap are stacked up in corners, labeled and taped for the move.

Seedling, infant, child, girl, woman, human, only occasionally and deeply afraid of that yet, having gone from one extreme to the other in so short a time it seemed to her, she was hardly waiting to make the bestseller list. If wife were simply an archetype, the way daughter and sister are, then whatever was she waiting for?

And yet, it was simply enough to pick up the paint brush, to bake the lemon meringue pie, enough to assert that clothes really do proclaim the woman. Worn merrily by sheep, once, grown in fields, planted and picked by unpaid or low-wage laborers, spun of worms, out of a heap of threads, a textile that carries the secret of its itinerary, that in Shakespeare's words, can "denote one truly." A garment can be just as instinctive as cartoon-o-journalism and just as limitless in scope. Wear it and declare it then, loud, against ubiquity. Become somebody, not somebody's.

Paulette eyes the two dresses again, but this time with something like rage. Oh, she is mad, crazy mad, hate-driven at her father who had always to be right and who dismissed her like she was always wrong. And now he is sacking Benjamin too. Always the cutter, when once she might abuse herself and relish the suffering, maybe even bask a little bit in her red misery, because to feel bad is to feel something fervent and familiar, now she is twisting those hairs, pulling on them one by one. There is nothing really vapid about clothes, not in an oral state where there is *tête-à-tête* about most all things. She would tell her father that, about Hamlet's "suits of solemn black." She supposed that he respected Shakespeare, at least.

Huhpp. Paulette holds the gulp of air inside her long enough to pass out. A silent existence is not an option for Benjamin. Knowing this calms the frenzy inside her and she is able to stretch again, to daydream and decode. In the march toward equality, gender and otherwise, Benjamin expects something weighty from Paulette and that makes her expect something from herself. Benjamin likes almonds and pumpernickel, mushroom soup and German chocolate cake. He chews clove gum, drinks prune juice, collects pennies, appreciates craftsman design, sips cognac, puts honey in his tea, wears a winter pea coat of caramel and cinnamon tweed without those arm patches and carries a shoulder bag of rubbed-up leather the color of French roast. He is solid, reliable and wistful, entitled, like her, to a little bohemianism, entrusted with giving society, and her, some reasons for its contemporary reality.

Sliding down an icy ski hill on a rubber inner tube seems relatively safe enough, considering the slope and the velocity and the proximity to the ground, but for the tree. Expressed as hackberry or hierarchy, it is all about the chain of command. Perceiving a way through that is essential to everything, everywhere, everywhen. This is the definition of what Benjamin really does, which cannot itself be reduced to a word that her father would appreciate, a word like professor. It is work she hopes to do too, and soon, somehow or other. Paulette exhales, settling up, settling down. Even though she'd stopped smoking a couple years back, her lungs suddenly feel fresher, larger and more open. She knows they will be back, those hiccups, but she can certainly sense them gone, for now. In a few hours, her makeup artist friend Henrietta will come paint her skin and her lips and lashes playful and delicate, though not weaker.

In the best of all worlds, then, unnatural as "moth-repellent" wool, though hardly as artificial as nylon, when considering the signs, the symbols and the sociology, Benjamin will most likely fancy the brown dress, she decides, finally. Even though the grey in the background of the other one is better suited for her eyes and her complexion and is in general more decorative, the real life of the party. Yet now that she has got the attention of an abundant man, now that she has got nothing and the entirety to hide, now that she is doing her best to draw some lines in the sand because in life, margins are quite essential, desire itself is spicing up her wardrobe, retaining only some of the flavor of the original. She lays the suitcase out flat on the bed, opens it, folds up and packs away the flirty pineapple dress with all its fresh juices amid the jive swing skirts, baggy jeans and her two-piece, high-waist bathing suits. She leaves the reassuring, frugal brown one with the seamless genetic material that's still on the hanger to her poetic intelligence, and to Benjamin's. Almost ready to depart, it is the chaos of the tropical night that's calling heaven and earth.

16.

Stain

As Paulette and Benjamin are married now for about 17 weeks and with their tropical honeymoon decidedly over, they are both feeling a bit on the verge of becoming jaded city dwellers, nestled temporarily in a rented dollhouse with smallish rooms and questionable plumbing, curtained with various ferns and flowers on West Washington Boulevard near Venice Beach.

Benjamin is rather pleased with his new place among the psycholinguists, pragmatists and the syntactic theorists as an associate professor of semiology at UCLA. His well-established meaning-making credentials paved his way, and his classes on metaphor and cultural symbolism are full. Overfull, one might say, with long waiting lists that he slogs quite hard to deal away with. His students are brainy and prodigious, the lot of them, majors in history and cultural anthropology, dynamic scholars who try to set social conventions aside and who happily take up the peace of growing new things. And Paulette has just finished the very last polish of her master's thesis and submitted it to her committee for final review.

So Benjamin has got an idea of how best to stir up the promise of their amalgam marriage, so to speak, to keep the luster from becoming lack. It's fresh, romantic, slightly erotic, a spectacle of sorts, and like their wedding, will be reminisced about for a very long time. "I promise to raise you up, to sanctify you," they had both said to one another in their vows beneath a silk *chuppah* stretched over four bamboo poles. "I promise to wake before the sun rises each morning and choose you," she said. And he: "To dare you. To defy you. To encounter you." And then the seven blessings recited over a cup of wine. And then the Romani band with their flamenco dance, friends' and family's hands from the world over clapped without even wanting to, hips prodded Andalusian too.

"Nothing very messy, I hope, my sweet husband," she says to Benjamin across the kitchen table, laminated green with a silver metal base that's only a bit rusty. She hadn't heard herself call him that much yet, but she liked the vibration of it. She hoped it would never sound lazy or silly the way she heard "other half," or "better half." Like nails on a chalkboard, that. It was never her ambition to become half of anything. Hard enough to become the rounded-out whole of herself, she reasons, with all of the robust peel. Working a tad more than part-time now for the ad agency organizing focus groups for market research, a people-person, she will impatiently stay put until something better comes along. For life's various evils there will always be the promise of a cure, a glinting Eden, and Paulette is crafty at that.

It wasn't that she was turning out badly. It was that she had not yet turned out. Hand-sewed her rushing river, though, just to the point where it flowed into the stream, like the one in Idyllwild, way back when. Shallow and muddy in parts. Impossible to remember the green-brown water, impossible to forget, she would rustle it all up as she went along. She sets her coffee cup down and smiles, rests her chin on her hazy purple manicured hand, slides her elbow across the table toward Benjamin. The vase in the middle of the Formica holds tulips, pert yellow ones. Benjamin had brought them home hidden behind his back. It was near the top of the mountain, Idyllwild, the peak of the planet.

"Living's good and messy," Benjamin answers, pushing the blooms aside, grabbing Paulette's elbow, stroking it. "Makes the world bigger, know-what-I-mean, the agony and the ecstasy." Yes, yes, she'd thought forever the very same way about most everything and everyone, just not about herself, about the way she had finally pulled it all impeccably together, fixed all the flaws, mended all the tears.

"Cirque du Soleil, this sort of French street theater in the guise of circus, it has this crazy mad show, *Nouvelle Expérience*, with fallen angels, spirits of disobedience, ruler of the corporation, us represented by an everyman. I hear buzz hype from students who saw it under a big tent pitched in a parking lot by the beach. Does this grab you?" It sure grabbed him and he wanted to share it with his wife.

For too long he had kept to himself. His affection for Paulette had grown gigantic. It filled him and it likely filled the whole planet.

"Where?" she asks, buoyed up. Musical theater was not at all her thing, nor was an event with elephants, but this sounded quite promising. She sits straight in the padded chair, shoulders held higher than before. He's the lime juice in that ruddy ceviche, and then some; grouper, sole, striped bass, a half-cup to one pound of it, in 20 minutes, pickles all.

"Las Vegas," he says, turning, looking out the sash window open a crack onto the sunny fall morning. The new day on the other side of the screen is buzzing. Kids in pullover sweaters off to school, cars speeding down streets toward offices, the gardener mowing the lawn next door and the noise is moderately annoying, but only to Benjamin. His lean fingers figuratively cover his ears, wedding band radiant as the anticipation. The pink gold was Paulette's idea.

The dress from the early '40s that quick pops into her mind to wear is oh so flimsy, though it seems just right for this sort of thing that sounds so frothy and fun and French, so *nouveau*. When she bought it recently at a vintage shop in Sherman Oaks for way more than she'd ever spent on any one dress, when she first touched it, the smooth, silky fiber that began its journey as wood pulp, that went full and long in the shape of a bell, way past the knees as others did before the wars, she knew it was not a worker bee but instead the queen. One hundred and sixty dollars, well, it seemed like almost nothing for such a great something. Needed some perking up, it said to her, will make voyeurs of the public. On sale from $190, before that $220; such a deal.

Roses wilt and die, lemons rot, people pass on, and from all of that dresses are not exempt. Sometimes though, one more than a half-century old remains impeccable—no spots, no tears, buttons all there, zipper with every one of its metal teeth, seams showing no signs of wear, nothing patched grey or yellowed by age. Yet it appears fragile, so gossamer and graceful in fact that you don't really want to have it anywhere around anything that will soil it. It is not about the impracticality of fringe on a sleeve that might drag across the platters of fricassee, or the solid light colors like fawn that show sloppy spots. It's about the translucence of the printed rayon chiffon, like a vague childhood memory, there, in particles of reality and rite, fleeting as a bursting cloud. Something theatrical and just out of focus, background to be coveted, obsessed over and conjured into foreground most carefully, draped, as one might a veil of all-pervading ease. Fine and ethereal as a raindrop shaping into itself, this dress, and just as elusive.

"We can fly if you like, spend the night after," Benjamin says with some mustered-up conviction. "Two nights even, visit the Grand Canyon if you want. I heard from my parents about this sweet buffet at the Rio where you can pick from all sorts of super cool ethnic things. Food under glass seem clean enough for you, Baby?" He certainly did not want to taunt her qualms or dismiss them in any way, only to help her move beyond them. She'd be so much freer, he reckoned. Quite fond of her rawness, though.

Yeah, she tells him, thinking that she would stay far away from the smokers in the casinos and the blue cocktails and the mounds of shrimp with red sauce. All the jellies and creams and icings, well, she'd been to Vegas before a few times and it was full of the things she feared for her dress and its faultless molecular order, yet it did match symbolically in kitschy and bastardized ways that she could never actually plan for, a city in its own glam get-up. If she puts on her touch-me-not visage, she will keep her distance from many of the dangers.

"It could be a kick, yeah, I suppose." She was not too sure about the buffet, though, since she never overate, not ever, and gluttony made her quite panicky yet, but Benjamin assured her that it would likely be petit-bourgeois art and she could simply awe on it; make it *nature morte* in her head. "Eat only what you want to be," he promised. Fed up almost always about something, now there was nothing.

Sublime, she thinks, cheery both with herself and with her husband, the very dream of clever. She might think to pinch herself but she is not the sort. Not prone to prayer or to actually counting her blessings much either.

The world is a beautiful mystery, though, for the both of them, worthy of reflection at every turn, of examining all that often goes without saying.

Impeccable still, the dress, and oh so pretty in its comfortable size 14 (read 8, today) posterity, and Paulette, zits all gone and no pockmarks left to speak of, and only the weight of the world left on her inner thighs and a few scars yet on her braceleted wrists, she just worshipped that. Why, Benjamin, he did too. New for old, and old for new, they both say, happiest with charming, prosaic things that still resemble the earth.

And the truth is, even though they bicker some now over small, silly things, the way he hangs his towel, for example, when the fold is slightly off, the way she leaves clean dishes in the drainer waiting for him to put away, she is not sure she isn't dreaming. They had become dialectically reconciled you might say; thesis, antithesis, synthesis. That was the way she saw it, some of the time.

While she had really little else in mind but Benjamin when she got the dress, except for the golden color of her sparkling tourmaline, and some precious chandelier earrings with pearls and champagne rhinestones that she'd found at a yard sale in Encino, that actually went with nothing else she had, the fact of the stylized green citrus pattern on transparent blush was simply quite enough. She'd walked around the shop three or four times to try to forget the thing, but simply could not let it go.

From the Arabic and French *lim* and traced all the way back to Babylonia, lime is a hybrid, used as an acidic accent to turn, the way the buttons on the front of the dress are like little emerald and white pinwheels, jewelry highlighting the bodice that turns tart sweet. Yet the cut of the V shirt-waist neckline is just a bit low and Paulette will need to pin it somehow so that her cleavage does not distract from the racy swag of the garment itself.

She is proud that they did not sag, her tits, and holds them in the air even more firmly now with good French push-up bras of the laciest variety. But they are not the star of this show.

Oh, with its rhythm and with its horizontal and vertical swing in just the right measure displacing the air, illuminating the snazzy female condition and its particularly curvy silhouette, and with of course the ending of her thesis, which in truth is sending her right over the deep end. Oh, more than enough, all of this, to make the whole key lime pie. A sprig of mint on the whipped cream center marks the very instant. Ah yes, the pretext. Very American, this.

"We've got so much to celebrate, my Love," Benjamin declares, "our unity, our altered fortunes. In every possible interpretation, your dress of sliced limes is so perfectly vital. It really should get out there," he says, chewing on that pencil as though it were a manifestation of his ideas. "Let the world give it a proper appraisal." Only halfway serious, him, though not her.

"Everyone wants to be noticed, Benjamin, don't you think?" she asks, staring at the grey of his green eyes, pulled in by their low-level black and high-level yellow melanin as if by force of a magnet. It was always foreplay, fingers sliding beneath her silky half-slip, his eye up. "Approved of, or maybe even disapproved of?" At work, at school, at clubs and bars, most everybody stares at her, and when they don't she wonders what is wrong with her. It has almost always been like taking a pill for shrinking, one with deadly side effects.

"Not everyone. Some of us actually want to blend in with the wallpaper," Benjamin answers, smirking, showing her his teeth marks on the wood. Hieroglyphics to one day be deciphered, those.

"Why," she asks, "would anyone want to do that?" trying to remember the last time she'd actually seen wallpaper. In somebody's banana leaf bathroom in Silver Lake; in a painting by Vuillard. Paulette is very near discovering her own secret zest. And while she has felt wallpaperish for most of her life, what she really wanted was to become the vivid declaration that actually jumped off the wall. Psychographic and intrusive and splendidly mottled, she did not want to blend in. A stain on the scene, though loved, like on her wedding dress.

Along this voyage to tame her self-loathing and to leaf and petal, become a conduit for something that actually flourishes notwithstanding the acidity, Paulette has clothed herself in the pin-up virtue of vintage beauty the way an expert stripper does with haughty on her nakedness.

It is what you don't see when you look at her but is actually very clear, the unripe coverings that distract attention from the more mundane, the more mortal. *Who does she look like?* people around her in this age of celebrity hum. She might be this one or that one; Olivia Newton-John, Lauren Bacall? Unlike big shot or artist or costumer, however, unlike object in disguise, which she knew quite well how to do, though, Paulette has found a certain creative success in the conceit of getting dressed each day, causing even her nobody self sometimes to pause and wonder.

Her idol Patti Smith, for her street style, her poetry and her shambolic hair, she might've cut off the sleeves of her white tuxedo shirts to perform the way a stripper stereotypes herself with gloves, but Paulette's sequins and fishnet stockings are rounded down. Not the way backwards clothing and neon bandannas, butterfly hair clips and eyebrows all the way plucked thin are rounded down, though. An old thing caked on as everyday cosmetic, then, smoothing over the new '90s bubbles with a fine glacé of personal liberty. Useless, unlike Patti Smith, except for coming to know and accept oneself wholly the way that some coming into vintage occasionally do.

No, she did not meet herself with bright blue glittery eyeshadow or a Rachel hairdo, and in this way she was rounded up; this gave her a certain satisfaction, a certain self-respect that she never really knew, that rendered her fearless and determined, and hopeful, worthy, voluminous even. Carried it around everywhere she went, this vanity, fit it in her purse like a compact by Max Factor with pressed powder, a soft puff and a very good mirror that, well, almost shimmered back.

Well, almost. Homeopathy acts like a remedy to only some of the doubts; protective varnish covers just so much for just so long before it peels off. Always, and never fully herself, oh, not really. When self-worth has its source entirely in the regard of other people, the discord only seems external. Modify the hair, alter the body, contour the cheekbones, apply false lashes, switch the garb. Semi-conscious now of her seclusion, she can no longer live contentedly through it.

Come late Saturday morning, now on the American Airlines flight to Vegas, Paulette unpresumptuously asks Benjamin to place her carry-on up above the seat, since stretching too much the dress might tear the under-arm fabric, the precarious seams after all these years. She hated and yet didn't asking him, though it was unpacked and then packed again for the Grand Canyon lightly enough. And while he was at it, the frail-looking older woman across the aisle, she needed hers put up there too.

"Is she your wife?" the woman asks, thanking him, gazing at and admiring Paulette the way her grandmother might have, her tawny makeup creasing in slight lines around the smile in her dark blue eyes. Her tortoiseshell bifocals are thick, with a solid line in the center of the lenses, but they do not hide the beam. When she takes them off they fall to hang from a necklace of fetching amethyst beads.

"She is, yes." Benjamin sits down on the aisle beside Paulette, rolls up the sleeves of his beat-up jean jacket, buckles his seatbelt, reclines in some swagger.

Honor plays a double role. Nearly five months already, they both say, in different ways, feeling a bit triumphant because of it. And things had for a time been looking up. Paulette liked herself okay, mostly, most days. And yet, she did not deep-down feel to be Benjamin's equal intellectually, considered that they were almost from different realms, attracting and repelling and thus canceling out. Not his fault, though, this, yet on par with electromagnetism in terms of its influence.

Life or death for her, this, like friction, rainbows, television and so many other things that deal with particles at rest and the ones charged. "That's not actually a real problem, Paulette, is it," her mother had asserted, after Paulette had summoned up the nerve and the intuition to actually chat with her about it. Metamorphic, this, and admitting it was like finally declaring you need glasses because you honestly cannot see, even though you have managed for years this way.

"Maybe not for you," Paulette had answered, following her mother's stray into shallowness and cliché. She wondered if her father ever made her mother feel foolish, though she was afraid to ask her. For as long as she could think back, she had been afraid to ask. And her mother, she never brought up such things. "Most girls with husbands like yours are stay-at-home moms anyway," her mother had told her, forgetting, it seemed to Paulette, the years she's struggled frantically to make some sense of it all, to move from electroweak to strong. At least her dresses recollected just fine, and her sturdy posture. Yakety yak, yakety yak.

And when she told her mother that Benjamin was whisking her away to Las Vegas for a weekend, it pleased her to no end. In fact, her mother wished it was she who was going instead. Compelled to tell her that their stay there would not include crap tables and dollar slots and cheap drinks and lounge singers in rooms full of cigarettes, the way she and her father had done things, even though they could have afforded fancy. Yet she thought better of it. Oh, a couple leisure-suited comedians might even be a hoot, Paulette admitted. A kind of social signal, laughter is after all a set of gestures and the making of sound—short, vowel-like notes recited every 210 milliseconds. Everybody can use a little comic relief, she'd thought, hopeful the lack of dispute with her mother was as contagious as laughter. Living with Benjamin had already showed her plenty. Even if she will always and forever hohoho to his hahaha.

"Her dress is like something that I wore back in my day, when I was about her age. I never looked like that in it, though. Mamma mia," the elderly woman says, clearing her throat, snapping closed her seatbelt, heavily sketched eyebrows raised higher than the rim of her spectacles. "Easy on the eyes," she says, shoving her leather pocketbook with a gold clasp under the seat, pushing it further beneath with her lace-up shoe.

Paulette glows like the moon on a very dark night. Almost full, that moon. "Oh, it is nothing, really. Anyone can do this," she says, dismissing the woman's compliment offhandedly, letting it evaporate instantly. Like an eclipse of that moon.

"I bet you looked just as beautiful," Benjamin tells the woman, putting his warm hand in Paulette's. Her mercurial state, it lately turns with the tides. What comes next for her, it is undoubtedly in the stars, and his kindness, his rationality, his patience, why, it can shift the constellations, all 13 of them, the serpent wrestler included into the *mazalot*. She had not entirely put out of her mind her father's contempt before their wedding, calling their scholarship intellectual garbage the way he did, even though she tried to overlook its nature and view it solely as history. His.

"Oh boy, I used to have a closetful, all different patterns and styles, cotton, silk and woolens, not like the cheap, unnatural stuff today," the woman confesses, shaking her head. "The girls all look like boys now, skinny, baggy. Funny how they now want to cover everything God gave 'em with big overalls. I used to dress like a proper lady, the way she does." Pointing her crooked forefinger at Paulette, she giggles out of a euphoria that makes her forget all the oxymora of her 83 years. It is a little brutal, she says, shaking her head again, to find the nowadays "so blind."

"Blind?" asks Paulette, wondering what she was missing. Why, sometimes it seems that Benjamin speaks with others, even with her, in cypher, and decoding it, well, it's not always easy. Just as muslin is a cheap and versatile textile, she thought her mind was like that, simple and effective. And Benjamin's, his was extraordinary, like antimatter, one of the most difficult materials to produce and the most expensive on Earth. Reactant with everything it touches, it cannot easily be contained. She feels sometimes a charged particle in Benjamin's electric field. Men do that to her, some of them, though less frequently now that she has pursued herself.

"Blissfully clear of the falsely obvious," the woman answers, explaining herself by way of a little wink. Benjamin laughs out loud at that. Hahaha. All told, the woman's career as a high school math teacher may have helped to further things along. Polynomials, square roots, radicals, whatnot. Only a little geometry intersecting in that, see, along the lines of the Cartesian plane. "Everything's plural nowadays. Nothing's singular," she says to the both of them. "The whole universe is today in algebraic form: $N = R^* \times f_p \times n_e \times f_l \times f_i \times f_c \times L$," she says, reeling it off from memory.

"Next might very well be extinction," she declares, breathing a deep and heavy sigh, shaking her silver head from side to side almost mechanically, her eyes fixed on something filling up and transmitting power of cosmological scale.

So much gets amplified when a plane takes off—thrill, wanderlust, fear. There is lift, thrust, drag. The next point has no dimensions, only position. "Extinction?" Paulette asks. "Hmm." She stares out the window into astonishingly rare empty space, exhales into it, in that place beyond the usual limits, potentially infinite. Not even a bird in sight. Not a cloud. Civilization, it all goes dim with a mysterious energy fluid filling it. Looking for life support, each one of them.

Some 67 minutes later after they have safely landed all the weight toward the Earth's center and taxied toward the gate, Paulette and Benjamin stand with the elderly woman and all the other passengers to disembark. Amid the fray of suitcases escaping overhead compartments and passengers stepping into the aisle in a great hurry to get to the slots and the shows and the spirits and to flush lucky beneath the neon lights, Paulette smooths out the wrinkles of her cloudy dress, repositions its belt so that the buckle is right in the center where it ought to be, directly below the jeweled buttons and right smack on the line that separates the two directions of the pattern; checks too to be sure its shoulder pads have not shifted during the flying.

Neither Paulette nor Benjamin seems in a rush. In fact, the holdup is what Paulette needs just now to equip herself. She moves aside to let the older woman go ahead of them. "My grandson will meet me at the gate," she says. "He deals cards in one of the casinos at Caesars Palace. Wait till I tell him about the two 'a you." Her leathery hands get raised like parentheses in a formulaic equation to solve, with unknown Paulette being the X. And then she picks up her small suitcase and moves along quickly, bent at the middle and looking down.

"What's a proper lady, Benjamin?" Paulette asks, wanting to talk for hours the way they always do. A young man with a tear tattooed on his cheek in the seat behind them chuckles. "Watch your cocktails," he says beneath his breath, stepping out into the aisle and moving ahead.

"Well, it is a gendered thing and not today so clear-cut. The pairing to gentleman? Hmm." He shakes his head no, definitely not.

Like those pursuing the hypothetical fifth force of nature, Benjamin keeps on trying. "One who staggers the edge between generic girly and feminine, but slips occasionally, I suppose, yet sets herself apart always, who maybe knocks the word 'ladylike' over and flits away. Good question, Paulette," Benjamin replies, though not as if it were in contrast to a bad question, shrugging his shoulders, thinking about it. "One with all sorts of ramifications. I have a request? Can the lady be a little improper?" he asks, cheery, drawing her body in that dress close with both hands, kissing her forehead with his lips and his eyes, even his breath. It is so gentle and loving, so force-carrying that it does not need a reply.

On the passageway toward the exit, Paulette will worry some about keeping her distance from any children with dirty hands and from strange men with dirty thoughts, be somewhat vigilant not to catch the dress' fabric on anything jabbing out into the aisle toward deterioration. Messiness, it will take maneuvering, practice, some letting go and valuing oneself and all those fascinating little imperfections that make it sole, that generate oddity, and stain, and Paulette, why, she is green as a new pickle yet. No quickles, Benjamin might playfully say.

In the outside world beyond the McCarran runway where there is at this moment the wispiest of desert rain, where luck be a lady and even the dark emits light, the impeccable dress of hybrid fruit like most everything else that actually is, with up-quarks and down-quarks and orbiting electrons, it can't possibly exist without some official date of birth, some cosmic moment when the sun and the inner and outer planets transited the sky, indicating the very instant it might be degraded by history and by time. Quite the way Paulette had been degraded by ignorance and loss and indifference, by being, actually. Rechristening the airy dress and herself in this galaxy and the next one, flying free of biography and autobiography, of the quantum spin and its angular momentum, of its gyroscopic precession, now.

Asking Jupiter please for a little less torque this afternoon. Asking Venus and Saturn for that too.

17.

- - - - - - - - - - - - - - - - - - - -

Who? What? When? Wear?

For near half of her surly existence, Paulette has been swayed by the past, by the stories woven into the fabric of her dresses, veiled in the identity they lent her, in the drama they disguised and drew out. She still shuns the vogue edicts that so many of those she knows dress by, but shares with plenty a uniformed longing to be of use somehow or other, to matter, some way. Equivalent, though not identical, unfastened someplace between things and words, like a halter top of dark lilac and grey-green figs unbuttoned down the back.

At 32 now her own work is a battle cry. Gesture, labor, nature, history, chutzpah, in that order—Paulette's opus: an evaluation of the effectiveness of using sexually explicit materials in HIV/AIDS education that targets gay men. And not just queer, but black, Latino, Asian, transsexual, with a diversity of norms, practices and values that reveal social context. Moving past the grammar and idiolect, entering the ethnography of dildos, dirty words, purple condoms, mutual masturbation—sex-positive health, not morality, not fear, though the diagnosis of AIDS is indeed a death sentence.

Yes, considering that a million Americans are now infected with HIV, including Magic Johnson, that Freddie Mercury has just died of AIDS, that a close friend from her gym died of it too, that some of the strategies for reaching those at risk have been censored, withdrawn, due to charges of obscenity, perverts attempting to entice perverted practices—considering that there is a brand new red ribbon of hope and compassion that people are actually wearing, it is time. Paulette knows it is her time too.

With urgency as its stimulus, the linguistics department, the med center and the School of Public Health became UCLA bedmates and found the federal money using the notion that to become truly effective as a tool, that is, to become genuinely proactive, education must not be subject to criteria discriminatory and homophobic. Confusing what might be valuable in dealing with risk-related behaviors with the promotion of a lifestyle reveals a deep prejudice against gay men—that homosexuality in and of itself is obscene. Any sexually explicit rendering of it in education is therefore pornographic.

Force everyone to speak the very same language, though, and the scope becomes random. Culturally inappropriate, blandly general, cleaned up and yet ineffective in reducing infection rates. Engage the viewer sexually and perhaps the conduct changes, making the education resourceful, is the very hypothesis to be tested. Dumb the message down, why, she had been doing that to herself, diminishing her own power in all sorts of ways, for years.

Shortly after it all coalesced, after the project manager gave her a plan, Paulette found herself wandering alone among the old shops along Pico Boulevard the way she did when she was younger. Contemplating the seriousness of the business she was about to become engaged in, she encountered that old-fashioned dark-haired mannequin with the curvy hips who first stirred her. She imagined her stepping right out of the old storefront window, right out of the era, right out of the morals and the manners and the measures, colliding head-on into modern existence, flawed and forlorn as it may be. With some surrealist reflections, Paulette thought to pull her by her long wavy ponytail, grab her stiff, jointed elbow to slow her down some so that she might indeed pass her by. At the corner crossing Robertson, she heard herself thank the mannequin profusely for showing her the way. Had her dad not left her there in the quiet, they might never have met.

Acquiring real confidence that straightens you up and out is an odd thing. It is the missing accessory in most outfits, though not the belt or the purse or the shoes. One might think it has got to do with money or with beauty, with the blue polka dots, the yellow boomerangs, or the pink Eiffel Towers, with the va-va-voom curves that plump up the zaftig paper doll, but that couldn't be farther away from the truth. Why, Paulette might have fully developed it sometime sooner, the way her body did when she began taking the pill, or at the end of college perhaps, or when she got a raise and applause for some linguistic research she fixed for a successful ad campaign, or when a very evolved young man fell off the map and into *amour* with her, but oh well, for the kind of boldness she hunted in herself, the kind that ascended outward from that dressmaker's dummy, better late than never.

That was how it went, her gene pool and the way she had grown quite accustomed to the sort of attention she got for her looks, and how she developed herself so incompletely around it. It became as dependable as a woolen pea coat that keeps one warm. When conflict is interior, though, darling or not, no coat will do. Paulette realized from writing her thesis on the pidgins and creoles that evolved in settlement colonies among non-European slaves, that to do herself some justice in any career worth its own salt, that in order to document, analyze or revitalize anything linguistically, she must first feel all right about herself and believe that she actually has something dynamic to contribute. That she, in some obscure Platonic sense, is a universal fashioner. Speak up, girl, it was something she just had to learn. The African slaves did it, so she had to ask herself, why can't she? Built of sounds, words, body language, clothing, customs, culture, breath, bone, blood, mind, spirit, matter, history—broken, like the dominant lexicon that spawned her, shards of glass everywhere, into something and somebody new.

Read, study, keep quiet, mull over, learn, debate and rework reality, reassess, then rock the boat off the coast of Gibraltar where the old world ends and the new one begins. It's really okay to fall off, Benjamin says. The Greeks and Phoenicians, they went without saying. It was not a vacancy Paulette yearned to fill, no, it was a calling.

"Actually, the term is 'demiurge,'" Benjamin had told her over Tito's Tacos in Culver City on a recent afternoon, "one who invents get-up-and-go, organically, posthumously, benevolently," the fresh red salsa dripping all over his hand, burning his hangnails.

"Is that what you are?" Paulette asked him while picking at some shredded lettuce and strings of shiny yellow cheese.

"My parents gave me wood building blocks, not plastic toy soldiers," he answered, wiping his fingers with a folded white paper napkin. "I stayed in close contact with the tree," he said, the hard corn shell crunching beneath his very straight white teeth.

Breaking off a piece of the shell, Paulette imagines the corn husk and the indigenous people, and the Earth before Columbus added tapas to the acorn, elk and sage-seed menu. Everything gets transformed by history, she said to Benjamin. "Even Tito's."

Whoop, there it is. Sounds simple enough, this Socratic lingo, almost like choosing a dress. Yet in doing that, like in learning a spoken language, it requires fluency, knowing which consonants go together in a word and how they go together, a whole series of patterns and components interacting with each other, mathematically, logistically, empirically. When you gawk with pleasure at a chalky pale woman with freckles, red hair and blue-grey eyes wearing a dark, grungy green and bamboo-yellow print, you can lose perspective, miss the thousand material and non-material decisions that went into the inventing, the fit, the length, the labradorite teardrop briolette beads and charcoal eyeliner that set it all confidently off.

The spontaneous life merely wants doing up, to create itself intuitively, to join wordlessly, and Paulette has learnt this too, all right. Conjugating verbs to communicate gender, mood and voice is only a very small part of whipping it up, only just the lip liner, the dangling earring. Learning what is obsolete and shifting among all the bits and bobs, and how exactly to transform it, that is the enduring red lipstick with the new novelty name on it.

Just as a doctor wears white to clothe sterility with words, a nervy thing then like the Québécoise Fucklamode to assume the reality, to wear for the gala that marks the start of a homoerotic literacy campaign rendering safe sex sexy. Her own coming-out party, of sorts, as she had overcome the odds. The dress Paulette has in her mind for the Friday night launch, since it is nearly summer and in full feather, is hand-painted, adorned by a Mexican artist along the Texas border for tourists in the '50s, and is just bursting with wildlife. A little bit like graffiti, she thinks, running her fingers over sequins that embellish the naïf fauna and flora design on thick, heavy black muslin, depressing as the '30s, iconoclastic as the Beats, somber as the coronary of this decade. Donkeys, horses, lions, rabbits, deer, roosters, snails, even bulls beside flowers, pineapples and palm trees.

It must have been silkscreen-printed first, she thinks, since some of the teeming images are lucidly duplicated without the aid of any industrial equipment to speak of. It was a couple hundred dollars, half-off, from a shop on Melrose. Seemed at the time like zilch for a work of original art. Fit her to a T. Fucklamode then, only dressier, the hand in play and vintage, she thinks, but of the same flickering kin, certainly.

The crowd will be made up mostly of gay activists from West Hollywood, academics and the local media types who are covering the crisis for the *L.A. Times, The Advocate, The Reader* and the *L.A. Weekly*. Since AIDS is largely considered a disease of men who have sex with men, or of those uncivilized in Africa, there's not a lot of ink devoted to its prevention at this moment, which is itself another part of the social context. How to drum up business, so to speak, is what Paulette must really do, bring the bulls and the lions together in yellow and orange and red fantasy and desire, and make some safe sense of it all.

"Hey, if you wear that, Baby," says Benjamin, eyeing Paulette as she holds the weighty dress up in front of her, "I will have to find something worthy. Maybe a zoot suit?"

The sweetheart neckline plunges deep, with extra fabric that acts like a drop collar, and darts accentuating the bust line into a sort of bullet point. She will need a balconette bra for its lift and cleavage, much different than the one recently designed by Jean Paul Gaultier for Madonna in the shape of a cone. The spirals of stitching to the nipple are pretty and erotic, especially if you are a pin-up sweater-girl type like the "Singin' Rage" Patti Page.

Madonna's *Blond Ambition* Tour has revived lots of interest in vintage, made the cost of it go up up up. Funny how real style hasn't got one thing to do with what's popular. And Paulette was naturally blonde before that was popular too. Madonna is the new Jackie O, icon-wise. She wonders how long that will last. A season, maybe three, until the new heartthrob glides on by just as in the *Tennessee Waltz*.

"Zoot suits are exaggerated and rebellious, kind of like you," Paulette says, standing next to their shared closet in the biggest bedroom of the little house, beneath a green glass chandelier that casts fractured colored light. Her liquid eyes shine like a cat's beneath it. "And since you are tall and bony, you can carry that off. A tad costumy for me, though, and yet on you, not a bit disrespectful of the culture and movement that spawned 'em."

Conscious of his ardent focus, she turns off the fixture. It is too harsh, she thinks, too real, and demystifying as touch.

"Swing jazz and bebop, like the Zazous in France," he says. "Got to really appreciate defiant clothing that was inspired by the trumpet. And you know that I'm keen on scarves," he says, still looking at her in the dim natural glow of early evening that moves through the small window overlooking the lawn. "Extravagance," he says, "it always pisses off the partisans."

Both of them are tired from the hours at the university, yet they might try to make a yoga class, a Vinyasa place they can walk to up the street. Benjamin meditates daily; Paulette is learning, but her mind does not always cooperate. Not yet, anyway. Leftover chicken noodle soup is simmering low on the stove. Right when she got home, Paulette added some cut-up pumpkin and cilantro, hot pepper too; tips from an Algerian girlfriend at school. The aroma of it flavors the entire house, leaves its sinuses quite runny the way Gaudi leaves a park bench runny.

"I always like it when you wear those scarves, the greys and the yellows, particularly, and the one that's like indigo peacock feathers. You are such a gorgeous man, Benjamin, especially when you express yourself with layers of color. They are the banners of your inner revolt." Her face turns red and flushed, radiates heat. It is like a rising pitch, pointing forward. "There's a little time before Friday. We can go looking on Third Street. By the way, I love that little goatee you got going." She runs her fingers along the new hairs growing consciously on the edge of his chin. "It's spicy," she says, fluttering her Chanel blue eyelashes.

He bends down over Paulette and the dress, kisses her cheeks, first one, then the other. Of all the codes available to human beings, the kiss transcends a single context, is the chief beneficiary of the primary centrality of communication. Under this condition, anyway, with the waning light and all, and with her sheer enthusiasm about most everything. The sun sets pinky-orange on the horizon nearby and Benjamin can feel it in the warmth of her cheeks.

"What did your father have to say about your new position?" he asks, still standing close, the gulf between them quite narrow. While he knows her pop, Benjamin is apprehensive. For his wife he is always a little bit on edge. Though it is bodiless, this anxiety transmits information the same way as DNA. When he first met Paulette, she gave her father an authority she offered no other man. He'd supposed that would change, but he couldn't be sure of it. He has tried to be jinks and jamb all these years of liaison, transmit that too.

Paulette smirks a little. "That it is not a real job." There, she'd said it, her pitch falling backward, closing the field. Everything her father believes, taking shape in a distinct little sentence with only a few words and a period. It stings some yet, but it doesn't cut the way it used to.

"What's a real job, in his book?" When Benjamin asks a question, and he does not ask that many, he stops to wait for the answer because for him no communication can be construed in advance. This is a starting point, and a starting-over point in all his vital relationships, and why he is so valued a professor by so many. Listening, he says, tedious and slow as it is, it's a lost art, like cursive writing; we must be diligent in reviving it.

"One with determined hours, I suppose, with an office, a phone extension, and a salary, with, you know, benefits: dental, eye, 401(k). Money-making, I guess, with a bit of security, like his, like yours," she answers, pointing to the small mid-century wooden desk where Benjamin sits to read papers and ponder concepts, write class notes, enter marks into his leather-bound grade-book. "You can imagine how he feels about me working to promote the health and welfare of gays." She laughs at that, inside and out.

"I can, oh yes. Particularly the more obvious ones." Benjamin smiles deep and broad, the curvature of his mouth fondling his fresh whiskers, caressing his entire face. While neither credit much to a higher form, it is a Gothic cathedral, his smile, one with gargoyles that scare away all the demons. In many European churches they are crumbling, missing eyes, horns, bits of their pointy tails. Those monsters, they sure put up a struggle. "I suppose he is rather disgusted, all that discourse about licking ice cream."

"Oh yes, he's irked, but my sisters are proud of me, the both of them," she says, a little bit sentimentalized. "I overheard them bragging to their friends about the significance of my work, and that felt pretty decent." Fate opened wide the future for all the daughters in her family. She would like to leave it at that, if she can, keep hold of the surface. The middle one became a geriatric nurse, the youngest a teacher with a literacy specialty she is working on in the inner city. Say what you will about the great family of man, somebody did something right.

Of course, on the other side of the Earth, where opportunity is scarce and suffering age-old, where the money's tight and the matrix uncommon—leave it at that, if she can. Consider instead the lyricism, the poetry of the cantina dress, and the French jet double-strand choker of faceted round and oval beads that practically pleads an audition.

"Not surprising," he says gently, "since both concern themselves with historical or sociological problems, and make service their mission. And your mother?" He'd called his yesterday to spread the news and she'd been delighted, for the both of them. "*Mazel Tov*," she'd said, more than one time. Yes, she was pleased, yet she was relieved too, since there was absolutely nothing inferior in Paulette's nature holding her back. She knew what it was herself to be a shooting star entering the atmosphere. Both she and Benjamin's father had been expecting sudden brilliance.

Another smirk. "Happy that I have got you!" When she says this she twists away from her husband. She's no good at hiding her disappointment and she really doesn't want him to see it. She is almost bored by her parents' regret, nearly over it. There is mostly coolness now between Paulette and her mother. They speak routinely on the phone, meet occasionally for coffee and allege conversation, but in all honestly hardly say a thing. When there's rain they talk plenty about that. Talk pours like that when it is needed, into an unspoken truce.

Paulette understands that when a rebellious life chooses you, to be at ease you must choose it too. It is about accepting oneself, after all, the natural beauty and the nastiness and everything else that's bombshell beneath the clothes. And the concessions you are forced to make are ones that may not be possible. To some degree it might be generational, her father's rigidity, but her mother's? Shouldn't Kari's daughter have picked up a little sass in her? Just as pants no longer signify masculinity as they once did because of who it is that wears them, society is not static. The planet spins, even when some don't want it to. That her parents cannot accept her, it actually shores her up. She hopes that she and Benjamin will bring a thinker into the world. A rebel, just like them.

The soul might very well be sexless, Benjamin tells himself, but the spirit of the moment between the two of them is anything but. In fact, it is near orgasmic. He'll pick up some chilled cava later after yoga. After they have given their doubts over to the universe and put their bodies into plank and chaturanga, they will drink to her say-so, at last.

On this stage of swag and scrub and sike, it is what sustains her, after all, that blue cloth she waves in lieu of the sea, that pillar of Hercules marking the frontiers of what's known. Peculiarities aside, become a warrior as AIDS becomes the number one cause of death for American men ages 25 to 44. It could be him, he thinks, panting, others he knew too. Vice and virtue, it is exactly the stuff of creation.

"And are you happy that you have me, isn't that the real question?" Benjamin asks as he walks across the room and sits down at the desk. He lets go of the heaviness into the chair, waiting to hear exactly what she wills herself to be.

He sees clearly the two ideologies of love, only one of them eternal, but is entangled nonetheless. It is a classic work in progress, untainted yet, mostly, like everything else about his delirious existence, and hers. As young women go, Paulette can be quite tragic. Then she plunges exaggeratedly into the whirlwind of her rare, timeworn dresses, expressed as beautiful and magical and transcendent, expressed as virtuosity.

As the machina advances, living with her has elements of Brecht, he thinks, smiling, pausing patiently, palms sweaty with anticipation, staring across the room at the garment. It is the physically touched and emotionally charged spectacle that she will wear to the kickoff, he admits. Such a skinny little waist and a skirt so joyously full. She'll wear it with agency and imperative like nobody else. And then again, she'll wear it with the *chi* of the ladies who wore it before her. All their ordinary extraordinary stories, he thinks, suffering now sweetly for hers.

When somebody at the university asked Benjamin about Paulette's ability, besides the way she worked the room like a drag queen, he mentioned in passing that nobody spoke better in terms of metaphor than she. And she did have a particular gusto for gay men, and they for her. Seems they share an urge for similar relics and might, at any time, impulsively and mischievously surge into high heels. Multilingual, she, and fitted by temperament, education and experience to use her skills in creating advertising to sell perhaps a safer X-rated practice. Right for the three-year government grant and its linguistic approach to health promotion, oh, he was never surer of anyone, anything. He could see it, the *Mons Calpe*, and further across the Strait and its rough waters to the African side. And that seed got carried off in the gale force, planted and just grew on its own. A flowering field about now, he imagines, red poppies atop lots of soaked-by-the-sun green.

"I am happy to have me, Benjamin. I give you that." Since she keeps her food down and eats when she is keen to, and she no longer needs to bleed herself. Since she sees now what she is when she looks in the mirror, rather than what she is not. From every grim moment in her dresses, there can be heard a gasp of emancipation. Each one of those come together, that is her opus too. And so when she says this effortless and honestly to Benjamin, she realizes that another man might sulk over it, might have his ego dashed, though not her husband, not Benjamin. For him, her answer is literature, yet entirely within his reach. He would not try to touch it, though, do nothing *a priori* to affect its value, except to get up from the chair quickly and rush across the room to kiss her, and it. His lips touch her neck delicately and she feels it sharp down in her ankles, in her toes. They are strung together like poses in a flow sequence, half mandala, or energizing solar.

Behind her visage, that real beauty she had restlessly grown into, from one vantage point or another à la Jean Cocteau, the vivid green and yellow and purple and orange sequins, hand-stitched with craft and care and singularity onto the festive old black dress, they dazzle in the fading light just the way all the little secrets inside Paulette dazzle.

Mythical bugs, berries, bongos, bunnies, backlash, bloodshot, brio, and for the time being, glitzy and wild and crude as they are, Benjamin, he cannot take his eyes off of them.

CPSIA information can be obtained
at www.ICGtesting.com
Printed in the USA
FSHW02n0128131018
52880FS

9 780990 696698